To Jesse B,

Enjoy the

Robert "Bob" Marx

REPLAGUE: THE NEANDERTHALS' REVENGE

by

Dr. Robert E. Marx

DORRANCE
PUBLISHING CO
EST. 1920
PITTSBURGH, PENNSYLVANIA 15238

Dorrance Publishing Co
585 Alpha Drive
Pittsburgh, PA 15238
Visit our website at *www.dorrancebookstore.com*

ISBN: 978-1-6386-7214-2
eISBN: 978-1-6386-7743-7

CHAPTER 1
THE HUNT

On a mildly breezy mid-August day with a fine mist of snowflakes blowing across the lightly forested tundra landscape, Turok places his palm down on the cold ground. All is silent as he senses an almost imperceptible vibration. His experience from years past tells him of a herd of caribou that he anticipates is about a half an hour away. He doesn't know what a half an hour is. However, he does know intervals and he does recognize herd behavior. Most importantly, he understands that a caribou or two will feed his weakened clan for a day or two. Turok is Neanderthal and together with Blort, they are a hunting party of two. At 26 seasons, Turok is a tested hunter and, by seniority and successful competition, the leader of a clan of thirty-five men. There are twenty-two females, who gather plants and wood, and they see to the basic needs of the clan, including eight younger than ten seasons, and four infants.

Turok lets out a series of grunts and clicks that inform Blort to move to a tall grass island in the pathway of the oncoming caribou herd. Though Neanderthals have not been blessed with the pre-frontal brain cortex to develop a complex language, artistry or writing, they nevertheless communicate effectively with grunts, clicks, screeches and gurgles akin to modern-day dolphins and chimpanzees. Turok relates a plan to seek out a lingering or injured mature caribou for their first kill followed by a less predictable but hoped for second kill at the tail end of the herd once it calms down and re-gathers from its most assured panic.

Blort positions himself in the tall grasses and crouches down low to be unseen. Just twenty yards opposite him, Turok hides behind a mound of dirt, grasses and boggy tundra. Although it is near freezing, their short stature, barrel chest, heavy musculature and abundant hair, together with light animal skins, insulate them from the cold temperatures of the last ice age. As a Neanderthal, Turok cannot think in the abstract or relate to symbols, but his memory and senses are keen. He quietly waits...but he senses that something is wrong. He listens carefully. Could the "others" be nearby? He listens again, only to be distracted by the audible snorting of the caribou herd coming into view in the distance.

The caribou herd approaches. The herd munch on the tender grasses and moss as they move slowly southward, away from the advancing ten-month winter of the last ice age in the territory of what now would be northeastern Spain. The herd marches between Turok and Blort. Each instinctively focuses on a big bull with a visible limp, probably injured in a rutting battle for alpha male mating rights. He was the loser and now the selectee of the hunters. The bull, with an impressive rack of antlers, comes over to the edge of the grass island hiding Blort. As the oblivious animal grazes on the grass strands, Blort jumps onto his back and twists in an effort the get the animal, more than 300 pounds, off of his feet. However, Blort underestimates the animal's strength and is carried along as a passenger as the caribou limps and bucks at the same time. As the rest of the herd scatters, Blort's wild ride ends when he is quickly thrown off. The more experienced hunter Turok pounces on the caribou's front shoulder and grabs the rack of antlers on each side. The end comes quickly as Turok's great strength twists the animal's neck and head. The neck snaps with an audible crack, severing the spinal cord. The caribou drops instantly to the ground, his tongue protruding from its mouth and eyes wide open. Blort returns from being thrown off and registers in his own mind the lesson he just learned from his elder about bringing down a caribou.

Turok and Blort look down on their kill with a sense of satisfaction and notice a light dusting of snow already gathering on the animal's fur. Turok looks up and sees that the herd is completely scattered. As he scans for signs of a lingering caribou to stalk, he hears a sickening moan coming from Blort and feels a warm liquid spatter on his face. He sees his co-hunter fall over the caribou carcass with a long spear entering his back and a finely sharpened stone spear point emerging from his upper chest. As Turok realizes the splatter to be is blood, he hears a *yip yip yip* howl. He then sees three "others" running at him from the only stand of trees fifty yards away.

The "others" are modern man-Homo sapiens, and are there to steal the kill. Turok, sensing that the spear is a good weapon, tries to pull it from Blort's body draped over the caribou carcass. However, the shaft breaks in the effort, leaving him without a matching weapon. He stands his ground not running away despite a three-against-one disadvantage. He has only an incomplete understanding of fear. The meat of the caribou is the priority, not just food, but survival for his clan.

The standoff begins. Turok and the tallest one of the "others" circle around, as the two other homosapiens start to remove Blort and drag away the caribou. Turok looks at his six-foot adversary. He looks strange to Turok, even ugly. His chin sticks out. His hair is braided. His face is painted with some type of ochre and burnt mammoth bone charcoal in a strange yet purposeful design. A bone pierces through his nose and a string of long bear claws hangs from his neck. His animal skins are thicker and tied together more tightly than Turok's as the sleeker homosapien's body habitus is less resistant to cold.

The "other," known as Blandeshar to his tribe, looks at his stocky barrel chested and shorter by half a foot adversary with a protruding forehead and no discernible chin. He thinks to himself that this is what the ugly primitive men look like up close. His only experience with Neanderthals is from the two female slaves captured years ago as adolescent girls, an unpleasant memory. He notices the worn teeth, broad nose, and dense, dark hair unkempt and blowing in the wind.

Blandeshar senses his advantage in weaponry and lunges his spear at Turok in an underestimation of Turok's agility. Turok side steps the spear and breaks the shaft with his hand. Blandeshar rushes in to overpower his shorter dim-witted adversary, a fatal miscalculation. Turok is not overpowered but greets his adversary in a bear hug. As he squeezes with strength far in excess of a homosapien, they are face to face. Turok notices for the first time the red dots and red papules over the exposed facial skin of the "other." He remembers the weakness and death that the red-dot signs mean. He has seen it in his own clan this season and knows all too well of the death it brings to his clan and other clans of his kind. However, his mind refocuses on tightening his grip. He can't let go. He squeezes tighter despite Blandeshar gouging at his eyes in vain as Turok's protruding forehead and thick bone over his eyebrows shields the eyes somewhat from his efforts. Then Blandeshar's ribs crack, his eyes bulge and a spurt of saliva mixed with blood and vomitus sprays onto Turok's face.

As Blandeshar's lifeless body drops to the ground, Turok wipes the human detritus off his thick mustache and beard to see the two "others" dragging the caribou carcass toward the lone strand of trees where they were hiding. Accustomed to fighting for food as well as mates, Turok races over to reclaim his kill. He grabs the caribou's antlers and, with the two "others" each grasping a back leg, a tug of war ensues. After just a few minutes, perhaps due to Turok's greater strength or perhaps due to his better grip on the antlers, he is able to pull the carcass free. However, one of the "others" quickly jumps on him and clutches his throat from behind pinning Turok's left arm under the caribou. Turok struggles to break free but his legs are being held down by the second "other." Turok feels the warm stale breath of his adversary on the back of his neck as he experiences his own air hunger. Gasping, he summons a final burst of strength to free his left arm. He breaks off one of the caribou's antlers and, by twisting toward the "other" behind him, violently pushes the top six inches of the antler through the right eye socket crushing it through the thin bones at the back of the eye and well into the brain. His adversary releases his grip instantly as he cries out in pain and convulses uncontrollably with blood pouring out of his eye socket and nose. The lone remaining "other," who is called Metander and is the younger brother of Blandeshar, witnesses this second gruesome sight, panics and flees.

Such is the hard and unforgiving life for both homosapiens and Neanderthals in Ice Age Europe. Each group knows that each day is a fight for survival and procreation. Little does scared young Metander, now fleeing over the tundra and between sparse pines and spruce to his tribe's camp, realize that his kind will win in the end. For better or worse, his species will expand its recent technologic leaps of harnessing fire and domesticating animals to become the dominant species on the planet as well as its apex predator.

Little does Turok, now recovered from his ordeal, realize that his kind is doomed and about to become extinct. Despite their better adaptation to the harsh ice age climate and their species success for the past 200,000 years, their numbers have been steadily declining. His own clan is one of the few remaining Neanderthal clans, one that has also seen its numbers reduced over the years due to the famine and the sickness brought about by the red-dot disease. The end of his clan will herald the conclusion of a striking effort in human evolution. The reasons for it will be much debated by their successor's millennia later.

CHAPTER 2

THE CLAN AND THE TRIBE

Turok looks at the caribou kill, now all his own, with a deep hunger. Although he would like to cut open a choice rump section with his handheld stone axe and help himself, he knows that the smell of open meat would encourage an attack by a cave lion or a pack of dire wolves during his four-mile trek back to his clans' encampment. Instead, he takes a nearby heavy stone, lifts it over his head and crashes it down on the lower leg of the dead "other" with the antler still protruding from his bloody eye socket. The lower leg bone cracks in half audibly. Turok immediately takes the lower half still attached to the animal skin-wrapped foot and sucks out the nutrient-rich bone marrow. It is still warm and satisfying to Turok but it is not enough. He then scoops as much marrow out of the other end still attached to the torso with the fingers of his bare hands. He repeats the same maneuver on the other leg and also rips off the calf muscle. He chews the calf muscle eagerly. His powerful jaws, with teeth worn flat from a coarse and gritty diet, easily pulverizes the muscle, skin, tendon complex. Knowing that his opening of the "other" and the blood around him from the three dead combatants would soon bring in predators, Turok grabs the two forelimbs of the caribou in his left hand and the two hind limbs in his right and proceeds to effortlessly hoist the more than 300 pounds of carcass over his head and onto the back of his shoulders and neck.

Adjusting its weight for an even balance, he heads off to the west to bring back the sustaining meat to his clan. However, before leaving the area, the seashell necklace and colored feathers on Blandeshar's body catch his eye. With the caribou carcass still on his shoulder, he stoops down to take each item. In his mind, he has a plan for them. He knows it will please his mates who in turn will reward him with their favors.

While Turok is just starting off on his trek to his clan's encampment, Metander has already put miles between himself and the bloody scene. He is still running scared through the open tundra, being careful to avoid the isolated stands of trees that may hide a cave lion. Different from modern-day lion prides, cave lions hunt alone and ambush their prey. Metander knows that. If he can stay in the open tundra, a cave lion would not have the stamina to sustain a long-distance chase. Tiring, Metander crouches down low to rest. He too is hungry. He pulls out of a pocket, neatly sewn into the upper covering of his animal hide, two strips of dried meat. He eats it hungrily. So much of his existence depends on the Yurok, an ancestor of modern-day cattle, from the meat that sustains him now to the sinews which the females use as sewing threads to create the pocket that stored his food. The domestication of animals, particularly the Yurok, the evolutionary, ancestor of modern-day cattle, has become a turning point in our species evolution from hunter-gatherers to what we are today.

Metander's rapid and heavy breathing slows. However, he remains afraid. He too is scared of a possible confrontation with a cave lion or a pack of dire wolves and also scared that the brutish "primitive" might be coming after him. However, he is mostly scared of how he will be treated by his tribe. He will return without his older brother and the other hunter. He will not bring back a kill for the tribe or items from a "primitive" indicating a victory over those evil beings. He will be asked why he returns and the rest of his hunting party does not. He will be looked upon as a coward. He will be shamed and ridiculed. He will be overlooked by females. He will be punished. The shaman will place an evil curse on him. As all these thoughts race through his mind, Metander begins to think of a story to avoid this fate.

Today's humans would call this saving face.

After three hours of rapid walking with the caribou carcass draped over his back, Turok approaches his clan's cave from the darkness. He sees the glow of several fires within the cave, as well as a larger fire warning predators away just outside of the opening. The members of the clan come out to greet him as he throws down the carcass next to the larger fire among grunts and howls of appreciation. His two mates register Neanderthal affection by rubbing their heads back and forth onto Turok's chest. He is pleased but weary. He clutches the gifts he has brought so that his mates cannot see them. There will be a better time later.

Four or five other clan women seize upon the carcass and immediately begin skinning it with their stone hand axes and opening the abdomen. They separate the internal organs to be eaten later. Nothing will go to waste. The empty abdomen cavity is then filled with roots and edible plants collected earlier that day. The women add skinned rabbits, and several plucked ptarmigans brought by other hunting parties to the fire alongside the caribou. Such is the beginning of a campfire feast, Neanderthal style.

As the flames periodically crackle and flare up when sinew or fat catches fire, the other clan men gather around Turok their leader. With gestures, grunts and whistles, he methodically relates the events of the hunt and his battle to retain their meal. He tells them of the death of Blort, which is met with an incompletely developed sense of sympathy. They know he is gone like the caribou but they do not know where. Neanderthals do not understand the concept of a supreme being or a deity. They do not paint elaborate images on their cave walls. They are part of nature like the lion the wolf and the bear. They live, they eat, and they produce new ones. Their kind continues like these other animals. Yet they feel a sense of grief when they lose one of their own that they don't fully understand. They appreciate kindness and gifts. They bury their dead not just to keep them from scavengers but to rest them along with a few of their more coveted possessions for reasons modern anthropologists don't yet fully understand.

Running most of the nearly twelve-mile distance to his tribe's encampment, Metander arrives after dark somewhat later than Turok arrived at his clan's cave. The homosapien camp also utilizes a cave but includes much more. Numerous huts are made of stacked mammoth bones and tusks, as well as bones and antlers from the other mega fauna of Ice Age Europe, and have been draped with various animal skins to adorn the area around the outside of the cave's opening. Fire pits are positioned within the cave and in front of most of the huts. A somewhat out-of-breath Metander stumbles into the encampment and is immediately surrounded by the men of the tribe. The elders interrogate Metander in an actual verbal language, the product of a speech center in their brain developed and improved over thousands of years.

Homosapiens are relative new comers to Ice Age Europe, a species that slowly trekked out of East Africa a mere 60,000 or perhaps 80,000 years ago.

Metander is pelted with questions: "Where is Blandeshar? Why are you running? Where is the kill you were to bring back?"

His own mother rushes in pushing the elders and other men aside to caress her own teenage son. "Where is your brother?" she asks. She suspects the worst. "Is your brother dead?"

Now, crying and holding on to his mother, he relates his story. "My brother killed the first caribou and I killed a second. We struck both through the heart as I was taught to be a good hunter. Then a band of primitives attacked us, twenty or more, throwing spears and rocks. They are evil, I tell you. They have evil magic. They summoned their wolves to attack us. The wolves killed my brother then his friend. They would have gotten me too but I killed the wolf leader and the pack turned away. The evil primitives then began chasing me, but I outran them."

The tall tale told by Metander will become characteristic of his species. It is accepted with wonderment by most but with dubiousness by some of the elders. However, the Chief has been eager to remove the "primitives" from what he sees as their land and recognizes this tale as a means of exciting his tribe to battle. However, he knows he must first get the approval and blessing of the Shaman.

The Chief takes Metander from his mother with a gruff and a stern look. He and the five true elders together take Metander into the cave. Metander enters the sacred cave for the first time in his life. A low fire in the middle reflects a flickering light on to the cave walls. There in the flickering light from the fire pit he believes he sees yuroks and antelope running across the cave walls. He sees images of his tribesmen chasing after them with spears in hand. He is entranced by the images of a hunt but before he can get closer for a more detailed look, a shadow comes over him blocking his view. It is the Shaman. This tall figure sports a wrinkled face and long, silver-streaked hair streaming down over his shoulders. Atop his head is the fur-covered skull of a cave bear with teeth glistening in the flickering light. The skin of the cave bear covers the Shaman's backside like a cape. The imposing figure of the Shaman is made even more imposing by a necklace of lion claws and a bib made of the dried heads of small animals. Behind him, two poles each brandish the dried head of a primitive. Metander is alarmed and awestruck at the same time. His eyes have been so focused on the Shaman and his surroundings that he has not until now seen four of his tribesmen sitting on animal skins around the fire. He examines them closely. They have red dots on their faces and exposed arms. They do not appear ill. None are moaning. Metander is then snapped back to reality by the deep raspy voice of the Shaman.

"Young Metander, these of our tribe have been afflicted by an evil spell. Stand away so that the evil spell does not strike you."

Metander now recalls that his perished older brother had the same red dots on him. He thinks it must be the evil spell from the primitives. In his mind, this reinforces his tall tale. Metander repeats the same story this time adding even more embellishments. The die is now cast. The Shaman gives his blessing for a war party then turns back to administer to the four with the red-dot disease. Reciting short incantations and shaking a rattle made of a Yurok's bladder filled with stones and small bones, he proceeds to administer his self-made potion. The potion is a mixture of several animal parts but primarily from the domesticated Yurok, a stroke of unintended good fortune for his species.

The Chief flanked by the elders comes to stand at the mouth of the cave shouting the blessing of the Shaman. Like a modern-day political rally, he proceeds to convince all who hear it of the noble purpose and tribal defense needs to eliminate the primitives and their evil magic. The tribesmen are whipped into a frenzy, repeatedly beating hollow logs at the cave's mouth and throwing themselves into a ritualistic dance featuring mostly mock spear jousting and chest thumping. Meanwhile, the elders select Valtron to lead tomorrow's raid and instruct him to begin at first light by sacrificing one of the two female primitives captured in a previous raid.

CHAPTER 3

THE CHASE

The next day, the raid doesn't go off as intended. The ritualistic dancing and frenzied rhetoric imploring the spirits of the earth, sun, and moon to be with them has left them exhausted and disorganized instead. By noon, Valtron is seen rousting his young warriors out of various sleepy and stuporous states, caused in part by the consumption of certain seeds and leaves thought to increase strength.

Experienced in raids, Valtron knows he must prepare carefully. He must plan for food and prepare enough spears, rock throwers and clubs for the battle to wipe out the primitives and maintain the commitment of his troops. He slows the pace down to adequately prepare, usually a wise tactical move but one, he will regret later.

Uneasy at the apparent closeness of a tribe of "others," Turok gathers his clan to move from their present location of only two months. It is unfortunate since they had planned a much longer stay. His grunts and gestures are clear to everyone. They are to move toward the frozen waters (North) even though the frozen waters themselves are drawing near as the cold season approaches. Turok knows all too well the murderous nature of the others and their desire to take their young and their mates. He knows the "others" are not as threatening or as fast in the cold, though he doesn't know why and is not capable of concerning himself about it anyway. It is just something he knows.

Turok leads his clan out of their cave, the men carrying only wooden tree limbs for clubs and longer straight tree limbs with tips sharpened to a point for spears. Female clan members carry leftover meat from last night's feast as well as edible roots, nuts and fruits bundled in animal skins that serve as rudimentary bags. Their feet covered with the thicker parts of the same animal skins are strapped to their lower legs using the tendons of their kills in traditional Neanderthal fashion. They plod northward.

Valtron spends the first day after Metander's return as well as the next in preparation. That evening, he, together with four of his lieutenants, approaches the steep pit that houses the two slave primitives. As each one lowers himself into the pit using vines tied into a nearby tree, the two captives race to the opposite end of the pit and hiss while cowering together. The first four men wait for the last man, Valtron, to get down. They know of the fierceness of primitive females. It requires that they stick together. They eye each female primitive with the thought of selecting the right one for the sacrifice. But first the five have another thought in mind.

The female primitives scatter in different directions. However, the group of men finally corner one, holding her down, not for a sacrifice selection but to satisfy their sexual yearnings. Three of the five take their turn with the unwilling primitive as she screeches, kicks and attempts to bite her adversaries to no avail. Having sated their urges, the group releases their prey and corners the other female after a second chase around the pit. This time the two unsatisfied restrainers of the first rape are the first to release their sexual tensions followed by Valtron who wants to attain a second round of pleasure. Laughing at their game, all five agree to sacrifice the second female primitive to ensure success in vanquishing others of her kind. They tie her tightly with vines and hoist her out of the pit then tie her to the trunk of a dead tree which has only one remaining branch.

The next morning, Valtron and twenty warriors are seated around a roaring fire fueled by the scarce amounts of wood available in the mostly tundra landscape and also by mammoth dung and ivory. They are prepared for two sacrifices this morning. The first sacrifice is that of a mighty and robust Yurok to give the warriors strength for the raid and to supply food on their quest. The second will be the female primitive as an image and symbol of their quarry as well as to gain the approval of the gods who rule the natural world.

The tethered Yurok is slaughtered matter-of-factly with a vicious club to the head. Next, the warriors cut open the beast and chunks of raw meat chopped from the shoulders and hind quarters with their own more advanced handheld stone axes. Each warrior grabs chunks of flesh. As each warrior eagerly chew and swallow large bites of the raw red meat, none are aware of the lumpy tumor like growths lodged in the neck of the dead animal. Even if they did notice, they would not know of the long-term consequences whether good or bad for their species.

After the feasting, the tied female primitive is next. Without remorse or sympathy, Valtron slices into her neck with a stone hand-knife, much sharper than a modern hunter would dream possible. The effort not quite but almost decapitates her. The blood pouring out of her severed carotid arteries and jugular veins initially spurts out as from a faucet then slows to a continual flow. The warriors scoop up handfuls from the pools of blood and drink as their tradition demands. With this, Valtron's recites their belief: "The blood of this primitive will guide us to the primitive's lair were we will slay them." Loud yelps of approval and the raising of spears follow his shout. The mood of his troops is now set. They are finally ready.

Valtron inspects each of his warriors as they leave their encampment. They follow Metander who knows where to pick up the trail leading to the primitive's cave. Although he is pleased to see their weapons and also their faces painted for battle and necklaces adorned with talons, claws and animal teeth enhancing their warrior image, he notes that eight have the red dots and red skin growths on their face and arms like Blandeshar had. He thinks to himself, *These warriors seem strong, they should not weaken in the battle to come*. He thinks further. *Blandeshar didn't weaken*. He cannot rationalize it further and proceeds to catch up with Metander to lead his band.

The two-and-a-half-day delay by Valtron's band gave Turok's clan the head start it needed. It also took Valtron's band almost an additional half-day for Metander to lead them to the site of the Caribou kill. There they found little if any remains of Blandeshar or his fallen team member. All had been scavenged except for three skulls, one missing the lower jaw and one with a caribou antler curiously protruding from the right eye socket. Another half-day was needed for Valtron's band to follow Turok's tracks to the now abandoned cave.

After three and a half days, Turok and his clan reach the steppes of the glacier-covered mountain. Although he is reluctant to scale the glacier, he knows both the cold and the view from above will give them an advantage over the "others" that will surely follow. He also knows he must find an accommodating cave for warmth, a shelter for his clan who are weak and tired. Even he feels a strange and never before realized weakness. He is worried about the small red dots he can now see on the skin of his arms between the scattered hairs. He wonders if red dots are on his face like they are on the faces of several of his clan members. A moment of complex thought flickers for an instant in the Neanderthal brain that otherwise focuses only on basic needs.

"What are these red dots? Did they come from the others he killed days ago? Why do they take away our strength?" That is the sum of introspective thought Turok can muster. He pushes his weakened clan up into the glacier-covered mountains.

CHAPTER 4

The Raid That Wasn't

Ten days have passed since the caribou kill. Turok's clan is holed up in a cave alongside the glacier. It is spacious enough for his entire clan and is surrounded by the ice and snow of the glacier. It also has a direct view to the south where Turok sees Valtron's raiding party approaching. The strategic location would normally comfort Turok, but he, as well as at least half of his clan, is weak and sick from the red-dot disease. Turok has lost weight. His big forehead burns with a heated fire. At times, he is dizzy. He surveys his clan gathered in the dimly lit cave where only a single fire burns. Some of his clan with the red-dots cannot stand up. They lie against a wall of the cave or some supporting rock in the middle. Turok would do the same except that he is their leader. He must show strength. He must stand. He must endure. He must lead them into the battle that is sure to come.

Valtron's men, thoroughly tired from a long trek that included often stopping to warm themselves up over a hastily built fire, are in much better condition. His troops with red-dots show only minor ill effects except for the red dots themselves, albeit now scattered on the faces of a few more. Valtron sees the trail of Turok's clan in the snow leading up to an opening in a rock face. The glow of a flickering fire pit above can be made out, confirming the location of the primitives. Valtron orders his men to build a shelter in the remaining two hours of daylight. He plans to follow the primitive's trail up the mountain tomorrow, avenge the death of Blandeshar and return the conquering hero. He thinks this will please the elders and the Shaman and place him in line to one day become the Chief of his tribe. With little natural resources in the tundra landscape, Valtron's men are only able to build a rudimentary lean-to out of rocks and the local grass to shield them from the wind. They huddle together under every animal skin they have brought and brace themselves for the cold night of the changing seasons.

The anticipation of the brutal, freezing darkness was realized and much more as a Northwester storm blew in pelting both groups first with freezing rain then with a massive blizzard-driven snow. The next morning finds Turok's cave opening sporting a five-foot snow drift with a blinding snowstorm adding to it and starting to even fill the inside of the cave. Valtron's band fared even worse. They are now covered with two feet of snow and are chilled to the bone. Maintaining a warming fire proves impossible and they are boxed in by the driving blizzard.

The storm lasts throughout the day and all through the night. By morning both groups can barely dig out to see that the snow continues, but at a reduced rate. Turok's clan is even weaker than before the storm as the red-dot disease overtook most and their food supply is exhausted. They sense their entrapment and possible doom.

Valtron senses something different. He senses a break in the storm, a chance at conquest and glory, as well as the opportunities it will bring him. Now is the time. He hurries his band to dig out and follow him up the snow covered tracks of Turok's clan.

Ignoring the cold and slugging through the three feet of snow, Valtron's men are more than ready for a conflict. Their pent-up boredom, their anger, their inherent hatred of the primitives rises to a peak. The band shouts war hoops louder and louder as they scale closer to the cave opening above.

Turok's himself and the few remaining clan members well enough to respond do so with war hoops and loud screeches of their own. They begin throwing many of the numerous rocks they stockpiled in the previous days. They roll a few boulders down as well. The combination of the war hoops, rocks, and boulders loosens the snow below Turok's cave creating an avalanche of not only the new fallen snow but also portions of the glacier. The combination of snow and ice crash down mercilessly on Valtron and his men. Some are physically crushed, while others are suffocated by more than twenty feet of snow and ice that descends upon them with a thunderous and echoing roar. Soon, Valtron and his raiding party is no more. Silence befalls the mountainside as the last echoes of the thundering avalanche finally subsides. It takes the ever- weakening Turok and the few tribe members left, many with emerging red dots, some time to understand what has happened.

They look at each other curiously and then look down the mountain slope. There are no rocks or grass. There is only snow and ice. The others are no more. Turok musters his strength to grunt and screech out the joyous news, a tragic mistake. As his remaining clan joins in his screeches, howls and stomping of feet, the ruckus triggers a second avalanche. This time, the massive snow pack piled above their cave lets loose. A thundering flow of snow rains down on them covering the cave mouth and filling the cave itself. Like Valtron's tribal band, the Neanderthal clan is entombed in a frozen grave. The clan has perished. Twenty-five thousand years ago, the ice age is still on its ascendance. Years, decades, centuries, and millennia pile more snow and ice on their frozen graves. When this most recent of our planet's five ice ages ends, 12,500 years ago, the thick ice cover and its altitude will continue to keep their buried secrets. These secrets will be a revelation to 21st-century anthropologists. At the same time, these same secrets will threaten the very survival of the species naturally selected to reign supreme over the earth.

CHAPTER 5

The Proclamation

General Diego de Almagro mounts his stately black stallion and rides out to greet and meet his old friend and territorial Governor Francisco Pizarro. For General de Almagro, it is a downhill trot of about a mile from his own encampment atop a rise before the majestic Andes mountain range begins to spread east in what today would be called Cusco, Peru. General de Almagro is a burly 50-something experienced soldier with a short reddish brown beard and a weathered complexion. He meets his old friend and together they ride ceremoniously back up the dirt road which is now flanked by the General's soldiers and accompanying staff of cooks, maids, weapons managers and managers tasked with the care of his bulldogs known as "War Dogs," as well as the several Spanish Mastiff's used as guard dogs. The triumphant procession of two is trailed by ten of the Governor's accompanying bodyguards. General de Almagro, dressed in his leather breast plates and iconic conquistador metal helmet known as a Morin, gives stark contrast to Governor Pizarro dressed in a regal red cape and adorned with a black silk hat from which two short white ostrich feathers emerge over his right ear. With his more slender body and his thick black mustache and a neatly trimmed protruding thick black 10-inch beard, he is the picture of Spanish authority and represents the royalty who commissioned him to conquer the Inca Empire.

As they stride between the rows of admiring soldiers who would have taken pictures of them if only cameras had been invented. Pizarro notices to his left a small pyramid of bodies stacked and another pile of bodies aflame and watched over by guards. He is all too familiar with the cleanup needed in the wake of a major battle.

Arriving at the summit, Francisco Pizarro stops in front of a small stone building hastily erected for the governor in the past week after the battle. He turns his stately black Stallion around to face the soldiers, managers and dogs who followed the procession up the hill. "By the authority of King Phillip II, I claim this land for the glory of Spain this day October 22 in the year of our Lord one thousand five hundred and thirty-six." Amidst cheers from the small crowd, Pizarro plants a long metal staff into the ground that bears the flag festooned with the bold red and white cross of the Spanish Empire.

Pizarro settles into the building and sits behind a stone table using a chair brought with him from his headquarters in what would be in present-day Lima, Peru. General de Almagro sits on a stone seat to his right facing the governor.

"Diego, you have done well again. What is your report?"

Diego de Almagro relates the customary battle report: "We killed over 2,000 of the savages and captured their Chief. He goes by the name of Atahualpa and continues to be uncooperative. However, we are working on that. We have sequestered the women and children in separate pens from the remaining men of their tribe, mostly old men. Some of their warriors escaped to the east into the mountains. We gather from some of the survivors that there is a large mountain fortress there, possibly with some religious significance. They call it Machu Picchu, meaning 'Old Mountain.' Should I go after them to complete our mission?"

"No, not at all," Pizarro replies. "Our mission is almost complete. The Queen herself sent us, not to conquer these savages, but rather to conquer the land for its gold and silver. You fought against our enemies in France and England, so you know that our country needs new ships, new weapons and more soldiers. The riches of this new world will allow our country to overtake our enemies and dominate Europe. In doing so, we will keep a tidy sum for ourselves, right Diego?"

Both let out a short but all-knowing laugh.

"By the way, what is your troop strength?"

"Governor, we remain strong," Diego answers. "Lost only fourteen in the battle. We have an infirmary with twenty-two incapacitated with diarrhea and another thirty with the pesky red skin sores and nodules. Most of those will be able to go back to duty in a week to ten days. That will leave us with a Garrison of nearly seven hundred. We brought donkeys to carry the gold and silver to your headquarters then North to Cartagena on the north coast and on to our ships bound for Spain. We also brought cattle, pigs and chickens that, together with the local game and the abundant fruits and vegetables, will sustain us indefinitely."

Pizarro smiles. He knows that Diego is not only a tough soldier and a clever tactician but also one who knows the logistical requirements and details beyond fighting battles that is critical when conducting a campaign in a foreign land. His only comment on Diego's report: "You brought those straggly cattle all the way from Spain to here?"

"Diego, keep the captives under control," he continues. "We will need the women to cook and do chores. We will need the men to teach your soldiers how to cultivate the land. If they don't cooperate, chop off their heads as a sign to the others. They'll cooperate after a few heads roll. We will be here for a while. I'll be sending for our excavators and diggers to extricate the gold and silver from these mountains. They will arrive next month. But excavation and mining takes time. For now, we will need to find where these savages have hidden the treasure of El Dorado. Bring their Chief to me now."

A half-hour later, two guards bring Chief Atahualpa through the opening of the small stone building to stand in front of Pizarro. He doesn't resist and shows no fear, staring straight ahead not looking at his capturer but seemingly beyond him. Pizarro smiles as he scrutinizes the man, who is his own general height and who wears a gold helmet lined with bright red feathers, a patch work fabric vest, a gold necklace holding a large gold amulet and forearm plates made of silver. Surely riches such as this must be strewn throughout his empire, Pizarro thinks. He also thinks that he is somewhat young to be a chief but is obviously a strong specimen projecting a stately appearance of authority. Pizarro immediately tries to interrogate him with no response. Is it that he doesn't understand Spanish or is he playing dumb? Pizarro cannot decide and gives up for now. He will focus on the immediate riches of gold and silver at the Sun Temple across the field from his new headquarters.

CHAPTER 6

The Breakdown – The Escape

Atahualpa's followers mimic his passive resistance approach. The women go about the chores required of them but do little else. The few remaining men till the fields under the watchful eye of the guards and do not attempt escape. This seemingly peaceful acceptance of their captors goes on for a full month as they watch their sacred sun temple being dismantled and hauled away by caravans of donkeys. However, the mingling of the conquistadors with their captives, which includes several beatings and several sexual excursions into the compound pens holding the younger women, begins to break the peaceful acceptance attitude. The captive women and a few of the older men begin to show open resistance.

More concerning to General de Almagro is that fewer of them are able to work due to weakness and fever. Many have developed the red sores and red nodules that had not been noted in any of the savages before. The red dots and nodules are similar to but more numerous than those of his soldiers. As days pass, the astute General notices that the captives seem to be affected worse than his soldiers. At first, he concludes that they must be faking but when six of them die he becomes concerned and reports his observations to Pizarro.

"Governor Pizarro, many of our captives have been stricken by the red sores and some have died," he says. "I am losing most of my work force. We may need to remove some from work details at the Sun Temple to till the fields and do camp chores."

The news hits Pizarro hard. He was sent by the Queen directly to produce gold, silver and other riches for the crown. His reputation and possible ascendency to royalty are at stake. He decides to up the ante. He brings Atahualpa in for the tenth time in a month. However, he now notices red sores on the face and arms of the Chief that he hadn't noticed before. He also notices that the Chief seems to have lost weight. Nevertheless, Atahualpa stands as stoic as before. Then out of either frustration or anger or both, Pizarro rips off the gold chain, and silver wrist braces then screams profanities into the face of the Chief as he yanks off his feathered gold helmet.

"I don't care whether you can understand me or not, you're going to tell me where the treasure of El Dorado is or I am going to behead one of your tribe for every day you don't."

With that, he tells Diego to bring in one of the women with red sores. In a few minutes, the General presents a short, brown-skinned woman in her mid-twenties. Wide-eyed with smooth facial skin, other than a few red sores she just developed that day, the girl presents the picture of young Inca womanhood. She and her Chief have no idea what is about to happen.

Angrily Pizarro holds up the gold necklaces and shouts, "Donde esta el tesoro de El Dorado?" in the Spanish neither understands.

When he gets no answer, he unsheathes his sword and, with his two hands and his full strength, he brings it down on the girl's neck with a sickening thud, severing her head and creating fountains of blood that spurts out of the fallen corps. Atahualpa's stoic stare disappears into a helpless sympathetic acceptance. He crouches down at the fallen corpse and looks up at Pizarro in astonishment. He realizes quickly that he has no choice. He has known all along of the conquistadors' thirst for the very same metal his tribe has worshipped for the past thousand years. This knowledge and tradition has been handed down to him by his father and his father before him and his father before him through the ages. He also knows Pizarro will continue to kill his people until he gives him want he wants. However, Atahualpa's dilemma is that there is no treasure of El Dorado. He knows that it is just a myth circulated by the Spanish soldiers who have taken his land. Atahualpa knows of other smaller sun temples scattered throughout the Inca Empire. As he stands by the now blood-drained corpse of one of his tribe, he uses gestures pointing to the west toward the Pacific Ocean then pointing to his gold chain and silver wrist bands held now by Pizarro then holding up three fingers to indicate the days to travel to get there. Between those gestures and what Diego de Almagro has learned of the language of the Incas, he tells Pizarro that riches of great proportions are within a temple close to the ocean three days away.

"Governor, I will take the Chief and five of my best men. We will find El Dorado."

A satisfied smile flickers across Pizarro's face. He thinks to himself, *I have broken the Chief's will. My best and most trusted General will find the great treasure of El Dorado. We will both return to Spain rich and will finally become vice royalty of the crown.*

That night, Atahualpa tells his six most trusted lieutenants that he will lead the General to the small shrine near the coast, one with only a small amount of gold and silver and one which serves only a small part of his kingdom. Atahualpa knows that the General will be disappointed and extract his revenge on him. He knows he will be killed and accepts his fate to enter the afterworld of the sun god. He instructs one special lieutenant to go ahead of them to warn the followers at this shrine and escape into the jungle. He chooses his closest lieutenant and bodyguard, Thupa. Atahualpa next instructs the other three to seek the right moment and take all who can run east to the old mountain fortress called Machu Picchu. With the General gone and a dark night with no moon in three days, his troops are not likely to follow the men into a land strange to them. They will be safe there. The remaining two will accompany Atahualpa to what they realize and gladly accept as a death mission.

The caravan consisting of General De Almagro and five of his men along with Chief Atahualpa and two of his own selected men leave the encampment at Cusco astride donkeys. Donkeys as compared to horses are far better suited to negotiate the rocky terrain of the Cusco area down toward the flatter and sandier area of the coastal Pacific basin, the anticipated location of El Dorado in the General's mind. Chief Atahualpa looks nothing like a regal chief as he rides tied to a donkey, stripped of his gold helmet, necklace, silver forearm plates and feathers. The only remaining hint of his stature is the patch-like fabric vest with a pattern only that a chief would wear, a reality unknown and unimportant to the General.

Indeed, the caravan takes three full days to reach the Pacific coast area, slowed progressively by the increasing heat and humidity that oppresses the men as they descended several thousand feet to the Pacific coast basin. They camp just one half-day distant. The cool of the night is a welcome relief from the stifling heat and humidity as well as the buzzing of insects that plagued the group once they left the altitude of the mountains.

In one corner of the camp, close to the small central fire that cooked the beef they brought along, General De Almagro and his men are savoring their meal. Opposite them, at a distance from the central fire but still within eye sight of the Spaniards sits, Chief Atahualpa and his two men with their legs tied together but with their hands free to eat the bananas, roots (known later as potatoes) and other fruits and nuts that they brought along. Inca tribes refused to eat the foreigner's meat. It was not natural to their land and tasted bad compared to their usual diets derived from the blessings of the gods to their native land.

General De Almagro is in a state of great anticipation but nevertheless methodically instructs his soldiers on the specifics of tomorrow's events. He reminds them that he and one other will take only a few samples of the treasure back to Governor Pizarro to prove they have found El Dorado. The others will remain at the site to guard the treasure. He appoints his most trusted soldier Jesus Gomez to lead the group.

"What are we to do with the Chief and his two men?" Gomez asks.

"Don't worry about them, Jesus. After tomorrow, they will be no more," the commander responds.

All five break out in all knowing laughter heard but not understood by Chief Atahualpa and his two men on the other side of the fire pit. Chief Atahualpa is somber yet businesslike and stoic once again. He tells his men that he will likely perish at the hands of their captors when they discover that the outpost temple is not El Dorado. He instructs them to run onto the sand of the beach and even into its waters if necessary. Their captors with their heavy boots, breastplates, and helmets will not be able to follow on the soft sand or in the water. They will be safe. He asks them to leave his body to nature rather than the resin embedding and entombment usually required for a Chief so that his spirit, looking as he had appeared in the kingdom, may ascent to join the gods.

The next morning breaks with the General's men untying their Inca captives, except Chief Atahualpa, so that they can hack through the dense coastal forest and lead them to the Shrine of El Dorado. As they do, Chief Atahualpa smiles knowing that his men will be able to escape along the beach running barefoot as they are accustomed once they get to the outpost sun temple.

The caravan arrives just as the sun is high in the sky. General De Almagro is at first surprised that the great shrine of El Dorado is so small and curiously resembles the one already completely looted at Francisco Pizarro's Cusco encampment. The seasoned General immediately becomes suspicious and orders his men to enter the temple. When they emerge to report that there is even less gold and silver there than the one that they left in the mountains, an angered General De Almagro turns to the Chief. As a knowing smile spreads over the Chief's face, the General realizes that he has been tricked and instantly exacts his revenge by running his sword through the chest of the Chief Atahualpa. The Chief's last gurgling and blood spattered words in his own language trigger his two lieutenants to speed down the beach toward the south. Just as the chief predicted, the heavily clothed and armor laden soldiers are unable to follow and get only a few yards down the beach before they give up.

Sensing a more intricate deception, the General calls his men back.

"We need to get back to headquarters immediately. I suspect an escape plan of those remaining. Let those two natives go. They are of no concern to us now and let the Chief rot right here by his temple. Quickly, take whatever gold and silver you can. We will be leaving soon."

Within half an hour, General De Almagro's men have taken the little gold and silver stored at the outpost sun temple and are on their way back to Pizarro's headquarters. It will take another three-day journey on the backs of the donkeys.

An hour later, Thupa, the man Chief Atahualpa sent ahead to warn the locals, peers through the overgrowth at the edge of the beach toward the outpost sun temple. He sees that Atahualpa's men are gone but, more important to his task, confirms that the General De Almagro and his men are gone. He also sees the lifeless body of his chief lying at the temple steps and cautiously approaches. He kneels down next to the body and slowly looks around in all directions.

Once he is convinced that the Spaniards are really gone, he looks down at his fallen chief. He kneels and places a hand on his patch worked vest, now soaked in blood. Tears well up in Thupa's eyes but before emotion overcomes him, he remembers the duty he must perform and the deeper reason he was sent ahead.

Thupa is the caretaker of the royalty and the appointed Deener in anticipation of a chief's death. He respectfully rolls Atahualpa's body onto a mat made of banana leaves and drags the corpse into the outpost sun temple, the resting place chosen by Chief Atahualpa a decade earlier. Thupa opens a trap door in the floor of the temple, one that went unnoticed by General De Almagro's hurried men looking only for booty. There in the storage place are the fabric wraps and clay pots containing the resin not to embalm the body but to seal it. He wraps the body in three resin-soaked cloths and then layers fresh resin over the covering again and again as each new layer dries.

Thupa works well into the next morning before he utters the final ceremony of prayer he has memorized and uses it to introduce Chief Atahualpa to the Sun God and afterlife. He then lowers him into the crypt below the trap door. Thupa completes his solemn duty by going outside to the sun temple and taking a large heavy tree limb in both hands. He uses it like a hammer to knock out the hidden wooden dowels that support the building and then stands back as the four walls collapse inward and the ceiling falls straight down in a manner so precise that it could rival today's dynamite implosions of city skyscrapers. There is little left remaining other than a heap of rubble and a dust cloud. Thupa walks away, heading back to his captured village.

CHAPTER 7

General De Almagro's Second Surprise

General De Almagro and his five lieutenants arrive well ahead of Thupa but it has taken them four days to ascend to the mountain encampment of Francisco Pizarro. Gone now one full week, he finds an angered and impatient territorial Governor.

"General, your guards have been lax," the man lambastes him. "Soon after you left, all the natives that were not too sick to walk escaped. Some of the sick ones have died but we managed to find out that all of the others were heading west to their mountain fortress they call Machu Picchu."

"My Governor, I must tell you even more bad news," Almagro responds. "The shrine of El Dorado was a hoax, there was only one satchel worth of gold and silver. That bastard of a chief tricked us."

"Well, bring him to me. I'll make him pay for his deception."

"I already did, Governor. His body now lays there rotting in the same sun he worshiped so dearly."

"You fool. Don't you think that all this deception allowing his people to escape to this Machu Picchu fortress was to lead us away from El Dorado? Machu Picchu is where we will find the treasure of El Dorado. How are we to find it without the chief?"

"Do not be concerned, my Governor. We will follow their trail to El Dorado. These natives may be clever but they cannot hide the trail left by over a hundred of them. I will assemble one hundred of my most fit and loyal troops to find this mountain fortress, slay those who escaped and bring back some of the treasure of El Dorado to prove it."

"Do not fail me, my old friend." These are the last words heard by the angry, revenge-minded General as he bolts out the door to start his mission.

As he expected, the General has no trouble finding the beaten down path leading out of the compound to the east. However, he and his troops find the rugged terrain and continued thinning of the air arduous. Their pace is slowed by the need to take periodic rest breaks. They also feel the need to shed some of their armor and weaponry to lighten their load as they transgress the 60-mile journey. This concerns the General, who now fears that his weakened troops with less weaponry may not be able to take the fortress. He is also troubled by the positional disadvantage of an enemy at a higher elevation than his troops particularly since he does not know the troop strength of his adversary.

Another three-day journey finds General De Almagro and his weary troops at the base of Machu Picchu. He rests his troops for two days as he surveys the well-designed and expertly put together fortress. However, he observes no activity. He hears no sounds. He is wary. He thinks, *These natives are more clever and deceptive than they seem.* A lesson he just recently learned. Is this another trick? Are he and his men to be met by an avalanche of boulders raining down on them? Are he and his men to be met by a thousand spears cutting them to pieces?

General De Almagro constructs a battle plan for the unique situation he has encountered. He plans to split his troops into five regimens of twenty each, all ascending at the same time. He feels this will avoid any single catastrophic event as well as confuse the native inhabitants.

The fateful day arrives and the ascent begins. Cautiously each regiment scales the steep incline. Still no response from above: no sounds, no spears, no rocks. General De Almagro finds this quiet unnerving. He puts aside a momentary thought of turning back. He presses on. Still nothing. As he reaches the plateau, he only hears the echoing sounds of his own troops clamoring over the edge but his nostrils are met with the stench of rotting flesh. He surveys the ground and stair-stepped slopes ahead. Bodies and more bodies. Some bloated and discolored. Some open and partially eaten by vultures and condors. The General notices for the first time the birds circling above. But all the bodies have the red-dot disease. Did they all die of the red-dot disease, he ponders? He knows it affects some of his own men and he knows the natives are affected much worse but to have all of them die from it? He finds no answer.

Concerned that the rotting flesh from several hundred of the inhabitants may be a risk for disease to spread to his own troops as much as to quell the foul stench he orders the bodies to be gathered and burned.

While the several funerary fires burn the lifeless inhabitants of a once thriving city in the mountains into mere ashes that blow away in the wind, the General's men search for the elusive gold and silver stash of El Dorado. Of course, they find none and the General returns to Pizarro emptyhanded once again. He leaves the fortress of Machu Picchu desolate and isolated for future explorers to find and debate what happened to the occupants of the magnificent city high in the mountains. Many theories will be advanced but the real reason will be lost in time.

As far as General De Almagro's fate goes, history notes that due to his failures to find the Treasure of El Dorado, he was sentenced to death by Pizarro, a task carried out by the replacement appointed by Pizarro.

History further notes that Francisco Pizarro never made it back to Spain to assume the vice royalty he so dearly coveted. Instead, five years later, on June 26, 1541, at the age of 69, twenty armed soldiers led by the son of General De Almagro burst into his palace in Lima during a dinner amongst his relatives and friends. Despite fighting off his assailants and killing three of them with a sword pulled off the wall from behind his chair, he was finally overcome and stabbed in the throat. This ended his ruthless and murderous reign over the already vanquished Inca Empire. However, before he succumbed, he painted the sign of the cross in his own blood on the floor and proudly kissed it as the final exclamation point to the hypocrisy of Spain's conquering the New World.

CHAPTER 8

RECORDED HISTORY'S FIRST BIOLOGIC WARFARE

"Captain Trent, there has been yet another attack on one of our settlements. Five families, including four men and two women, are dead. The heathens took three of the wives and two of their daughters captive. We found one man alive and two young boys hiding in a brush pile. The man is in pretty bad shape. The boys are seven and nine. They're all right. I have them in the dining hall. Captain they scalped all the dead ones and burnt their cabins. It was the smoke from the burning cabins that drew our attention. When my troops got there, the savages ran off like cowards."

"What tribe is responsible for this disgraceful act?"

"That's just it, Captain. It seemed to be warriors from more than one tribe, mostly Delaware but I also recognized Seneca, Lenape and Huron."

"Lieutenant, they are not cowards. They're clever. They ran off because you outnumbered them. They don't fight unless they know they can win. Their strategy is to pick off small settlements and groups that I don't have the manpower or weaponry to protect."

Captain William Trent has command of the frontier fort called Fort Pitt. His troop strength is reduced and many are incapacitated from the latest outbreak of smallpox. His 240-troop strength has been reduced to only 192. Only two have died but forty-six are weak and are quarantined in the infirmary. It is the start of a hot summer during early June in what will later become the State of Pennsylvania. With his red vest unbuttoned and perspiration beading from his brow causing his sandy brown hair to become stuck to his forehead, he pens a plea to Britain's North American Commander-in-Chief, Jeffery Amherst.

"Baron Amherst, I am duty bound to inform you of a growing threat to the settlements in and about Fort Pitt. The heathen savages have grown increasingly murderous and I suspect their numbers are increasing. My troops continue to fall ill and although not fatal the smallpox renders them unfit for our defense. On behalf of our families, I beseech you to send additional troops lest I fear being overwhelmed by these savages sent from the devil himself."

Trent sends his most trusted enlistee Corporal Winston Agarn to courier his note at great speed to Commander Amherst and to wait for his written reply before returning. Corporal Agarn grew up with the Delaware tribe during a more peaceful time and knows their ways and their language. Although he sees the reasons for the Indian's bloody attacks and empathizes with their loss of land and the ravages of "White Man's Disease" on their numbers, he is nevertheless a soldier and a loyal British subject. He masterfully negotiates the two-way trip to Amherst's headquarters and back without being noticed by the several tribes now coming into the area.

Arriving back at Fort Pitt within three days, he hands the response from Amherst to the anxiously awaiting Trent. Trent tears open the wax sealed envelope bearing the seal of the Britain's North American Commander and begins to read the handwritten note within: "Cannot supply support, troops or materials. You will do well to try to inoculate the Indians by means of hospital blankets as well as to try every other method that can serve to extirpate this execrable race." It is signed: Jeffery Amherst.

The next day Captain Trent pays a visit to the infirmary. With a red cloth held to his mouth and nose to avoid the contagion, he reviews his stricken troops. Indeed, most all within the crowded and dimly lit infirmary are stricken with smallpox made worse by the stifling heat and crowded conditions so that the lone doctor assigned to the Fort cannot trace the origin of their fever. He sees the raised red nodules and numerous red dots located mostly on their faces. He sees some with open sores oozing a clear amber colored liquid. He just then recalls that the Indians call it the "running face sickness." He now knows why. However, he knows that most of his troops will slowly recover and with proper food, rations and water many will get back to duty. He also knows that the Indians lack the strength to fight smallpox and most die or never recover fully. He attributes this weakness to their lack of Christian beliefs. The words of Amherst now resonate in his mind. At first, hesitant due to his own Christian beliefs, he ultimately decides to follow Amherst's orders and rationalizes what will be later known as the first recorded act of biologic warfare as a necessary means of ridding the world of these devil savages.

Later that day, Trent sends corporal Agarn to relay a message to the Delaware Chief Maumaulette. The verbal message corporal Agarn relates is to meet at the center of the open field five kilometers from the Fort. The chief is to bring two warriors to match the number to that of the white man including Agarn and platoon commander Bristol. Chief Maumaulette trusts the young man he has known since youth and accepts the invitation with a return message that they will meet the next day when the sun is high in the sky.

Promptly, at around noon the next day, Chief Maumaulette and his two most senior warriors, turtleneck and Growling Bear, approach the three white men already waiting in the center of the open field devoid of brush and with only short grasses bending in the breezy mid-day sun. Despite the hot mid-June day, the Chief and his two warriors are clothed in animal skin leggings, their traditional moccasins and an ornate chevron patterned short-sleeved vests. Each has a single eagle's feather protruding upward from the back of his head affixed with a red headband contrasting against their raven black hair.

Chief Maumaulette is older than his two warriors. He is said to be the elder of his tribe but the number of his "seasons" is unknown. Nevertheless, he approaches with an air of dignity and stern purpose with a warrior on each side. As he approaches the three white men fully clothed in the official red vest and white pants of the British Army and adorned with the traditional British high-brimmed red cap not unlike today's baseball caps, the Chief notices a single horse-drawn cart behind them. At first, the chief is suspicious of a possible white man's trick but once he notices the small size of the cart and its contents of neatly folded blankets, he begins talking to Captain Trent in his own native Algonquian language. Corporal Agarn interprets sentence by sentence for Trent.

"Chief Maumaulette welcomes this chance for two leaders to meet in this place with the hope of avoiding further war and death. He warns that a great number of warriors from many tribes are gathering to attack the fort. He begs you to remove your people while there is still time. He pledges that they will not be harmed."

Captain Trent is taken aback by the directness of the Chief's warning but is not surprised by the announced threat. He has been aware of the growing number of Indians in the territory and the increasing boldness of the younger warriors. He looks into the eyes of the old Chief and sees the honesty of the warning and the sincerity of his offer to allow his people to leave unharmed. However, perhaps naïve or worse, too trusting, the Chief does not see the deceit and trickery on the rehearsed face of Captain Trent.

Captain Trent responds through Corporal Agarn who unwittingly contributes to the ruse by also believing in the sincerity of the words he is translating.

"It is with great reluctance but with the noble purpose to avoid the unnecessary deaths of your people and mine that I accept your offer. I ask you to instruct your warriors to allow us one full cycle of the moon to make necessary preparations to leave. For this grace, we offer you these blankets to warm your loved ones in the cold months yet to come and this special cloth as a token of our respect."

Somehow, Trent maintains a straight face of sincerity as the Chief and his warriors accept the gifts not knowing of their source from the beds of the smallpox victims who have the greatest number of open sores. Later that day, history notes the following entry in William Trent's journal at Fort Pitt: "Out of our regard to them, we gave them two blankets and a linen handkerchief out of the smallpox hospital. I hope it will have the desired effect."

Indeed, William Trent's hope was realized. The chief and his two warriors contracted smallpox directly from the blankets as did other Indians who unwittingly came into contact with those already infected. Without the inherent immunity to smallpox that existed in the European invaders, either protecting them altogether or lessening the severity, the smallpox epidemic cut through, not only the Delaware, Seneca, Lepane and Huron tribes in 1763, but the entire Indian nations in North and South America later. The massive gathering of Indians aimed at attacking Fort Pitt never occurred. An 80% death rate from smallpox devastated each tribe affecting men, women, and children. Needless to say, Trent never left Fort Pitt in 1763. By the 1890s, history recorded other devastating Native American depopulation statistics such as that of the Mexican Native Indians reduction from 25 million to three million in just the fifty years after Cortes' invasion. In Florida alone, the Native American population decreased from seven hundred thousand in 1520 to only two thousand by 1700, mostly due to smallpox.

CHAPTER 9

The Chance Meeting in the Sky

The first-class cabin on American Airlines flight 54 Miami to London finds Dr. Robert Merriweather and his fiancé Heather Bellaire settling in after the inflight meal, each with a glass of Pinot Noir in hand.

"Well, is this going to be the honeymoon before the honeymoon or are you going to find a bunch of your colleagues and work the entire week?"

"Not at all, Heather. After the British Medical Association Awards ceremony I am all yours. We will be typical tourists for a change. Buckingham Palace, the Big Ferris Wheel, the home of Charles Dickens and Big Ben. Remember, now, Big Ben is a clock, not a guy," Merriweather joked.

With that, Heather gives Robert a playful slap on the shoulder and a smile which he returns with a soft laugh and smile of his own.

As Robert and Heather review options for their after-the-ceremony mini vacation, a slender man of medium height dressed in khaki cargo pants and a pocketed khaki vest overlying a checkered shirt taps Robert who is sitting on the aisle seat on his left shoulder.

"Bobby Merriweather, it's really you?"

Dr. Merriweather looks up and in astonishment recognizes one of his best college friends from over thirty years ago.

"Ralph-Ralph Earlandson, I'll be damned. You look the same as when we last saw each other. As I remember, it was when you finished your doctorate in archeology at the University of Chicago and I just finished my

Dental School years at Northwestern. As broke as we were then, we celebrated at a Lou Malnnati's pizza place. Remember?"

"I remember it well, Bob. Say, I've read about you several times. You have become quite a well-known tumor surgeon and stem cell guy. I've read some glowing reports about you. I've also read about your confrontations with the corruption in the pharmaceutical industry. That's the Bob Merriweather I remember, always looking to expose lies and wrong doing."

"Ralph, you've done pretty well for yourself too. I read your latest article about the debate concerning the extinction of the Neanderthals. How you feel they were murdered off clan by clan over a 40,000-year period rather than being merely outcompeted by modern man or being absorbed by inter species mating. You see, I have read about you too. It is too bad that we fell out of contact. I am sure it's the demands of each of our professions. You know, I agree with you. The demise of the Neanderthals was probably the genocide from early humans. We only need to remember Hitler, Pol Pot, Stalin, Rwanda, Kosovo, the Vikings, Genghis Kahn, and the likes to remind us of our species inherent brutality."

Now, kneeling down in the aisle next to Merriweather, Ralph Earlandson responds.

"Bob, you sound just like me. This is like we are back at old Northwestern all over again."

"Well, I guess I should just accept being ignored," interjects Heather.

"Oh my gosh. I am so sorry. Ralph, this is my fiancé, Heather Bellaire. I worked for many years with Heather when she was the Chief Editor for the El Cid Medical Book Publishing Company. She's now a freelance science and medical writer. I sort of stole her away."

"Nice to meet you, Ms. Bellaire. You must be very good if you have been working with this guy. As I recall, he can be very demanding."

"Aha, you are right, Dr. Earlandson. In fact, we are heading to London to receive the British Medical Association's book of the year award for a pediatric head and neck pathology book Bob wrote with his coauthor Robert Greer, one that I edited. Both of those guys were picky and exacting of every detail. They drove me crazy at times, but I guess it paid off."

"Ralph, so now you know why Heather and I are heading to London. What were you doing in Miami and why are you now heading to London? The last I heard you were still at the University of Chicago."

"It is somewhat of a long story. Yes, I am still at U of C and am sponsored by the Field Museum for a dig in the Pyrenes Mountain glacier range in

Northeastern Spain. I stopped in Miami to pick up some gear and some specialized, extra-rugged photographic equipment. London is just a stop-off point where I will connect with two other archeologists. One is from the University of Madrid and the other from the Lycee Boudin University in Northern France. They are sharing the expenses and supplying the crew and an intimate knowledge of the Pyrenees glacier."

"Impressive, Ralph, but what is it all about?"

"Funny you should mention Neanderthals and modern man. It seems that two summers in a row of above-average temperatures and mild winters, perhaps aided by global warming, has resulted in a recession of the glacier and revealed some well-preserved tools of ancient man."

"Now, that is interesting. What are these tools?"

"That's just it. One is a six-foot hardwood spear with a perfectly honed stone spearhead precisely strapped to it. It's in perfect condition and is like those found at other sites. It is from modern man about 25,000 to 30,000 years ago."

Bob and Heather look at each other in genuine astonishment. They are wide-eyed and present a body language of wanting to hear more.

"Ralph, that's amazing. You mean to say that this spear is the real thing not a fossil and it is complete?"

"Indeed it is, but there's even more. A more crudely chipped hand axe and a foot covering of animal skin were also found. The exciting thing is that these items are definitely Neanderthal. This area and this glacier have other artifacts from both modern man and Neanderthals that can be dated to the same time period. That's the time period when Neanderthals were thought to be on the verge of extinction. I am hoping that this could be a battle site. Wouldn't that be something? Proof that our species brought a competing group to extinction by actual war, not friendly competitions or crossbreeding."

A little turbulence prompts the pilot to instruct all passengers to take their seats and put their seatbelts on. Robert and Ralph conclude their discussion and reunion of sorts with a promise to keep in touch. However, before returning to his seat Ralph asks for Heather's business card as well as Robert's.

"Ms. Bellaire, I am not much of a writer. Bob here pulled me through English literature classes back at Northwestern. May I contact you for help if I am asked to write another piece for *Discover* or *National Geographic*?"

"Certainly, I'd be glad to help. It is what I hope to be doing now that we're getting married."

As his old college friend takes his seat a couple of rows forward, Robert turns to Heather with a smile but says nothing. He thinks to himself, *Yes, it is the right decision to get remarried at 55*. Heather, the statuesque brunette ten years his junior and an accomplished professional writer, is ideally suited to him at this stage in his life. They have already been successful with several of Robert's textbooks and scientific articles but, more than the professional relationship, there is a profound friendship and genuine love and romance. Robert wonders why the guilt he felt and still somewhat lingers about the divorce from Veronica, his first wife, took so long to reconcile. He accepts that it was his fault, his focus on his surgeries and his research caused a neglected wife to finally want to let go. Until now, he reconciled the loss as best for Veronica, thinking that she deserved the chance to pursue her own passion for animal rescue. It was his dedication to his own work and his greater attention to their three sons that blinded him to their drifting apart. He vows to himself that it will not happen again. He smiles again at Heather.

Heather smiles back not realizing the thoughts that have raced through the mind of the man she loves.

Federico Civantos looks over his nine months of data collection from Machu Picchu. As professor of antiquities at the Universidad Central del Peru in Lima, Peru, he is dismayed at how little he learned and how little data he collected during his nine-month field trip. The short, burly, heavyset man with a short, full beard of dark but graying hair and similarly tinted hair combed straight back and overlying his ears ponders over his notes and the photographs strewn about the desk in his small but tidy office on the third floor. He stops for a minute and stares out his westward facing window as the early morning sun begins to reflect off the soccer field and small buildings below not completely shaded by his own building. He looks beyond them not looking for anything in particular but thinking that these past nine months were probably a waste.

Frustrated by the ever-present tourists at Machu Picchu, the need to conduct private tours to help finance his trip and the government's restrictions about digging and removing any artifacts, he has little to show for his efforts. He has some evidence that the magnificent structure was built around 1450 and also knows that it was not built by extraterrestrial aliens as too many of the obnoxious tourists believe and insist. Indeed, the materials and craftsmanship suggested local artisans of the pre-Colombian era, although highly skilled ones with a large manual workforce.

What happened to the estimated five thousand inhabitants remains the number-one mystery. No burial sites, no bones and no signs of warfare. The consensus among historians is that it was built as a palace for Inca Chief Pachacuti, and then abandoned later due to lack of interest. However, Professor Civantos thinks differently. Something occurred. No one would leave such a place. What happened to them? It was the most common question asked of the tourists. One he could not answer.

Poring over the photographs again looking for clues he might have missed, he doesn't see the faded charring on stones at various locations indicating a long-ago local fire. Had he noticed, he probably would have thought that it was caused by a cooking fire rather than its real purpose anyway. He is then interrupted by two of his graduate assistants who spent the two weeks after their post Machu Picchu field trip on vacation in the coastal city of Arequipa south of Lima. Pablo Hernandez and Enrique Colon almost simultaneously and excitedly blurt out.

"Professor, look at these photographs we took. Heavy rains and winds washed away some of the vegetation and soil off what was thought to be just a mound at the edge of the beach where the jungle ends."

Professor Civantos looks up at the two men, both in their mid-twenties and dressed casually in sneakers and jeans, one in a tan and the other in a blue short-sleeved shirt. Despite being displeased by the interruption of the more important task of deciphering the enigma of Machu Picchu, he humors the two and takes the photos in hand. Casually glancing over each of the three images, he is at first unimpressed. Then something catches his eye. A stone remnant of a building with some type of an image on it. He scrambles through two of his desk drawers to find a magnifying glass. Focusing on the small portion of the black-and-white photograph before him, he sees the image of a figure wearing a regal headdress and carved out wrist bracelets on arms holding a rod with radiations indicating light at its end. The figure is looking up at a rendition of the sun illustrated by equally spaced straight radiant beams carved into the stone. Civantos looks up at his two assistants.

"Pablo, Enrique, this was a sun temple, probably an outpost temple before the demise of the Inca empire. You have made a significant finding here."

"Professor, we think so too, but look at the third picture."

Curiosity and a mounting excitement overtakes the usually well-in-control professor. Once again, with the magnifying glass, he sees something he recognizes but does not quite believe. He sees a leftover and torn section of wrapping material, the kind he recognizes as what was used to bury nobility. His suspicions and even hopes are confirmed when he looks closer and sees a broken vase with hardened clumps of material on its edge. He recognizes the telltale look of resin.

Now, wide-eyed and energized, he looks straight at the two assistants and says, "You have found a sun temple. The wrapping material and the resin vase indicate that a noble person is likely buried there. It may be a Chief, members of a Chief's family or a special warrior. We must explore it and organize a complete excavation. You must tell me, where is this sun temple?"

"Professor, it is only fifty-five kilometers north of Arequipa. It is very reachable by all-terrain vehicles and Land Rovers if we travel along the shore."

"Indeed, I will get the necessary university and government clearance. You get our equipment and at least ten laborers to Arequipa. We will set out from there in one month."

The die is now cast. Two excavations that will reverberate through the world are about to start six thousand miles apart. Both have well-meaning intentions and great expectations of answering the mysteries of the past, but at what cost?

CHAPTER 10

THE FIRST EXPEDITION

Federico Civantos expedition gets off quicker than that of Ralph Earlandson, due in part to the close proximity of Lima and Arequipa to the site, the favorable terrain and the abundance of laborers eager to work. By contrast, Professor Earlandson's expedition is delayed by two annoying misfortunes. First, cargo dispatchers have misdirected his gear (including mountain hiking gear; waterproof, heavy-duty tents; and ice-excavating equipment and simple chainsaws) to Finland. This, despite clear instructions pointing to Madrid, including the stickers on the crates that read "For use on the Pyrenees Glacier." However, the geographically challenged dispatcher was unaware that a glacier actually exists in the mountain range separating Spain and France. Aware only of glaciers that exist in Scandinavian countries, Greenland, and Russia, the clerk sent the crates 2,000 miles away from their intended destination.

Further annoying the usually mild-tempered Earlandson is that his French counterpart Jacque Rousseau texted him that his group could not join them for three weeks. It seems that he and most of his group did not want to miss the upcoming Crepe's Festival in Paris.

"My God. It is mid-August. We need to get started ASAP or else we will be delayed into next May. We will be forced off the mountain by November first, if not sooner."

Earlandson's frustration mounts.

"We have an opportunity to uncover the greatest archeological find in history and we are blocked by some ass-clown who doesn't know Madrid is in Spain and so we sit twiddling our thumbs. And, of course, the French, as usual, are focused more on food and festivals than an important scientific finding. Louis Pasteur would roll over in his grave if he knew of this."

Seeing the frustration boiling over in his mentor, John Marshall, his understudy and veteran of several archeological digs involving prehistoric man, breaks the ice

"Well, we can hope the French bring their chef. At least we will all eat gourmet."

The professor falls silent, as does everyone else. As all look straight at Professor Earlandson, they see his frown of frustration slowly turn into a smile and a spittle-spraying laugh of acceptance to endure these delays without further angst. All join him in boisterous laughter.

By the time the Earlandson expeditions finally collect all the required gear and manpower in Madrid to begin its move to the second level of staging in the town of Ordino at the base of the Pyrenees glacier, the Civantos expedition has already begun its excavation.

Although the Earlandson expedition hurries up to the glacier to begin and, hopefully make some important finds before winter sets in, Civantos has no such concerns. He is close to the equator. It is always warm, even hot, requiring a four-hour siesta break in midafternoon.

It is mid-September and Civantos' crew has already set up a 50-foot-by-50-foot grid of strings supported by ten-foot posts over the temple site ruin. To the casual observer, it would seem to be nothing more than a small mound of dirt. The large square is further sectioned off by strings placed one foot apart to create 2,500 one-foot squares. This grid is photographed by a camera that has been suspended by wires from adjacent trees and two posts placed into the ground by the laborers. The camera is positioned in the center of the square and will photograph each artifact as it is removed. By coordinating each find to a designated one-foot square, the workers will be able to create later a two-dimensional reconstruction of the original position of each artifact. This is the standard archeological "dig protocol" dutifully followed by Civantos. However, it takes all of his patience to resist just tearing into the mound so he can search for what he knows to be within: the mummified body of an Inca nobleman. He is not even thinking of the possible riches in the ruins, but Pablo and Enrique are.

In less than one week, the dirt and foliage cover that accumulated over the past 486 years have been removed, as have the stones and pillars that once formed the roof and walls. Six of Civantos' men are needed to remove the cover stone of the crypt in the center of the old temple. Civantos uses the camera remote to snap the required pictures he hopes will capture his greatest find. Civantos looks down into the crypt three feet below him. The dust plume kicked up by his men as they removed the cover stone finally settles. Before him is a well-preserved figure. A man fully clothed. He stands back and uses the remote to snap several more pictures in a burst mode. He peers into the depths again. The semi-opaque resin obscures details but he can make out that there is a figure within. It is without the head ornament or wrist plates indicating nobility. The figure looks like an ordinary Inca native from the 1520-1550 era. It's still a great find but not the one he had hoped it to be. Then Civantos looks again. He sees the vest, the ornate checkered pattern vest. Only Inca Chiefs were allowed to wear it. It was considered a uniform of sorts and demanded respect for anyone who wore it. Civantos excitement and anticipation returns. He instructs his laborers and also Pablo and Enrique to carefully remove five cm of dirt under the resin-encased corpse in a right to left pattern to create eight parallel trenches under the body. He then asks Pablo and Enrique specifically to insert wires through each trench under the body. He then gives them long wide cloth strips to attach to the wires. He instructs them to draw the wires slowly and steadily under the body to pull the string cloth strips through the trenches and then detach the wires. Pablo and Enrique are amazed. In all of their graduate studies, they have never seen such a field technique to hoist a fragile mummified body out of a crypt. Each now gets a closer look at their prize. Through the haze of the semi-opaque resin, they look eagerly for the expected silver wrist plates, gold chains and gold head ornaments.

To their great disappointment, they see none. They gently place the resin/corpse composite they just lifted from the crypt onto a waiting foam-rubber lined cot.

Civantos now gets a chance to examine the body more closely. He observes that the resin is thinnest in the areas of the chest and of the face where prominent contours exist such as the nose and forehead ridges. He notices the Chief's vest is stained with a purple color in a billowing pattern that today's forensic pathologists would immediately recognize as a blood flow from a sharp object. Civantos does not recognize the pattern and moves on to the nose and forehead ridge. There the resin is thin and clearer. He notes the red-purple nodules and sores on both the nose and forehead skin, but he does not recognize them as smallpox sores that would immediately make a trained forensic pathologist suspicious and concerned. Instead, Civantos shows his observations to Pablo and Enrique. They too do not recognize each observation for what they actually are. Instead, they conclude that the person must have died from old age like most chiefs and the sores were from insect bites. They point to several welts on their own skin and relate the constant swatting of insects by all in their camp that has become commonplace in the past few weeks. Civantos accepts their theory for now and begins to make plans to relocate his prize back to his lab in Lima. But first, he must complete the excavation of the ruins in which he hopes to find clues as to the identity of the mummified body and his place in the hierarchy in the Inca Empire.

CHAPTER 11

THE SECOND EXPEDITION

Enduring the delays puts the Earlandson expedition more than a month behind that of the Civantos expedition. It is October 2nd and his team is finally camped at the foot of the glacier, a good distance above and remote from the soon to open ski resorts. He has already dismissed the inclination to turn back and postpone the expedition to the following May. However, he is now pushed on with a sense of urgency knowing that he must bring back some evidence of a Neanderthal-Modern man confrontation before November 15th at the latest.

The local Spanish-speaking alpine hikers who found the original artifacts together with Dr. Marco Morales, Chairman of Archeology at the University of Madrid, and some of his crew, lead Earlandson to the site of their find. Ralph buttons the last button on his parka and dons a wool head cap rather than flipping the hood of his parka over his head. He wants to maintain as much peripheral vision as possible even though the breeze flowing down from the glacier is colder than at his base camp located two miles down the gradual slope. Although the breeze of a 40°F temperature brings the wind chill factor into the low-20s, Ralph welcomes it. He hopes it will blow away any loose snow or ultra-fine crushed rock produced by the force and weight of the glacier itself.

Taking charge as the expedition leader, he instructs Dr. Morales to have his men spread out and comb the ice around the original find. By combing the glacier, he means not only to have Dr. Morales' crew spread out but also to sweep and polish the ice surface to allow them to see any artifact encased within.

After several hours of combing, they have found only a variety of rocks and boulders within the glacier ice. Dr. Earlandson begins to suspect that the rocks were placed there purposefully. He is well aware that rocks and even huge multi-ton boulders are often carried miles by the slow advance of a glacier. But that is just it. These are not huge boulders. Most of the stones are the same size and the number and proximity of the stones suggested that they have been arranged rather than caught up naturally in a glacier. He thinks to himself. Emitting a small white cloud of breath into the cold air as he talks to himself he mutters, "This just may be a battlesight. The stones would be the likely weapons of Neanderthals." However, his voice is too soft for anyone other than himself to hear. "These rocks were placed here by someone. NO! NO! These were thrown here from above. They had to be."

Just as Ralph's epiphany sinks in to direct his gaze upward, he hears someone shouting in excited Spanish.

"Profesor Morales, ven aquí, apurase, encontramos algo."

Professor Morales quickly goes over to his graduate student, falling down twice in his haste despite the spiked boots specifically designed for walking on a glacier. Professor Morales shouts.

"Es una persona y una anza congelada en el hielo," which he quickly translates into English for Dr. Earlandson that there is a person frozen in the ice and that there is a spear lying next to him.

Earlandson and the entire crew, sixteen in all, gather about the site. At first, all are quiet as they observe the obscure but recognizable figure of a man fully clothed in heavy animal fur including a fur cap. They can make out some type of stitching on the headwear. The face is turned down and not visible but the spear is close to the surface with its details more visible. Ralph and Dr. Morales immediately recognize its fine point and sharp edge identifying the skilled knapping of modern man in the 20,000 to 30,000 B.C. era. The expert wedging of the sharp tip into the hard spear shaft and the detailed tying of the stone point to the spear shaft confirms the time period and the source from modern man (homosapiens).

The quiet ends with chatter amongst the workers and the sound of back slapping from the two professors embracing in a hug. Each tries to speak at the same time with Earlandson finally talking louder and even faster than the usually fast-speaking Spaniard.

"This is a perfectly preserved ancient human. The oldest non-fossilized specimen ever found, I'd guess. It is the find of the century! We must remove it en-block and keep it frozen for detailed studies. Don't you agree, Dr. Morales?"

"My friend, I certainly do agree. I am without words in your language or in mine. We must tag it for now and continue our research. We need to make plans on how to remove a section of the ice containing the person inside and move it to the freezer in our laboratory. We won't be able to study it up here next month when winter begins."

That night, the crew celebrates with "glacieritas," that is, margaritas chilled with glacier ice and, of course, salt. Even the French contingent forgoes their wine and downs the glacieritas as a celebratory party atmosphere pervades their tent camp. The more serious and contemplative Ralph Earlandson leaves the party atmosphere of the main tent and adjourns to his private tent, which is warmed nicely by a small propane heater.

Ralph puts together the findings of the day, the best day of his archeological career. However, his joy is tempered by the thoughts running through his mind. As an experienced archeologist of ancient man and his habitat, Ralph partially puts together the scene that unfolded between Turok and Valtron 25,000 years ago. Although he doesn't know the two leaders' names, he infers that the frozen modern man found today was not on a hunt. He was there for a battle. He can deduce that from the number of similarly sized rocks strewn around the body, which his fellow archeologist failed to understand were probably thrown from above. He knows he must go higher on the glacier. He must exert the additional effort and of course the increased cold and risk. He asks himself, "Am I right? Will there be artifacts up there? Is this the site of tribal warfare between two competing bands of modern man or will we discover Neanderthals up higher?"

After all, there were no spears or battle tools pointed down the slope, only up the slope at some adversary. And the rocks would be the likely weapon of a Neanderthal clan. Professor Earlandson continues to talk himself into believing he found a Neanderthal/modern man battleground. He drifts off to sleep to pictures of a great battle conjured in his imagination.

Over the next four days, Dr. Morales and his group set about using chainsaws and crowbars in an attempt to extricate their prize. At the same time, Dr. Earlandson and the French contingent have begun exploring the glacier area above, which has a thicker ice shield and several dangerous crevasses. They return emptyhanded.

The quiet ends with chatter amongst the workers in a mixture of French and English. They summon Professor Earlandson and Professor Rousseaux to an ice mound from which they have already removed the snow cover. Both Professors had been comparing ideas about where they are most likely to find another frozen artifact or, better yet, a whole person. Each trudges carefully along the slope toward the ice mound. Each feels the colder wind of this higher altitude and each registers concern about a possible cold front heading their way. The cold bites through their ski masks and even their fur parkas as they reach the ice mound. Both men try to speak at the same time with the crowd of six French workers huddled around the ice mound gesturing and excitedly chattering in French, which Earlandson only partly understands even though he speaks French fluently. The workers are speaking too fast and the howling of the cold wind permits only a few of their words to be heard. However, he senses a combination of excitement, curiosity and speculation from their tone. He and Professor Rousseau separate two of the workers and peer upon the object causing their excitement for the first time.

Earlandson removes his tinted ski glasses and is instantly confronted with the intense brightness of the sun and its reflection off the ice and snow, which belies the ever-decreasing temperature. It takes him and Jacque Rousseau each a full minute and a half to adjust their eyes. They are speechless and amazed at what they see. There before them they spot the shadowy form of a man fully clothed in animal skins. He is bent over so that his back and only one side of his turned head is visible through the clear blue glacier ice. The thickness of the ice is about eight inches, speculates Earlandson. The thickness of the ice obscures the details he seeks. However, he recognizes that the figure has a full black beard and long black hair but most important of all is that the figure is facing downward toward the site of the find of the original spear from modern man and of their own more recent find of a whole frozen member of the homosapien family. Cautiously, he ponders, "Is this too good to be true? Is my speculation that this is a battlesight with an adversary at this height reigning down those boulders and rocks I saw the other day?"

Earlandson's excitement grows as these thoughts and hopes race through his mind. He reaches for one of the ice shavers held by a French worker and proceeds to frantically scrape off ice as if preparing flavored shaved ice treats for some carnival. Over the next twenty minutes, the exhausted and heavily breathing Professor Earlandson has managed to shave off almost two inches of ice. Kneeling close to what seems to be the head of the entombed figure, Earlandson polishes the scrape marks smooth with his bulky fur-lined gloves. He peers intently at the head of the figure now slightly more visible than before. There it is. He sees it. It is the forehead, a big protruding forehead and eyebrows overlying what must be the thick bone underneath known as a supra-orbital ridge (a ridge of bone as the upper part of the eye socket). The figure is undoubtedly Neanderthal. This is more than Professor Earlandson could hope for. It is a likely a battlesight between two early species of man. He looks up at his counterpart Jacque Rousseau and asks him if he also interprets this figure as Neanderthal. Have they discovered the archeologic find of a lifetime, a battlesight between Neanderthals and homosapiens? Rousseau, excited as well, agrees and is about to begin a discussion on how to remove the ice block around the figure and down the glacier when both hear an echoing scream. It seems to come from about 200 feet below them and off to the right as they gaze down the mountain slope. The workers around the ice mound hurriedly but cautiously shuffle through the snow covering the ice of the glacier. Earlandson and Rousseau follow them using a similarly awkward gait toward the original scream which now has turned into repeated desperate cries for help echoing up from a large crevasse in the glacier. The group cautiously inches up to two other French workers tightly and expertly holding onto to a pole wedged in the ice, which has a rope stretched 10 feet across the snow then disappearing down the crevasse.

It seems that this group of three were looking for artifacts and frozen figures like everyone else. They were roped together using six-foot-long sharp pointed poles to test ahead for the very type of abyss that swallowed up the lead worker. The two workers were initially pulled toward the chasm themselves by the weight of their coworker as he plunged through the crevasse opening covered by a foot of snow. They only escaped certain death when the third in line thought and acted quickly enough to slam his pole as deeply into the glacier ice as he could and to dig his spiked boots in as well. It was apparently enough to stop the fall of the lead worker and to prevent the middle worker in the tandem from joining him. Now, the two are clinging to the pole with one hand and unsuccessfully trying to pull the lead worker up from his precarious position 50 feet down into the crevasse.

The experience of the French workers, who are actually an experienced mountain glacier team, takes root as they move to attach a rope with a buckle onto the belt of the worker third in line, who is still holding on to the now mobile pole. That pole is also slowly working itself loose and out of the ice. However, just before the head man of this team of eight can attach the buckle, the pole gives way. The weight of the dangling worker in the icy rift pulls the two on the surface toward the gaping cavern in the ice only slowed down by the digging of their spiked boots into the snow-covered glacier and then instinctively spreading their arms to create a meager resistance to the force pulling them and their dangling cohort to their doom. The chaos is punctuated by fearful screams from the three in peril echoing around the glacier and by shouts of concern and orders issued from the French glacier team. Quickly, the eight Frenchmen drop to the snow and crawl on their bellies quicker than one could imagine in a single file toward the belt of the third worker. They intend to have the lead man latch on to the buckle. The lead man finally stretches out to latch on to the elusive buckle. Each of the rescue team quickly digs in their spiked boots and one by one are able to stand. Now, with sufficient manpower and leverage, they begin pulling the stranded trio to safety. As the three are dragged along the surface and through the snow of the glacier, each can be seen praying and making the sign of the cross. When they are dragged sufficiently far from the mouth of the ice cavern and the rescue team had stopped pulling them, all three lay motionless looking up at the sky with blank stares. Their expressions quickly turn to exhausted gratitude amidst hugs and pats on the back from everyone, including Professor Rousseau and Earlandson.

Although the harrowing episode ends without a tragedy, it has confronted both Professors with the stark reality of the dangers inherent when working on a glacier. Distracted by the rescue efforts, they don't notice that the temperature has dropped further and the winds have continued to increase. Indeed, a cold front is approaching. Enough excitement for today. They go back to the ice mound that encapsulates the figure of what must assuredly be a Neanderthal, frozen in time, to mark its location before descending to their camp below and plan the removal of their find.

The entire expedition celebrates again. However, it is one more solemn than the previous evening's festivities. They feel the relief to have escaped danger and now are focused on the desire to quickly complete their mission, take home their prizes, and leave the glacier before more calamities can befall them or a winter storm arrives to trap them.

Professor Earlandson pays tribute to the rescue team and offers his gratitude and wishes for the safety of the group. Thinking the same as the workers, he instructs them to use their chain saws to cut out the block of ice around the apparent Neanderthal and place multiple straps around the block to ease it and the other block of ice containing the modern man down the glacier where he plans to place both into refrigerated trucks. He announces to the group that the work should be done in just four more days after which they can return to their homes and families with guaranteed payment and a small bonus courtesy of his research grant. The announcement is met with resounding cheers and turns the solemn celebration into one with toasts to the three professors and impromptu renditions of the national anthems of Spain and France.

Spurred on by thoughts of leaving the treacherous glacier, returning home and the promised bonus the workers extract the frozen warrior's en-block and carefully negotiate both of them down to the very edge of the Pyrenees glacier. In two pickup trucks arranged by Earlandson, they take them to the town of Ordino where they load them onto two separate and special refrigeration trucks with the capability of maintaining a temperature of 10 degrees Fahrenheit (-11.2 Celsius).

The last night together finds Professors Earlandson, Morales and Rousseau seated at the back wall of a local tavern in the town of Ordino. Each is as relived to be off the glacier as their workers and all are also looking forward to studying of their finds. Amidst the too warm tavern air, stale with the mixed smell of beer and wine, Earlandson takes the lead. He tells Morales and Rousseau to work together on the frozen modern man at the facility of Rousseau in Paris and tells them that he will do the same on the frozen Neanderthal at his lab at the University of Chicago. They each agree to keep their specimens frozen and, at first only take photographs, x-rays, blood and tissue samples without deforming the bodies. They also agree to touch base every three days and begin simultaneously when Ralph gets his specimen back via a special air transport.

As the three men part amidst hugs and respectful back slaps, Morales and Rousseau leave the pub together with a sense of accomplishment and relief. Earlandson stays behind, feeling a sense of accomplishment but also a sense of incompleteness, a sense that this archeological dig leaves more to be found. Ever the person planning the next move and one with a greater knowledge and field experience than his contemporaries, he knows what causes ice crevasses to develop. He knows that the great cracks like the one close to his Neanderthal find are caused by irregularities in the ground level as the glacier slowly advances. Irregularities like mounds, ridges and caves. He surmises that a formation is just what Neanderthals would use as a makeshift fortress 25,000 years ago to defend against an imminent attack. Yes, indeed, there must be more Neanderthals up there. The confirmation of his theory will prove that the extinction of this early species of man was the result of the aggression and brutality of their successors, us.

Satisfied with the finds of this trip and looking forward to being the first to view and study a whole Neanderthal in the flesh, not just a scattered few fossilized bones, he is content for now but his plans for returning next season remain cemented in his mind. After the last few sips of his beer in the warm, dimly lit ale house, he braves the cold northern wind blowing down from the glacier to return to his room at a local inn.

While the Earlandson-Morales-Rousseau team was just starting its ascent up the glacier, Civantos had already finished his excavation of the sun temple, secured the ruins for a potential return excavation and relocated the resin-encased body of Chief Atahualpa to his lab in Lima.

Civantos' lab has been prepared much like one in a medical examiner's office ready for autopsies. On a Saturday morning, the resin-encased body lays just on an autopsy table complete with a suction machine, water faucets and spray nozzles. With the resin block laying on a special non-reflective cloth, Professor Civantos and his two graduate students, Pablo and Enrique, don masks and gowns, head covers and special eye shields to protect them from an errant reflection from the cutting laser they are about to use. Civantos chose a laser, which has the advantage of depth control which will allow him to cut through the resin without cutting into the Chief's body below. He plans to remove the layers of resin in one piece in order to lift it off the body, similar to opening the coffins of an Egyptian mummy. He then can replace the lid he created and reseal the resin with the addition of a single port to which he plans to suction out the air introduced by opening the resin in order to keep the body preserved between study sessions.

Civantos looks around the sterile, grey, windowless walls of his lab, adorned only with old x-ray viewing boxes. In the cool dry air of the high-ceilinged room containing four rows of fluorescent lighting, he gives the nod to the laser technician to begin. The bright, straight, green beam of the laser seems to bubble and melt a thin line around the circumference of the resin. After just a few minutes, the top is ready to be pried off. Now, Pablo and Enrique wedge two beveled wood slates each into the left and ride sides and pull down simultaneously. The top of the resin block pops off easily in a single piece as Civantos is heard to say, "Archimedes would be proud," referring to his famous quote: "Give a lever and I could move the world."

The body Civantos hopes and readily suspects may be that of the last Great Chief of the Inca Empire, Atahualpa, lays before them. All three first note that, other than some dryness and thinning of the skin due to loss of water, the body seems as if the person died just yesterday. They note the patchwork vest and the tear from a stab wound in the mid-chest area. They now realize that the purple red stain on the vest is blood, telling a story of murder. However, they fail to notice the red papules and sores on the exposed hands, forearms and face. Civantos immediately examines the vest and confirms the patchwork design to be that of a Chief. He removes his gloves to feel the texture of the vest and contacts the dried blood. He recognized that the thickness of the fabric and its tight weave is consistent with royal attire. He doesn't realize that microscopic particles have adhered to his skin. Excitedly, he runs off to pore over the descriptions and the few authenticated drawings of Inca Chiefs to verify what he hopes to be Atahualpa himself.

Left alone to take photographs, tissue and blood samples, Pablo and Enrique notice the one thing that Pizarro did not take off of Atahualpa before the trip to the sun temple 486 years earlier, a silver ring on the middle finger of each hand.

CHAPTER 12

Vectors of Transmission

Tuesday, at 6:00 P.M., Pablo and Enrique are putting the last of their fútbol party together in their apartment in Cusco.

Shouting from the TV area, Pablo directs his voice toward the kitchen, "Enrique, what kind of beer have we got?"

Enrique, in a similar loud tone, answers, "We have the usual Peruvian Cristal but I also got some Funky Buddha. You know the girls like that one."

"Good thinking. What else did you get? I hope you didn't buy any of those crappy kale chips again. They were awful the last time and nearly ruined the whole party."

"Very funny. I got Doritos, Sun Chips, and Ruffles plus dips, chicken wings and, of course, a little ceviche and some wine for the girls if they don't want beer."

Pablo and Enrique are enjoying the week off that Professor Civantos gave them as a reward for their hard work at the excavation site. At least, that's the reason he cited for the enforced break. Actually, Civantos needed some time alone without satisfying the impetuous curiosity of his two graduate students, who want to hurriedly dig into their discovery in hopes of finding riches. Instead, Civantos wants to concentrate on the design of the patchwork vest that may confirm that this is the body of Atahualpa. This find would garner him worldwide acclaim if he can just prove it.

For Pablo and Enrique, it is time to spend with their long-time girlfriends, Adriana and Ariana, from the undergraduate school at Pontifical Universidad Catholica del Peru. Both of the girls are now tour directors at Machu Picchu and, as fortune would have it, are on their week off in a three-week-on-one-week-off schedule. They also invited Pablo's brother Fernando and his date Consuela. They plan to watch the fútbol contest between Peru and neighboring Chile. Not only a rivalry game for each team but one they hope will ignite some excitement and passion in the girls they haven't seen in the past three months.

Just before game time at seven, all four guests arrive at once. A kiss on the cheek for each girl and a handshake and pat on the back for Brother Fernando. The group settles in quickly with everyone holding their choice of the two beers, Funky Buddha for Adrianna and Ariana and Cristal for the others as they sit on a large sofa and adjacent cushioned chairs in front of and adjacent to the big-screen television of the two bachelors. As South Americans, they intently watch and hang on each move and play set up in the slow-paced soccer game that would make North American football fans yawn and busy themselves with their cellphones. Their absorption in the game is sufficient that no one notices the gaudy silver ring on the middle finger of the left hand of Pablo and also one on that of Enrique. At least no one notices until Peru scores the first goal, just before the halfway mark, off a side kick from the left side and a header that whizzed past the goalie despite his getting a fingertip on the ball.

All five stand up to cheer and embrace each other. Pablo holds Adrianna by her head to steal a kiss, and the thick silver ring on his left middle finger runs across her cheek. She doesn't notice the beginning of small red sores on his cheek and upper lip.

"Pablo! Where did you get that ring? It's beautiful. It looks like it's an antique."

She now ignores the soccer game, as do the others. Working for the past year and half at Machu Picchu, she has become somewhat experienced and knowledgeable about the ancient Incan culture.

"Its designs are Incan and they are very intricate. Is this some tourist knockoff or did you get this from an antiquity dealer?"

Enrique breaks in now showing off his ring as well.

"Neither, we got these at our excavation site. They're the real things."

Lying smoothly to avoid the admission that he took the ring from a 484-year-old corpse, he continues.

"Pablo and I each found one among the rubble at this new excavation site that Professor Civantos thinks might be an old sun temple from the time of Chief Atahualpa."

All three girls and Fernando are wide-eyed and curious. The two graduate students are more than happy to add to their excitement. They take off the rings and let the others try it on. The fútbol game becomes a forgotten distraction as each guest places a ring first on one hand and then the other, admiring themselves in the hallway mirror. Pablo and Enrique tell how they originally found the excavation site and the details of the dig as well as Civantos great excitement of the find and hopes that it is the burial site of Atahualpa himself. Two more hours go by with all the attention focused on the rings, their possible history, and of course their worth. No one notices that Peru won the fútbol game 2 to 0. Nevertheless, it seems the rings achieved the intended purpose of the fútbol game anyway. As Fernando and Consuela bid their appreciation and goodbyes, Adrianna and Arianna stay for the night.

The Tuesday of his graduate student's fútbol game gathering will become a fateful day in the history of South American Archeology in more ways than one. After spending most of the weekend and all day Monday examining the corpse of the unknown Inca nobleman, Civantos finally finds the key to his identity. In what will become a serious and unrecognized mistake, Professor Civantos removes some of the dried blood from the patchwork vest. In doing so, perspiration from his brow falls onto the vest and then, after wetting the dried blood, a small amount came into contact with one of the vinyl gloves dutifully worn by the Professor to prevent just such contamination. However, while hastily removing the glove in his excitement to connect the newly seen image to known descriptions of the vest, the unseen viral particles come into contact with the Professors forearm skin. They then are unconsciously inhaled as he brings his wristwatch closer to check the time. The first domino has now fallen in a series of events that will have dire consequences yet to take place.

It seems Professor Civantos hastily removed his gloves because his saw a distinctive sun god image with six rays of light radiating from the image rather than the standard five.

It wasn't until Tuesday, while Pablo and Enrique were telling their altered version of the excavation that Civantos' diligent and pain-staking library research finds the proof he sought. In the old Spanish archives of that era, the scribe of General De Almagro noted the details of his massacre of Atahualpa's city and his capture also noted in what then probably seemed as an insignificant detail: "The stately Chief Atahualpa, not showing either fear or humility, stood before our triumphant General adorned with silver rings, gold helmet and silver forearm plates undaunted. His chest pushed out in defiance with his vest clearly showing the sun god image at its center with his personal signature of six rays of light pointing to the heavens. The General addressed the Chief…."

That was it, definite proof. He found Chief Atahualpa. History will be rewritten. The Chief did not die by strangulation while being ransomed for his treasure by Pizarro at Cajamarca as previously thought. Instead, he died in battle near this Sun Temple. An end to Atahualpa, more fitting of the noble Chief and one that will restore some pride in Peru's heritage. The image of the sun god and the lack of decomposition of the body proves both. He must have died close to the outpost temple and been preserved there soon after where they found the remains of the resin containing vases and wraps that preserved him.

That was Tuesday. Now, it is Saturday, the time for his celebratory dinner ordered by the President of the University and attended by the Chairpersons of each department, twenty in all. It is a singular honor and a stepping-stone to national acclaim. It is likely the first of many to come as the archeological world will be coming to him for his story. It is something that he has coveted for many years but never would have thought it to occur so rapidly after announcing his discovery and showing its proof just this past Wednesday morning.

Nothing could ruin this night of praise and adulation except the weakness and fever that had begun to plague him just this morning. Fighting off and trying to ignore these symptoms, he attributes it to a beginning cold or even the flu. He has stuffed himself with ibuprofen and Vitamin C to get through the night. Afterward, he will take it easy to "get over this annoying cold."

Seated at the center of the speakers table, to the right of the podium alongside the University President and the Deans of the Liberal Arts College and Archeology Department, Civantos is all smiles in his tuxedo even as he fights back the burning sensation in his forehead and the aching that ripples through his body that he attributes to poor body posture while working over the resin coffin. Civantos' immediate supervisor, the Dean of the College of

Liberal Arts, and longtime friend, introduces him to his fellow Chairpersons and other special invited guests seated around round tables a short distance from the podium.

After a brief congratulatory and gratuitous introduction, Civantos is invited to the podium. Clearing his throat with a deep rattling cough that would be distressing to medical experts, he approaches the microphone. Fighting off the fever and weakness that his home remedies have only partially blunted, he relates the excavation details and relates his feelings of joy and further curiosity as each artifact was uncovered. His story, punctuated by photographs at each step, concludes with the picture of Atahualpa's body alongside the scribe's actual wording from the archives, followed by a closeup on the image of the sun god emanating the six rays of Atahualpa's personal signature. Somewhat brief but directly to the point with picture proof, the presentation impresses his colleagues. They stand in unison for a long standing ovation. It is just the excitement and pride of the moment that allows Civantos to get through the dinner that follows and the rest of the evening.

The evening culminates with Civantos and the others that were seated at the head table being positioned in a receiving line at the door of the faculty club. Each guest approaches Civantos offering congratulations and words of respect, none noticing the four small red dots on the grizzled and partially bearded face of the archeologist. Of course, Civantos responds to each with a short response of thanks and a promise of keeping them updated on the other findings of the dig, all the while emitting a fine mist containing unintended and unseen viral particles to each of his unwary guests.

Just 30 hours later, it is 6:30 A.M. Monday morning in Miami, Florida, where the residents in oral and maxillofacial surgery are presenting last week's surgery cases and planning for upcoming cases this week with the faculty and the Chief of Service Dr. Robert Merriweather. Seated in the small second-floor modern auditorium in the central building at their flagship hospital Jackson Memorial, noted as one of the country's best Level I Trauma Centers (The Ryder Trauma Center), as well as a center of expertise for HIV/AIDS research and patient care, the presenting resident knows to present each case in detail and to prepare for the faculty's probing questions, particularly those from Dr. Merriweather.

With his computer open at the podium and his cases downloaded from a thumb drive, Chief Resident Shadi Alzahrani begins. He spent most of Sunday preparing slides that outline the case's history, as well as presenting clinical and radiographic findings followed by pictures of the actual patient and the actual outcome of the treatment. He is a particularly sharp and detail-oriented resident. Motivated by a scholarship from his native country, Saudi Arabia, he has diligently worked to master the intricacies of all aspects of Oral and Maxillofacial Surgery (OMFS), as it is called. However, his goal and true passion is to gain a fellowship in tumor and reconstructive surgery which will land him a promised important position in one of the large hospitals in Saudi Arabia when he returns. It is all part of an effort to westernize Saudi medical/surgical care and seed into each city well-trained individuals to pass on advanced education, procedures and best practices. Shadi intends to be the right person, in the right place, at the right time.

Shadi talks through the first three cases; one of a fracture at the joint of the lower jaw (mandible) from a fall during a patient's intoxicated state, another a left cheekbone (zygoma) fracture caused by a right cross from the patient's opponent acquired during a fistfight at a local bar and the third a major fracture of the upper jaw (maxilla), eye sockets (orbits) and nasal bridge area (naso-ethmoidal fracture) created when the patient's boat hit a bridge abutment as he misgauged the level of the spring tide and its current.

The results of this third complex fracture generated a welcome voice of approval from Dr. Merriweather. He notes that residency director and section chief for oral and maxillofacial trauma "Dr. Samanka did a great job on this case and of training you well."

Shadi then begins presenting the next case with a stunning photograph. It shows a young man with a shaved head and a blank faraway look in his eyes. To say he has a shaved head is actually a misnomer as the picture shows a stubbled hair growth, signifying that it was a surgical head shave by the neurosurgical team. Actually, the head is only somewhat of a half-head as the picture shows the left side of his skull with bone apparently missing, marked with a significant indent on the left side of the scalp. Shadi relates that the man is 33 years old and was a helmetless motorcyclist who, police reported, lost control of his motorcycle while weaving between cars. He and the motorcycle skidded about 150 feet, ending with both crashing into a divider wall on I95. The rider flew head first onto the abutment. He was helicoptered onto the roof of the Ryder Trauma Center and brought directly to the emergency bays, stabilized, CT scanned, and hurried to the operating room to salvage as much brain function as possible. Shadi goes on to relate that the cyclist is otherwise healthy but is aphasic (cannot speak), requires a gastric feeding tube, and has a Glasgow Coma Scale of four, compared to a normal rating of 15.

The Glasgow coma scale, the current and very useful scale relating the degree of neurologic function, can be easily assessed at bedside each day to gauge upward or downward trends. Here, the Glasgow coma scale has been steady since he was brought in one week ago. Shadi relates that the neurosurgery service consulted Dr. Merriweather's service due to a non-healing scalp wound created as the cyclist's head skidded along the pavement for a long distance.

Of course, Dr. Merriweather asks what Shadi and his OMFS trauma team plans to do about the large, unhealed wound.

"Well, we have already debrided the gravel and road particles out of the wound and dressed it with wet to dry dressings. He is on two antibiotics, one of the cephalosporin type for skin infections and the other clindamycin to cover anaerobes for the past week. However, the wound still doesn't look good and is not healing."

Dr. Merriweather breaks in.

"You did the right basic things but remember that open wounds in a hospital setting for a week or longer become colonized or even infected by pseudomonas organisms which are ubiquitous is large busy hospitals and trauma centers. I suggest you re-culture the wound and empirically add either IV gentamycin 160 mg three times daily to the current antibiotic regimen or tobramycin at 1 mg/kg diluted in 100 ml saline three times daily. That will cover pseudomonas. I also suggest that you replace the wet to dry dressings with a petroleum- lubricated dressing. At this stage, the removal of the previously wet but now dry dressing will pull off early healing blood vessels and tissue, which would be counterproductive."

Having shared his wisdom born of long experience, Dr. Merriweather follows with a question to the group.

"What criteria are you going to look for to tell if this open wound is actually turning around?"

Third-year resident Josh Blanton jumps right in.

"Granulation tissue buds (new blood vessel pods) will start to form from the edges of the wound so that it will begin to shrink in size."

With a smile of approval Dr. Merriweather responds.

"That's right, but can you do anything to accelerate the healing?"

"I would use PRP (Platelet Rich Plasma)," Blanton responds unwaveringly.

"Right again. You are sharp today, Josh. Go on. What is in PRP that accelerates the healing?"

"As I understand it, the growth factors from the concentrated platelets will increase new blood vessel formation and cellular ingrowth into the wound and the cell adhesion molecules in the plasma, like fibrin, will act as a scaffold for healing."

"Not bad, Josh. I see you have been doing your reading. Listen, everybody, this is how you need to answer the questions when you sit for the oral examination from the American Board of Oral and Maxillofacial Surgery. The questions that I and the faculty asks you each week are not meant to be annoying or mean, as you may think, but are intended to prepare you to pass that important milestone in your careers with ease.

"For now, this is certainly an extremely sad case with a poor long-term prognosis, a case that will require high-level long-term care, and even with that a greatly shortened lifespan. It is certainly a poster for a motorcycle helmet law that is long overdue. But let's move on with our other cases."

The remaining grand rounds move ahead with the intended case reviews and learning opportunities. Then, one case in particular sparks another round of questions. This time, senior resident (third year of a four-year curriculum) Andrew Stiles presents a case that requires a small bone graft and several dental implants in an HIV positive 58-year-old man.

Dr. Stiles related his plan to bone graft the upper jaw using the stem cell protocol of Dr. Merriweather so that sufficient bone can be regenerated without using any of the patient's own bone in order to place the six dental implants required in this man's case. He related that the man has been on a regimen of four anti-viral drugs that includes atazanavir, darunavir, fosamprenavir and indinavir, and is known as Highly Active Antiretroviral Therapy (HAART). It intends to maintain his current CD4 count at 600 cells/dl and his viral load at zero.

Dr. Samanka takes the lead in questioning this time.

"Dr. Stiles, what does the CD4 count and viral load each indicate?"

Dr. Stiles is as sharp and well-read as Shadi. He is also well-known as the resident computer geek. He responds immediately.

"The CD4 count is an index of the degree of HIV infection. The CD4 lymphocyte is the cell primarily attacked by the HIV virus. A CD4 count of 600 cells/dl is actually close to normal and is very good. It suggests that this man is no more prone to a graft infection or wound opening than anyone else."

Dr. Samanka, not unlike Dr. Merriweather, nods a gesture of approval but immediately continues the questioning.

"What CD4 count would be concerning to you?"

"A CD4 count of less than 200 cells/dl would indicate an actual clinical AIDS picture so that I would then defer any elective surgery and have the infectious disease team reassess their treatment."

"Okay, then, Andrew, what about the viral load?"

"Again, this man's viral load of zero viral copies is a very good sign. The viral load in HIV, to my understanding, is the speed at which the HIV infection is progressing. A viral load of zero tells me that the HIV is all but eradicated from his system, even though we cannot be absolutely sure."

Dr. Merriweather and Dr. Samanka look at each other in near disbelief but with a great sense of pride as well. "Well, I guess Dr. Samanka and I can just go fishing from now on," Dr. Merriweather then announces. "You all seemed to be ready for your boards." This declaration is followed by a somewhat muted laugh from everyone.

Just then, the constant reader and thinker Dr. Stiles fires a question back at Dr. Merriweather.

"Dr. Merriweather, the reports of the HIV-AIDS cases from the nineteen eighties were more aggressive and most progressed to death within two to six years. Yet, today, we see people like the former NBA star Magic Johnson diagnosed with AIDS back in the 1990s and is still alive today and actually in robust good health. Not only that, the new cases of HIV infection today are well controlled by these antiviral drugs without resistance but even untreated HIV cases hardly progress to actual AIDS or do so much slower than the reports from the 1980s and 1990s. Is it all due to the HAART anti-viral drugs?"

"A long question but a very good one, Dr. Stiles. The short answer is much of it but not all of it. That is, we faculty have tried to teach you to always incorporate biologic science in your patient care. As I have said before, we all need to be 'physiologic surgeons.' To do that, you need to understand some of the basics established in historical medicine. No doubt the HAART anti-viral medications have had a direct impact on the course and transmission of HIV infection, allowing active HIV cases like that seen in Magic Johnson and several celebrities, for all intents and purposes to have been cured. That treatment has been a consistent gain and response to all those who can afford the expense of HAART or avail themselves of philanthropically or governmentally supported programs like we have here in the South Florida AIDS network. HAART certainly can also explain the reduction in the death rate, as well as the stability rate of HIV. Further, the reduced promiscuity in the gay men community, which reduces the transmission rate and has had an impact, as well. However, it cannot explain the less virulent, the less clinically aggressive, and slower progress of HIV infection treated or untreated. However, evolution can.

"You should all remember reading about Alexander Fleming's discovery of a green mold that blew into his lab through an open window and landed on one of his culture plates back in 1929. That green mold was a penicillin mold and the bacterial growth on the culture plate that it inhibited was staphylococcus aureus. It launched the era of penicillin based antibiotics but, just 50 years later in 1979, all staphylococcus aureus had become resistant to penicillin and even some of the modified penicillins, such as methicillin, were found to be ineffective. That gave rise to the name of the most resistant forms of staphylococcus aureus known as Methicillin Resistant Staphylococcus Aureus or MRSA."

Dr. Merriweather's impromptu lecture continues.

"We have to realize that viruses and bacteria evolve constantly and, in 50 years like that seen with MRSA, evolve as much as mankind has done in its four million years of existence from primitive hominids to us standing here today. Viruses can mutate even faster and the HIV virus itself is known to mutate one percent per year. That means that, since 1980, the HIV virus may or may not have mutated as much as 40% away from its original genome. Mutations in viruses can make them more virulent and clinically more aggressive or perhaps create a less aggressive form as a response to new drugs and new conditions. Mutations can go both ways. I would suggest to you that the HARRT concept of four anti-viral drugs simultaneously combined with often exchanging new anti-viral drugs into the mix has reduced the viral counts in so many patients that resistant forms and a mutational drive toward greater virulence has been suppressed. It can be explained with simple mathematics. That is, if a viral load of four million copies/dl as was common in the early years of HIV has a one percent mutational rate that would be 0.01 x 4,000,000 which 40,000 mutated viruses in that individual per deciliter (dl) of blood. The chances that one or more of the more virulent mutated virus would take over and control the severity and progression of the disease is much greater than in those with lower viral counts, especially to the zero viral load counts we can achieve today. Essentially, targeted medicines and even natural defenses over time reduce the transmission and severity of a disease. This was graphically noted in the SARS epidemic in the 2003 and 2005 era where after 2005 the SARS virus without the development of a vaccine was less pathogenic to man."

Dr. Merriweather finishes. He scans the group of residents and fellows to look for signs of boredom or indications that the dialog may have gone over their heads. He sees no signs of either, only noticing that some are still typing notes on their lap top computers or iPads. He finishes by saying:

"Evolution is not just an archeological discussion. It involves the infectious diseases we treat and also the cancers we treat which is a topic for a future discussion."

Grand rounds breaks up with the residents and fellows scattering to operating rooms and clinic assignments. Dr. Merriweather and Dr. Samanka leave together to indulge in an hour of planning concerning the upcoming graduation ceremonies of the outgoing class and the orientation of the incoming new resident class, scheduled for just four weeks ahead in late June.

After the planning session with Dr. Samanka and Dr. Brewster who joined them, Dr. Merriweather is found heading South on Dixie Highway (U.S.-1), toward his primary office at Jackson South and the two surgeries he has scheduled that afternoon. His feeling of contentment with his resident's progress is complimented by the background radio music of the oldies 60s and 70s channel playing his favorite (Beach Boys and Jay and The Americans) classics. A telephone call coming in with a +44 area code from Europe that he recognizes is from London interrupts his musings.

"Bob Merriweather, are you there?"

"Yes, this is Dr. Merriweather. I am afraid I don't recognize your voice. You don't seem to have a British accent but I can tell from my phone that you're calling from the UK."

"Bob, it's me, Ralph, Ralph Earlandson."

"Ralph, my goodness! It is good to hear from you. I am sorry that I didn't recognize your voice. You're coming in on my Bluetooth car speakerphone which can be garbled at times. What's happening with your planned expedition last fall that we talked about on the plane to London?"

"That's it, Bob. We did it. We really did it. The expedition found a fully frozen modern man from about 25,000 years ago and guess what?"

Without giving Dr. Merriweather even a microsecond to offer a guess, Ralph Earlandson goes on.

"We also found a complete fully frozen adult Neanderthal. Not only that but both have spears with them and the surrounding terrain is highly suggestive of a confrontation."

Cutting in quickly, Dr. Merriweather interjects.

"Ralph, that is stupendous. Wow, wow and wow again. Where are these frozen specimens and what are your plans for them?"

"Well, the modern man specimen is in The National Museum of Archeology just 12 miles west of Paris, where my colleagues Dr. Morales and Dr. Rousseau are awaiting clearance by the French government to modify an existing lab into a below freezing at 10° Fahrenheit lab in order to keep the specimen frozen while working on it."

"Yes, yes, Ralph, but where is that specimen now and where is yours?"

"That specimen is in an industrial freezer awaiting the modifications. Mine is in a similar industrial freezer here in London but my lab at the University of Chicago is already modified and ready to go. I will be traveling with it and beginning my work on it by mid-June."

"Ralph, what are you actually going to do?"

"Bob, I am going to take a slow and careful scientific approach step by step starting with CT scans, blood and DNA testing before opening up this rare specimen for stomach contents and organ analysis. That is actually my main reason for calling. Your fiancé Heather, are you two still together? Are you married yet?"

"The answer is yes, we are still together and, no, we are not married yet, probably by the fall but we are in no hurry. Why do you ask?"

"This is the find of the century! I concluded the expedition in November of last year. It has taken me the last six months to get my own lab up to specifications and secure the necessary approvals to transport a frozen human specimen, at least human of sorts. I took notes in a diary every day back in my tent. I am anxious to get started but I want a writer to chronicle this effort every step of the way and write it up for me targeting the best scientific journals and lay publications. With your fiancé's experience and track record of success in medical publications, she might be ideal. Do you think she would be interested? Of course, I would pay her from my grant."

"Ralph, I think she would be chomping at the bit to be part of your historic find. She is as good as you surmise. I can attest to that. I'll tell you what. I will call her tonight and relay your find and your proposal to her. She will call you tomorrow. After that, it is up to you two."

The telephone call concludes as Dr. Merriweather enters the hospital parking lot. He relates his final wishes for continued great scientific finds to his old college buddy. The Bluetooth connection drops as he opens the car door. He walks briskly toward his office with plans to lay down his briefcase and proceed directly to the operating room. As he does, he mutters to himself, "What a beginning to the day." Little does he realize what has really just begun.

CHAPTER 13

THE OUTBREAK

While Dr. Merriweather gives his grand rounds dissertation on the evolution and mutational rate of HIV to his residents, Professor Civantos lays bedridden miles to the South in Lima, Peru. His plans to resume the study on what he knows and has announced as Inca Chief Atahualpa in his resin-encased tomb have been put aside for now. Professor Civantos is sick. He feels sick. Although he cannot see that most of his face is now covered with red sores, some of the red sores are open and weeping a clear yellow fluid while others have a yellow reddish crust. He is able to see the eruptions on his arms and wonders what they are. His body aches all over. He is weak and drifts in and out of a sleepy, almost stuporous state. He finally admits to himself that he needs help, but he is reluctant to call 911. Old school in the extreme, he feels 911 calls are only for heart attacks and life-threatening emergencies. Certainly, he is not that bad off. Instead, he first calls Pablo then Enrique but neither of them answer. He thinks to himself that they should be back from Cusco and ready to help him with Atahualpa again. "Where are they?" he mutters to himself. He finally gets through to his next-door neighbor and implores him to be taken to the university hospital's emergency room. Fortunately, Álvaro works a late shift as administrator of the radiology unit at the University Hospital where Civantos needs to be taken and receives the midday call.

Álvaro comes over and helps the weakened Civantos into the back seat of his car, noticing his neighbors sores and his general weakened condition as well as the weight loss that has occurred since he saw him last.

Arriving at the emergency room, Álvaro needs to assist his neighbor into a wheel chair and register him at the emergency room desk. During these ministrations, he finds his own hands and arms have become coated with the secretions coming from the sores of the other man. He knows he needs to wash off the exudate but waits until he returns home to do so, a miscalculation on his part.

Civantos waits 45 minutes, with a growing fever and worsening body aches, before being seen. To him, it seemed even longer. The first to see Civantos is a nurse who notes a fever of 40.2° C (104.3°F), a weak pulse at 56 beats per minute, and a low blood pressure at 90/60 mm Hg. She sees the disheveled appearance of the professor with his untrimmed beard, uncombed hair and the red sores, mostly clustered about the face and two forearms but actually everywhere, and thinks he is one of the homeless folks that frequently find their way into the emergency room. She takes blood samples and schedules a chest x-ray before reporting her findings to one of the emergency room physicians on call.

Somewhat alarmed by the nurse's report, the emergency room physician on call sees Civantos immediately and, despite the disfiguring red sores and straggly appearance, recognizes the professor from Saturday's newspaper reports about finding Atahualpa. He has also seen the man occasionally about the university campus. The physician doesn't recognize the disease before him but immediately starts an IV for fluids and admits him for further testing and consultation with the Chief of Infectious Disease, Dr. Juan Ulloa.

In Cusco, a similar scenario is playing out. Pablo and Enrique are bedridden in their apartment. Their girlfriends failed to show up for their tour duties at Machu Picchu. They are holed up in their own apartment, afraid to be seen with all the red sores on their faces. Fernando and Consuela are in similar straits as the two girls. Pablo and Enrique, who came into contact with the virus sooner, are unable to get out of bed. They are both feverish and weak.

Over the course of the week, the six fútbol partygoers progress to the stage of Civantos that Monday morning. Civantos remains ill but stable with IV fluid support, nutritional supplements and antipyretics to reduce his high fevers. By now, Dr. Ulloa has diagnosed "an infectious disease of unknown cause" with anemia, hypotension, fever and cutaneous nodules as its signs and symptoms. He does not recognize it as smallpox. Smallpox is extinct and, if ever regenerated, it would likely be seen in a poor person, a homeless person or from a lab accident, certainly not in a University Professor of Antiquities, Dr. Ulloa dismisses even the faintest thought of this case being smallpox and focuses his attention on other diseases and syndromes known to produce red sores, such as measles, staph infections, chicken pox, scabies, and a whole host of others. It is just too early to tell now. Nevertheless, being the humble and diligent infectious disease specialist that he is known to be, he has already sent scrapings of the sores and blood samples to Peter Fowler, Chief of Immunology and Infectious Diseases at the Center for Disease Control in Atlanta, Georgia.

Over the next few days, the emergency room at the University Hospital, as well as nearly every hospital in Lima and Cusco, have been overrun with patients bearing the same symptoms and complaints seen originally in Civantos. While Civantos' condition is stable, it is not improving. The same can be said for Pablo and Enrique and their four guests, who are now hospitalized as well. However, older patients, those with other medical conditions draining their energy and will to fight it as well as infants are doing much worse. Some are barely clinging to life only one week after their symptoms began.

Dr. Ulloa, realizing an epidemic is at hand, tries to contact Peter Fowler at the Center for Disease Control (CDC), with no luck at first. He then calls the main desk at the CDC and registers his most serious concern of a communicable outbreak related to the specimens he sent a week ago. He implores the operator to contact Dr. Fowler immediately and gives her his personal cellphone number for a call back.

Apparently, Dr. Ulloa's dire message got through, prompting Peter Fowler to return the call. Somewhat apologetically, Dr. Fowler M.D., Ph.D., only began processing the specimens yesterday sheepishly explaining the delay was caused by the lab safety reports and government compliance standards audit he was required to do. He asks Dr. Ulloa to send him pictures of several of the stricken individuals right away via digital download. While still on the phone with Dr. Ulloa, Dr. Fowler is immediately alarmed by what he sees. His experience and knowledge of historical medicine makes him immediately concerned about a smallpox epidemic. He asks himself, how? Why? But true to his scientific discipline tells Dr. Ulloa to quarantine all patients immediately and observe strict aseptic protocols. He directs him to isolate all present and any new patients with similar symptoms then excuses himself to attend to the specimens he neglected for more than four days.

Peter Fowler rushes to his lab and pushes the Lima specimens in front of the Polymerase Chain Reaction (PCR) technician and orders him to stop all other projects and do this one right now. Fowler knows that the PCR can match the genome profile of the specimen with known genomes (DNA) of numerous viruses, bacteria, parasites and even specimens containing human DNA. He needs to know if the PCR profile of the Lima specimen is a match for the variola virus known as smallpox. He also hand carries another portion of the Lima specimen to the Electron Microscope (EM) room two floors down. He instructs the EM technician to obtain transmission electron microscopy images from several sections of this specimen. He wants pictures. While Peter Fowler waits the processing of these now top-priority specimens, the hospitals in Lima and Cusco are above capacity. Patients other than those with the symptoms like that of Civantos are discharged and or sent to nursing facilities and even hotels where they can be cared for by any available hospital personnel. All hospitals are now using all waiting rooms, conference rooms, and even unused office space to house the continual ingress of new patients with red sores, fever and weakness. All hospital personnel are called back from vacations or educational courses to handle the patient overflow but it is still not enough. Some patients are neglected, not by choice but by the demands of the situation and that of more critical patients. These are the tough choices made during an epidemic.

Within just a few hours Fowler has his answer, a complete PCR match for the variola virus that causes smallpox. He views the EM black-and-white pictures and is taken aback by the number of viruses and their clustering on each image. He calls for an immediate emergency meeting of the heads of each department to report his results and immediately calls Dr. Ulloa to let him know of his diagnosis and of the dire consequences that a smallpox epidemic can cause moving through a mobile modern society. Dr. Ulloa is already knee deep into at least some of these consequences.

Over the next few days, a team of physicians and administrators from the U.S. fly into Lima and Cusco, while smaller teams travel to surrounding cities and towns, several hundred in all. With the help of the Peruvian government, all airports into Peru have been closed down and the country is on complete lockdown with military law enforcement. Gates across the roads into neighboring countries have been established and are guarded by gun bearing Peruvian military.

The epidemiologist's initial survey of the outbreak indicated 72% of Peruvians and foreigners trapped within the county have contracted smallpox.

The five-percent death rate can be traced mostly from the elderly, those with comorbid conditions and children under the age of five. However, with resources becoming scarce despite some supplies being flown from the U.S. and neighboring countries, the epidemic continues.

Back at the CDC, the plea for possible leftover stores of smallpox vaccine has been answered by only one pharmaceutical company, the Apollo Drug Co. It seems they were the only ones with an expansive enough facility to store the vaccines and happened to have a sufficient stock to begin a vaccination program in Peru. They are also willing to develop more vaccine from their original stock of substrate virus in their Morris Plains, New Jersey, facility. Because the Apollo Drug Co. has leftover vaccine that has been tested and found to be at full-strength against the smallpox virus, it can gear up quickly to produce more. In this knowledge, the CDC gives the company exclusive rights to manufacture more vaccine from their stores of antigen.

The vaccine stores and rapid production arrived just in time to help address the small outbreaks that began in neighboring Chile and Ecuador as well as Brazil, Argentina and almost every country throughout South America. A massive immunization campaign is started throughout South America. Anyone entering or leaving South America is required to be vaccinated, including those from the United States and Europe. The gated roadblocks are repurposed to be vaccination stations.

Within two weeks, the number of new cases has fallen to less than five percent and those who were vaccinated in the early stages of the outbreak have responded quickly to a complete cure. Even those such as Civantos, Pablo, and Enrique who developed a full-blown case of smallpox, all recovered due to their baseline good health and physiological reserve with the supportive care and the vaccine they received.

The epidemic was quelled within one country and prevented in dozens of other countries throughout South America. No cases reached the United States or Europe. The CDC vaccinated over 1.2 billion people with the Apollo Drug Co.'s vaccines. Dr. Juan Ulloa was honored for his diligence and efforts to find the cause of this modern epidemic and bring it under control before it affected even more victims than it already had. Dr. Peter Fowler was recognized as a hero. The man who diagnosed a disease previously labeled as extinct was given an honorary membership in the Peruvian Medical Association and honored as a candidate for Physician of the Year in the United States. However, the press anointed Apollo Drug Co. as the true hero and savior of millions. The company that had the foresight to retain a vaccine thought to obsolete and the facility moved to rapidly meet the demand for more than a billion more doses. Apollo's stock soared. This darling of the media was envied by the entire pharmaceutical industry and enjoyed huge financial gains from the exclusive sales for the high-demand medicine.

CHAPTER 14

THE AFTERMATH OF A QUELLED EPIDEMIC

The cellphone on the nightstand in a Brownstone apartment in the Upper West Side of New York rings and a sleepy Heather Bellaire looks at the caller ID: "Bob." True to his promise to his old college friend Ralph Earlandson, he calls Heather to give her the news.

"I am sorry if I woke you but I'm heading for the operating room and won't have a chance to talk to you the rest of the day."

"You're going to the operating room now? It's 6:30 A.M."

"Yes, the OR on Wednesday starts at 7:00 A.M. and I will need to talk to the patient and her family before we take her in. Let me get to the reason I am calling you this early. Do you remember my archeology friend Ralph Earlandson? The guy we met last year on the plane to London?"

"Yeah, I even have his card somewhere here in my files. He was excited about some frozen caveman artifacts in the Pyrenees glacier. What about him?"

"That's just it. He found a whole frozen Neanderthal and he is taking it back to his modified refrigerated lab at the University of Chicago. It's the find of his career and probably such an important find that it will garner worldwide attention. And you're going to like this. Heather, he wants you to chronicle the details of the glacier expedition from his memory and notes. He also wants you to be present annotating and capturing every forensic test and study on the Neanderthal."

Heather can't quite believe what she is hearing and, for a moment, thinks it might be one of Robert's practical jokes. But at 6:30 A.M.? *It's not April's Fools Day,* she thinks to herself before responding.

"You're not kidding me, are you?"

"No, not this time, sweetheart. It's for real. I think this is a great opportunity for you. This is just what you have been planning, a transition from medical books to freelance writing of important stories. Few would be as important as this one. Are you interested?"

"Certainly, I am, Bob. What should I do now?"

"I told him that you would call him sometime this week and discuss the details. I will text you his number in London. He is still there and will fly back with the frozen Neanderthal directly to Chicago next week or the week after. You two work out the details. He says he would like to have you there when he gets off the plane and with him every minute that he is working on the specimen. Can you do that?"

"Bob, this is just sinking in. I can't thank you enough. It really is a great opportunity for me to get started as a freelance writer. I'll do whatever it takes."

"Great, I knew you would but, look, I need to get to the OR in a few minutes. You know that you will need to take a camera. Take lots of pictures. You will also need to get a place near the University of Chicago campus. Ralph says he can pay you but if you need extra money to relocate to my old hometown Chicago, let me know. I'll be glad to help you. I'm thinking, too, that this might delay our wedding."

"Oh, I guess it might. I am sorry. How do you feel about that, Bob?"

"I am okay with it. We've waited long enough already. A little longer won't matter much, particularly if my bride will be a famous freelance writer when we say I do."

"So, it's okay with you?"

"Certainly, it is but remember no hanky-panky while you're in Chicago."

Taken aback and somewhat shocked, Heather quickly retorts.

"How can you say that? You have always trusted me and Dr. Earlandson is your friend!"

"I wasn't talking about Dr. Earlandson, I was talking about the Neanderthal. I know how much you like older men," he says with a smile in his voice.

"Oh, brother," she exhales with a little laugh. "I guess I fell for that one. I suppose I will have to put up with this kind of humor after we are married."

"You bet you will. But, now, I really have to go."

As Dr. Merriweather moves his own cellphone from his ear, he hears a faint "I really love you, you know" before he clicks it off.

Later that same day finds Peter Fowler, M.D., Ph.D., and Chief of Immunology and Infectious Diseases at the Center for Disease Control, seated next to David Epstein, CEO of Apollo Drug Co., at a hearing before the United States Senate Committee on Health, Education, Labor and Pensions. The group requested a hearing to discuss a national smallpox vaccination campaign. The request has been deemed so important that it was directly bumped up to this supervising committee from the Congressional Health and Human Resources Committee in the House of Representatives.

Peter Fowler, dressed in a blue suit with a white shirt and red and blue striped tie, sits at the microphone in the center directly in front of the committee. He is flanked by David Epstein, dressed almost identically, at his right. He looks straight ahead at the two-tiered rows of seats in the Everett Dirksen 430 Committee Room where the committee members are taking their seats.

Dr. Fowler and David Epstein have researched the political affiliations, past interviews, and voting records of the committee, which consists of 22 members, including 12 Republicans and 10 Democrats. Despite the rancor between the two political parties, their track record of support for health initiatives, particularly toward opioid control and vaccines, has been refreshing in terms of cooperation and consensus.

Seated in the middle and flanked on both sides by ranking members of the committee, the Chairman bangs his gavel somewhat softly and announces.

"Members of the Committee and invited experts. We are here today to discuss the request by the Center for Disease Control to initiate a national campaign to vaccinate our citizens against smallpox. Dr. Fowler, we thank you for appearing before this committee. We are familiar with the request and your impeccable credentials in this matter. Please give us the background reasons and implementation plans of your request."

Fowler proceeds with a prepared statement.

"Mr. Chairman and Committee Members, until just six weeks ago, no cases of smallpox have occurred since 1977. In fact, the World Health Agency now called the World Health Organization officially declared smallpox eradicated worldwide in 1980. This has held up until the recent outbreak centered in Lima and Cusco, Peru, occurred. I know you have been briefed about that. Due to available stocks of vaccine and the marshaling of prompt supportive care from several sources, the outbreak was controlled and contained. Nevertheless, in Lima and Cusco, 736,211 deaths were recorded which is five percent of the population. Those were mostly in children under five years of age and the elderly, particularly those elderly with comorbidities such as diabetes, heavy smokers, heart disease, and other diseases that would weaken the person's general health. Senators, although this is a large number of deaths, the five-percent death toll is very low when considering any epidemic. In addition, to Lima and Cusco, nearly every town and city developed smallpox cases and every country in South American reported at least 100 cases. We are concerned by these statistics and are requesting a national smallpox vaccination campaign here in the United States. We will be presenting a similar appeal to the World Health Organization next week. You see, even with isolation and containment efforts, spread of an epidemic is inevitable particularly one such as smallpox, which is easily transmitted and is transmissible during the entire course of the disease which lasts two weeks and usually longer, with an average clinical course of about four weeks.

"These realities were evident in this epidemic. Many vectors of transmission went unrealized. Private aircraft, back roads out of Peru, boats down rivers and along the coast, not to mention commercial airliners, all unknowingly transported early smallpox cases to neighboring countries."

Conversation buzzes between the seated committee members but Dr. Fowler cannot hear their words. Then the committee chairman clicks his microphone on.

"Dr. Fowler, my colleagues and I have several questions. My first is, are you sure that this outbreak came from a 500-year-old mummy and was not an act of spillage from some bioterrorism lab hidden away in the Andes?"

"Mr. Chairman, we are absolutely sure," the doctor answers. "We traced it to patient zero, there were actually three patient zeros. All had direct contamination from the preserved Inca Chieftain. We traced the source directly to them. It was in a simple university lab with no advanced protective equipment. There were no signs of bioterrorism."

"I have one more question before I turn the microphone over to my colleagues. Where is this Inca Chieftain now and is it secure?"

"It is. We have encased him in a sealed tomb and have relocated it to our own storage area for communicable diseases at the CDC."

"The floor is now open to questions from the committee members," announces the Chairman with a tone of both leadership and respect for his fellow committee members. The senior-ranking senator from Iowa advances the first questions.

"Dr. Fowler, are we prepared for a nationwide vaccination campaign?"

"Senator, I will let Mr. David Epstein, here to my right, answer that question."

David Epstein, the 48-year-old clean-cut-appearing CEO of Apollo Drug Company, has been waiting for just that question. He eagerly clicks on the microphone in front of him.

"Madam Senator, Chairman, and fellow committee members, I am David Epstein, CEO of Apollo Drug Co. Years ago when smallpox was declared extinct, my predecessor George Apollonia had the foresight to preserve not only a somewhat large stock pile of smallpox vaccine but also the antigen to which the vaccine can be resynthesized, I must say, rather quickly. In fact, we used 80% of the stock-piled vaccine in our response to the Peruvian epidemic and have already replaced all of that and more."

"Mr. Epstein, is your vaccine still 100% effective?"

"It is difficult to prove, but I can say that it was the agent that stopped the spread of the South American epidemic."

"Dr. Fowler, can you testify that no one who received the vaccine came down with smallpox?"

Dr. Fowler breaks in without waiting and, holding his microphone close, he reports.

"That is true. The vaccine prevented smallpox, even in people in close contact with those who had active disease."

Another Committee person puts forth a question.

"Dr. Fowler and Mr. Epstein, the United States has close to 400 million citizens and people coming across our borders all the time. How do you propose to vaccinate so many people?"

Dr. Fowler takes the lead on this one. "It would certainly be a challenging task but one that is very achievable. Vaccines are easily administered by doctors, nurses, physician's assistants and others. It is a simple intramuscular injection. I propose that we begin in the schools and nursing homes, then move on to hospital personnel and every person entering a hospital, and finally to every workplace. We will need to marshal a large medical workforce but that is something we already have. The consequences of an uncontrolled epidemic are unthinkable. If the U.S. population of close to 400 million, as you noted, experienced the same death rate of five percent, it would total 20 million deaths."

With that sobering figure, the committee members are first silent then begin to look at each other to gauge the level of concern in their colleagues. Then, the ranking Republican leans over and whispers in the ear of the ranking Democrat committee person. After a few minutes of quiet, while nearly everyone is watching them, they break apart and look at David Epstein. The senior Democrat takes the lead.

"Mr. Epstein, what is the cost of your vaccine?"

"The production of the vaccine, sterile packaging, labor and shipping would be about $50 per dose."

The Republican Senator responds.

"Mr. Epstein, applying my third-grade arithmetic that comes to 20 billion dollars. That's quite a pretty penny, isn't it?"

David Epstein, always the CEO, is prepared and advances his cost analysis.

"Yes, 20 billion is a large sum but think of the medical cost if even half the United States population develops smallpox and the impact it would also have on the workplace with a 50% absenteeism. That cost would be in the multi-trillions. The country would grind to a halt."

The Committee Chairman now breaks in.

"Your point is well taken, Mr. Epstein, but I recall some dark times for your company. I recall your painkiller problem where your company's painkiller ended up causing heart attacks in our citizens and your company had to retract the drug and pay off nearly a billion in lawsuits. I also recall your osteoporosis drug Bone Protect, which caused violent murderous psychiatric reactions in the post-menopausal women using it. Can we trust you?"

Dr. Fowler jumps in to save the situation and David Epstein.

"Mr. Chairman, we are talking about a vaccine, a proven vaccine as you just heard, not a painkiller or a drug to harden bone. As part of my proposal, I requested an oversight committee at the CDC to monitor safety and effectiveness. This oversight committee will be made up of those experts across the fields of medicine and nursing. They will ensure the efficacy and safety of a project we cannot turn our backs on."

Dr. Fowler's very organized and planned-out proposal, as well as his strong closing words, reassures the chairman and the 21 other members of the committee. They approved the proposal and forwarded an emergency request to the Senate Budget and Finance Committee.

After the committee meeting, Dr. Fowler packs up his papers to catch a late plane back to the CDC where he will prepare a similar presentation to the World Health Organization.

David Epstein, on the other hand, arranges for a quiet, private dinner meeting with his marketing director, Richard Bloom. In a private room at Bobby Vans, a high-end steakhouse, they compare notes over the restaurants highly touted seafood medley appetizer.

After taking in several tempura shrimp, Richard Bloom begins the discussion.

"David, it was tense there for a while but they bought the whole thing. We got $50 per dose. Those political schmucks don't realize that our production costs are only six dollars per dose. They didn't even do their homework. The flu shot we sell, even at our prices, is only $23.50 per dose and the shot for shingles only $26.70 per dose. No wonder our country is trillions in debt."

David Epstein responds with a chuckle and is soon joined by Richard Bloom. They clink their glasses together as the door opens and the unmistakable aroma and sound of two sizzling ribeye steaks gets their attention. After the waiters refill their glasses with the best cabernet from their wine cellar, they continue.

"Yes, Richard, it was quite a win for Apollo today. I must confess I was sweating a bit when they brought up Dolor Not and, worse, the Bone Protect fiasco. At that time, I could only think about goddamned Merriweather. We would never have been linked to that mess if it wasn't for him. I'm glad smallpox is not a jaw problem. He can leave saving the world to us and, of course, our making a sizeable profit in the meantime."

"Well, good old Fowler came to our defense and put it over the top. Do you think you can talk Fowler into including one of our guys to chair the committee?"

"Richard, I am one step ahead of you. Already done. In fact, I have even selected someone for the position."

"Who?"

"David Connors."

"David Connors? David, he's head of our logistics division. He doesn't know a damn thing about medicine, let alone smallpox or vaccines."

"Right, but he is loyal and ambitious. He wants to climb the ladder at Apollo. He will be our eyes and ears into the committee. He is very manipulative and will steer those brainiac doctors and researchers where we want them to go, just as I convinced Fowler that a non-medical chairperson would be the ideal balance for the committee."

"David, you are good. You are really good."

Laughter punctuates the end to their conversation and their dinner starts with smiles and gloating between them.

CHAPTER 15

The Vaccination Campaign

Eight-year-old Richard Snyder is fourth in line, waiting his turn to "get a shot." He sees his three classmates Yvonne Jackson, Doris Wickstrum and Ken Vespermen in front of him. He puts on a third-grader's brave-boy front to conceal his fear of the inoculation. He was told that it will prevent him from getting sick but he doesn't understand how or why. He just wants to get the ordeal that has been preying on his mind for the past two days over. He doesn't want to cry. That would blow his tough-guy image and subject him to teasing from all those who hadn't cried. He peers around Ken and Doris as Ivonne steps up to the nurse and her assistant in front of a table full of boxes. He sees the syringes and looks for the needles he has heard about. He sees one. He is momentarily relieved to see it is short and thin. He says to himself, *A small needle. That can't hurt too much.*

Yvonne, a rather tall for her age African-American girl who sits across from Richard in class, steps up to the nurse. She grits her teeth and braces herself and, as he watches, Richard feels the bead of sweat on his own forehead and feels his heart pound in his chest. He is breathing fast as he sees the needle enter the skin of Yvonne's upper arm. Her grimace goes away and a smile of relief becomes apparent. She doesn't cry. She gets a strawberry-flavored lollipop as a reward for cooperation and skips away happily. Richard, not completely relieved by the apparent lack of pain, remains concerned about his image. *If a girl doesn't cry and I cry, everyone will tease me and call me a wimp,* he thinks. His nervousness continues to grow.

Next, Doris moves toward the table. She is already crying in anticipation of the pain she knows will surely come. The nurse and her assistant console her and try to calm her down but without success. Doris' crying slows to a whimper as she closes her eyes to endure the needle stick. As she feels the needle enter her skin, she shrieks in a high-pitched tone that heightens the concern of Richard and all those in line, both behind and in front of him.

Clearly, Doris shrieked more from fear and anticipation than real pain caused by the needle. Doris eyes dry up instantly as she like Yvonne before her skips away with her strawberry-flavored treat.

Next up, Kenny Vespermen. Like Richard, he is considered one of the brave (macho) boys of the third grade. He tenses and is relieved that the slight sting didn't hurt at all and walks away afterward with a slight swagger in his gait, looking straight at Richard as he does.

Richard's anticipation continues to ebb and flow. *Doris cried and yelled. It must be painful,* he thinks. *Ken didn't cry and took it.* Heart pounding and visible perspiration on his brow and in his armpits, he approaches the nurse. He turns his head away from those in line behind him and grits his teeth. His face is contorted in a tight grimace. He feels the cool alcohol on the skin of his upper arm. The nurse slaps his skin causing Richard to turn his head wondering why she slapped him. He sees the needle coming out of his skin. He didn't even know it had entered.

"It is over. I didn't cry. I am fine."

His masculine image preserved, he walks away with a treat in hand, recapitulating Ken's swagger.

The relived Richard Snyder doesn't know that the slap on the arm served to excite nerve fibers transmitting touch to counterbalance and overwhelm the pain fibers going to his brain so that he would not even feel the pain of the needle. He also doesn't know or realize that the stuff that was injected into his muscle is already being taken up in his bloodstream and being engulfed by cells called antigen processing cells. That these cells will present the protein chemical structure of the attenuated or killed viral particles on its surface as a sign to be read by cells that know the language. These cells, called B-lymphocytes, will not only identify the virus when presented but also develop their own protein to break it up and destroy it. These attack proteins, called antibodies once fully developed over the next three to seven days, will stay in Richard's blood indefinitely, ready to attack any invader with a uniform bearing the name of smallpox. In addition, some of the lymphocytes will remember the precise words and produce new attack proteins if the body becomes invaded by small pox again in the future.

Of course, third-grader Richard Snyder doesn't know or really care about such complex biology at his age. Perhaps, he might, someday if he becomes a medical student or perhaps even one of Dr. Merriweather's OMFS residents. For now, he is only concerned with the after-school baseball game and tomorrow's spelling test.

Scenes like these, reminiscent of the diphtheria vaccination programs of the 1920s and the polio vaccination programs of the 1950s and early 1960s, with minor variations, are repeated in every school and every grade level from pre-K to graduate school in every state. Additionally, as Peter Fowler outlined, nursing homes, hospitals, drug stores, airports, offices, and factories are visited by teams of providers vaccinating everyone present to prevent a possible but unlikely smallpox outbreak. The yellow vaccination cards, hardly used anymore, are reinstated and required as proof of smallpox vaccination. The stamp on the card must be shown at airports and when embarking on any form of transportation within and out of the United States.

The mobility of modern society creates a risk for a rapid and worldwide spread from this type of virus. That same mobility, with an organized team effort by trained personnel, can vaccinate nearly everyone in a country within two weeks, assuming sufficient vaccination doses are available. The Apollo Drug Co. made sure there are.

After the first two weeks of the vaccination campaign, Apollo Drug Co. continues to produce the smallpox vaccine in the standard dose of 1 x $10^{7.8}$ plaque-forming units per milliliter (78 million pfu/ml) at a rapid pace. Now that about 348,652,212 doses have been injected in U.S. citizens, Apollo looks forward to using their already available vaccine and their recent notoriety to compete in the European and Asian Markets. Both of these markets would prefer to use their own drug companies but none has the necessary production capability. More billions of dollars await Apollo.

On a Wednesday afternoon, David Epstein is seated at the head of a large mahogany table in the second-floor boardroom of Apollo's headquarters in Morris Plains, New Jersey. With Richard Bloom seated to his right, he looks over the 14 board members seated seven on each side. Only one person is absent. She is off in Asia somewhere. However, the fact that fourteen of fifteen members of the board of trustees are present for a somewhat quickly called meeting is way above the norm. In fact, each board member is more than anxious to hear the details of Apollo's newfound credibility and reputation in the marketplace, as well as to get eyes on the company's financial report.

David Epstein stands up in front of the nine men and five women, all neatly dressed in appropriate business attire. He announces, "As you might be anticipating, the news is all good. First, we are now the talk of the nation with quickly increasing respect and admiration from the populous, the industry, the Congress and, most importantly, the FDA. Our quick and effective response to the South American epidemic has brought us national and international acclaim and attention."

David Epstein holds up first a copy *Time* magazine with his picture on the front cover, arranged in a stately pose. Then, from a stack of magazines in front of him, he holds up *Newsweek, BusinessWeek, Scientific American* and *Discover,* followed by several other well-known newsstand titles. Next, he then holds up articles from *The Wall Street Journal, Washington Post, New York Times, Los Angeles Times, San Francisco Chronicle* and two other newspapers before he concludes for fear of "boring the board," as he calls it.

"This positive press has made everybody forget about out past problems with Dolor Not and Bone Protect. We are ahead of every drug company on the planet," he crows.

The seated board members smile and applaud with several shaking their heads in positive reinforcement of Epstein's words.

"I will now let Richard Bloom review the financials with you. I am sure you will be impressed."

"Ladies and gentlemen, you all know me so I will get straight to the good news. Two months ago, Apollo stock was sitting at $36.5 per share. As of opening this morning, it had soared to $122.75 per share and, when I looked at my smart phone's app while David was talking to you, it was up another $3.25 per share for an even $126 per share."

The Board members interrupt with another round of applause along with a few fist pumps, a few hear, hears and a lone yahoo.

Bloom and Epstein are wreathed in smiles.

"It is incredible but the government pays promptly unlike insurance companies with their crazy HMOs and PPOs. We have been paid for every one of the 348,652,212 doses administered. That puts total sales at $17,432,610,600 to be exact, ladies and gentlemen."

This time, the board members all stand in unison for a standing ovation, which both Richard and David lap up, nodding their heads in approval.

The meeting winds down with David Epstein outlining his plans to enter the European and Asian marketplace by working with various drug companies in each country to create distribution hubs worldwide. He sums up the plan: "They get their local prestige, we get most of the money."

In Miami, Dr. Merriweather is in line in the hallway to get his own smallpox vaccination. As he finishes, the nurse stamps his card and hands him a lapel button saying, "I'm protected from smallpox." Unfortunately, there is no strawberry treat for him. Such is the price of being an adult. Just then, he hears his cellphone ring with his favorite science-fiction tune and sees that Heather is calling.

"Hi, lady of my life. What are you doing?"

"I'm just calling you to tell you that your friend, Dr. Earlandson, and I have touched base and I will be working with him from the start. It's really exciting!"

"Great, I knew you two would work it out. Tell me the plans."

Dr. Merriweather, dressed in his customary white coat, slacks and tie, listens to her while leaning against the wall, close to a window to combat the dead spots created by the hospital's reinforced, thick walls.

"Dr. Earlandson will be arriving with the frozen Neanderthal three weeks from now. I helped him arrange a refrigerated truck to transport the specimen from the cargo hanger of American Airlines to his lab at the University of Chicago. I have already moved out of New York and am actually living in Chicago already, coordinating things for his arrival.

"He plans to start right away, first with scans and x-rays after they chip away the ice. Bob, this is really exciting. He sent me his entry log and a summary of the Pyrenees glacier expedition. I am working on chronicling that in the time period before he arrives. The issues he ran into with the expedition were fascinating. The French delayed the whole thing to attend a crepes festival. One of the explorers fell into a crevasse and had to be rescued. Several developed first bite. It was really something."

"I can see you are pumped up. I will want to read every article you write. I will try to break away here and come up to Chicago one of the weekends before Ralph arrives and you get really busy."

"If you fly up to Chicago just to see me, I will certainly make time to be with you."

"Actually, Lou Malnati's pizza is the real motivation."

"Okay, okay, I know I have to live with that kind of humor from now on."

Both chuckle and express a smile unseen by the other. They disconnect their cellphones. Heather goes back to writing about the Pyrenees glacier expedition and Robert goes on to the medical executive committee meeting.

CHAPTER 16

The Last Tango in Chicago

True to his promise to Heather, Dr. Robert Merriweather boards American Airlines Flight 1476 to Chicago early on a Thursday morning.

In another week, Heather is scheduled to meet archeologist Ralph Earlandson and his frozen Neanderthal prize, and, in two weeks, he himself must host his residents/fellows graduation ceremonies. These early days in June are the best time for a romantic weekend together. Besides, it's also a beautiful time of year in terms of Chicago's weather.

Dr. Merriweather has already made it through TSA security and, for the first time, he shows his stamped vaccination card, despite the global entry card that gained him TSA pre-check privileges.

Sitting in bulkhead window seat 8F, he is not disappointed by the lack of an upgrade, something he hopes for because of his platinum frequent flyer status. Instead, he is just glad to be able to catch a break from his busy surgical and teaching schedule of the past few months and looks forward to being with Heather before she gets completely engrossed in her upcoming freelance writing project. It is just a good time to relax and enjoy their time together.

On this trip, he is not Dr. Robert A. Merriweather, Professor of Surgery, but just Bob, a civilian of sorts. On this flight, he has not brought along any chart work, research data or book writing projects. As the plane reaches cruising altitude, he settles into a daydream of his childhood and teen years growing up in Chicago. He recalls the bitter cold and gray skies of the

Chicago winters, and particularly walking along the Lake Michigan lakefront. He would traverse the walk way leading from a far-distant parking lot to the Northwestern Dental Medical School complex. In particular, he recalls that the cold, damp wind would create mini icicles on his mustache that he would have to knock off after entering the heated building.

Bob Merriweather thinks further back to his high school days at Lane Tech High School. Then an all-boys school emphasizing shop works to prepare young men for factory jobs that were in such high demand then, it is now a coed college prep school. He wonders how he escaped becoming a factory worker like his father, despite taking auto shop, machine shop, aviation shop, woodshop, and foundry classes. He now thinks it is a miracle that he ended up in the dental/medical discipline and, with a touch of melancholy, thanks his father, Nicholas A. Merriweather, who encouraged his studies of the biologic medical sciences that have served him so very well in his career.

A smile crosses his face next as he recalls his upstart baseball career hopes at Lane Tech. How it had been his little league boyhood ambition to one day pitch for the Chicago White Sox, despite growing up close to Wrigley Field, the home of the Chicago Cubs. This paradox was courtesy of his older brother of 18 years Nicholas Merriweather Jr. (Nick). His brother spent a time in the White Sox minor leagues and became a rabid, lifelong White Sox fan. Needless to say, big brother Nick corrupted "Bobbie" and his older brother, Carl, to the "Dark Side" of the baseball force and into White Sox Fandom.

In particular, he recalls spring baseball tryouts as a freshman at Lane Tech. One day, the accomplished and well-respected baseball coach, Al Manasian, came over to inspect the pitchers. All the boys who hoped to make the team as a pitcher were throwing warmups to those students trying out for catcher. The serious and stern fully uniformed coach with a midriff paunch and a stocky figure wearing his wool baseball cap sporting a prominent "L" was an intimidating figure. Continuing his daydreaming remembrance of the day, he recalls how the gum-chewing coach came up to him specifically and said, "Merriweather, show me your stuff—show me your curve ball." Dr. Merriweather recalls I did. I twisted my wrist and put the best spin on the ball that I could. The ball curved and dropped, a beauty. The coach then barked, "Show me your slider." I did that too from a partial side arm delivery. It was another beauty. The coach barked back,

"Now, show me your sinker ball." Ah, that was my specialty. I could throw two types of sinkers. I demonstrated both. A look of acceptance came over the coach's face. I thought I was a shoe-in. I just knew I had nabbed the position of a starting pitcher for Lane Tech, a known football and baseball powerhouse among the city public schools. Then a disaster occurred. The coach barked out, again, "Now, show me your fastball." I reared back and threw the ball hard as I could. I looked up at the coach, knowing full well it was not the blazing fastball delivered by the likes of Nolan Ryan. With a momentary pause, he recalls the coaches piercing words, "Nice change-up. I could have clocked that pitch with a calendar." I responded by saying frantically, "Let me try again!" I wound up with a high kick of the likes of Juan Marichal and threw the ball a foot and half into the dirt in front of the catcher. The coach was not impressed. "Merriweather, that is a great 59-foot fastball but the plate is 60 feet six inches from you." Adding insult to injury, the coach said, "You can be a relief pitcher," as he walked away. So I never became a starter and got into only a few games as a reliever. However, from then on I was known as Merriweather, "the 59-foot junk ball pitcher."

Bob Merriweather laughs into the airplanes window loud enough to be heard by those close to him. He decides to stop his daydreaming and sleep for the rest of the flight.

Sinking further into being just Bob Merriweather and dressed more casually than usual, he finds Heather waiting for him at baggage claim at O'Hare Airport. A short kiss and tight embrace stimulates thoughts of greater intimacy to come for both, but, for now, in light of the crowd around the baggage carousel that is all that is possible.

After gathering up his single bag, the couple moves toward the exit. The five-foot-eight-inch statuesque brunette is also dressed casually in a knee-length khaki skirt and, curiously, in a white t-shirt with a Cubs emblem on it. Bob looks at it curiously and doesn't particularly note that Heathers car is parked on the fourth floor of the garage designated as the "White Sox" level. However, he does notice that Heather heads out of the O'Hare Airport and proceeds southward toward the University of Chicago on the city's far South Side but then exits at Irving Park Road on the North Side.

"Heather, why did you have me fly into O'Hare, when Midway Airport is so much closer to where you are staying at the University of Chicago? And why are we getting off here at Irving Park and heading east?"

“Oh, you will see. It is only 10:30 in the morning. I have a special weekend planned for you.”

“I thought something was up. Well, I am all in for pleasant surprises,” Robert says with a grin. “It will be pleasant, won’t it?”

Heather turns off at Paulina Street and goes around the block onto a one-way street then stops in front of a particular house.

“Heather, you brought me to the house I grew up on North Hermitage Avenue. As a little kid I remember repeating my address over and over so that if I got lost, I could tell people where I lived. My father bought it in 1950 for $6,000, which was a significance stretch for a factory worker back then. Now, this neighborhood is called ‘Wrigleyville’ and the house is worth a whole lot despite its small size and small yard.”

Bob and Heather get out and spend 20 minutes looking over the outside and backyard of his old home, not wanting to bother the current occupants. Bob, of course, tells Heather some of his best memories of his family and pets throughout the years. He then tells her how surprised he is and how wonderful it is for her to have thought of this. They indulge in a short kiss.

Heather ushers Robert back into her car and turns right on Irving Park Road and then right again on Paulina Street, heading south. Robert wonders what she is up to next then recognizes the route he walked to school every day. They cross busy Addison Avenue, which has streams of people walking east, a fact that Robert fails to recognize as significant though he should. The car pulls up one block South of Addison Avenue, stopping in front of a brick stone elementary school.

“Okay, I get it, Heather. You’re bringing me down memory lane, but why? This is Hamilton Elementary School, where I went from kindergarten through eighth grade. How did you know? And why are we here?”

“Well, I am a writer with confidential sources that I can’t disclose, of course. I wanted to learn more about the boyhood of Bobbie Merriweather, since I already know about the adult, the straight-laced, punctual, detailed-oriented oral and maxillofacial surgeon I am going to marry.”

“Heather, this is spooky. I must confess I was daydreaming about my high school years and dental school years on the plane up here. Now, you’re bringing back memories of my grade school years.”

“Well, what do you remember?”

“Actually, a lot of things. Most of which are embarrassing.”

Standing in front of the seemingly unchanged brick and stone four-story building with a six-foot-tall, green wrought-iron fence surrounding it, Robert thinks back. He shakes his head and points to the north playground with its basketball standards, swings, monkey bars, etc.

"See that beautiful well-equipped playground? Well, when I entered first grade it was a gravel field, affectionately known as the tackling field. Back then, boys and girls had separate playgrounds and recesses. The culture of the boys' area was that you were either a runner or a tackler. Most little guys like me, from grades one to three, were runners and the bigger guys or older guys were tacklers like my older brother Carl. We knew no other game or activity. If you were a runner, you were supposed to run the length of the tackling field without being tackled. We almost never made it. Tacklers were supposed to tackle any and every runner you could, with or without the help of fellow tacklers. I recall kids coming in from recess with gravel in their hair, bruises, abrasions, and whatnot. No one cared, including us. It was just something you were supposed to do. It ended just before I got to fifth grade when they paved our beloved tackling field to build an actual real playground. Unbelievable, I cannot believe that was our favorite game. I wonder what the school boards and PTA would say about it today."

"Well, now I know why you're such a tough guy," Heather responds with a smile and a got-you poke to Robert's chest.

"I actually never got to be a tackler, darn it," he responds with a grin then continues. "I can tell you the tough-guy image is something all of us guys wore on our sleeve. It was the expected thing then. Boys were tough, girls were not—wow, has time proven that one wrong! I remember my buddies and I bragging to the girls about how our polio shots didn't hurt a bit. Remember, the polio vaccine was by injection then. Now, it is served on a sugar cube. By the way, you did get your smallpox vaccine, didn't you?"

"Yes, of course, even we non-tough girls know enough to stand up to the pain of an injection."

"I see my warped sense of humor is already rubbing off on you. Thanks for taking me to my old school. I have a lot more memories, as I am sure you do about your youth. We will have many years to tell them to the other. However, I am somewhat embarrassed to say I haven't been back since I left for high school. But, I can sense by the mischievous look in your eyes that you have something more planned."

"Yes, I have. Follow me."

Heather leaves their car parked across from the schoolyard, empty since it's late Saturday morning. They proceed to walk north back to Addison Avenue arm in arm. They join the gathering throngs of people, mostly families, walking east on both sides of the street.

"Heather, these people are walking to Wrigley Field for a Cubs game. Wrigley Field is only a half-mile from here."

They step to their right, allowing the throngs of fans walking to the game to pass them by.

"Oh, brother, how dense of me. I should have known by your Cubs t-shirt. We're going to see the Cubs, aren't we?"

With the biggest smile ever, Heather pulls out four box seat tickets for the Cubs game that day and waves them in front of Robert's face.

Shaking his head in astonishment. "Heather, you really went all out. What a treat, what a weekend, and, what a wife you're going to be. But, you know, I am still a White Sox fan even though they never drafted me."

"Hey, look who the Cubs are playing, big boy!"

Robert looks at the tickets now in detail. Yes, the Cubs—White Sox city series, a natural rivalry through the years. He then notices that there are four tickets and looks up at Heather with a quizzical look. Before he can blurt out his question, he feels a slap on the back and hears, "It's about time you came back to Chi Town for something other than a medical conference."

Robert turns and instantly recognizes his two cousins, Chuck and John Burger. In his younger days, he would frequently meet these two at this very spot and walk to Wrigley Field for a Cubs game. Now, fully civilian, his doctor role put away for the moment, Robert embraces each of his cousins, who he had called Chuckie and Johnny as kids, while Heather looks on smiling. They engage in a brief remembrance of their rousing racquetball games and past Cubs games before Heather breaks in and tells them that they still have a half-mile walk ahead of them. However, before they start out, Robert looks straight at Heather, "Now, I know your confidential sources."

The game proceeds with the usual intensity of a city rivalry, a close game that goes into extra innings. Despite the greater fan support of the Cubs, including Heather, Chuckie and Johnny, the White Sox won in the 12th inning seven to six, with Robert gloating over the others.

After returning to Heather's parked car, the four top off the day with Robert's favorite, a Lou Malnati's Pizza. After, he bids a hug-filled farewell to Chuckie and Johnny with a promise to keep in touch more regularly.

Robert and Heather then head north for Heather's last surprise of the weekend, a night at the romantic French Country Inn at the Illinois-Wisconsin border in Geneva, Wisconsin.

After a two-and-a-half-hour drive, they check in and unpack in a suite overlooking a lake. As Robert looks out over the lake, Heather comes behind him, kisses his neck and leans her head on his shoulder.

"So, you still love me after my team won and your team lost?" Robert says playfully.

"I guess a modern tough girl can deal with that, particularly if she is with the right man."

"Well, I might not be the right man. Look over the lake. On the other side is the Playboy Mansion, you know, and that boat down there at the dock is ready to go. Do you worry that I might be tempted?"

"I'm not concerned at all. I know you well enough to realize that you would get halfway across the lake and start fishing instead."

Robert turns around and smiles, then laughs, kissing her forehead and then her lips, as he finds the bottom edge of her t-shirt and pulls it up over her head. He then does the same with her bra before kissing each breast.

"You're right, I would rather fish than consort with a Playboy Bunny, but consorting with you is a very different story," he murmurs. He then unbuttons her khaki skirt and lets it fall to the floor, as he guides her to the bed where they begin to enjoy each other leisurely, because they know they have the whole night ahead of them.

The next morning, before Robert has to return to Miami, Robert holds both Heather's hands across the breakfast table.

"Heather, I can't believe you arranged such a great weekend. I hate to see it end. It made me realize a contentment I lost when Veronica divorced me. I hope we can have many of these kinds of weekends in the years to come. Next time, I'll plan it."

Each remains silent content to just hold hands. Visible tears stand in Heather's eyes and a little mist glazes Robert's eyes as well. That's something a tough guy from Hamilton Elementary and Lane Tech would never admit.

CHAPTER 17

The Beginning of Epidemic #2

A week after Dr. Merriweather's return, he begins his usual Monday morning teaching rounds at the main Jackson Hospital in Miami. Twelve hundred miles to the Northwest, Heather and Dr. Ralph Earlandson are supervising the loading of the crate containing the frozen Neanderthal into the freezer truck that Heather had arranged to cover all the necessary details a week before. While Dr. Earlandson completes the necessary forms required to ship "human" biologic specimens at the cargo area desk of Midway Airport, his two assistants Steve Cotini and Bill Reynolds secure the crate for the 18-mile travel to the lab that Dr. Earlandson has prepared in the basement of the Oriental Museum Annex at the University of Chicago. Although the mid-June Chicago temperature is 82° F, the refrigerated truck is up to the task and set at 10° F. Dr. Earlandson wants to take no chances of a thaw. He has read about the smallpox epidemic that broke out and was quickly quelled in South America and doesn't want to take any chances on a repeat. He is not specifically concerned about smallpox because his readings have indicated smallpox first appeared in the historical records in ancient Egypt long after Neanderthals became extinct. However, he is concerned about any unknown disease that a different species might carry. That is why he plans to keep the specimen frozen and use gloves, PPE gowns, and the N95 respirator masks for any work in the "freeze room." He also arranged the room to comply with the airborne infection isolation (AIIR) standard accepted by the CDC and WHO.

Arriving at the annex building, graduate assistants Cotini and Reynolds recruit several building maintenance men to help load the crate on to a forklift, which will be able negotiate the slightly sloped ramp to the outer door of the freeze room. Heather and Dr. Earlandson observe the forklift through the outer office separated by a sealed door and a long glass window from the freeze room. Similar to a CT scan station in most hospitals, this outer room is maintained at 68° F temperature and is equipped with computers, counter space, filing cabinets, and chairs. There is also a panel remotely controlling the center console and even a CT scanner within the large freezer room.

As the door opens, Dr. Earlandson and Heather are met with a blast of frigid air so much so that they first retreat back into the outer room to don the heavy jackets and fur caps awaiting them on separate hangers. Cotini and Reynolds do the same. They then guide the forklift to gently set the specimen down on a clean stainless-steel table that is similar to an autopsy table.

Once the specimen, which looks more like a seven-foot-by-four-foot rectangular block of ice with some dark but an indiscernible object blurring its center, is safely atop the table, the forklift and its operator are hurried out of the freeze room and back up the ramp to the outside. The forklift operator couldn't be happier to get out of the cold.

Heather, now swathed in a thick parka and fur-lined pants, enters the cold room and starts taking pictures of the ice block from every angle including the floor drain, which leads to a special trap that will sterilize any liquid melt that is taken up. The cold air vents and the CT scanner are pointed toward the far end of the room. Heather takes more pictures. All the instruments Dr. Earlandson brought are already laid out on a table along the nearest wall. She also has the presence of mind to take pictures looking back at the outer room from the freezer room, taking it at an angle to avoid a reflection of the flash off the glass. Dr. Earlandson planned the outer room to be a sort of control room and meeting room. What Heather can't take a picture of is the cold. However, she senses the excitement as Dr. Earlandson instructs his two graduate assistants on how to chip away the ice without cutting into the body. As luck would have it, each of the two had done some ice carvings for hotels and wedding receptions in their undergraduate college years so that they have at least a minimal understanding of how to do it, perhaps more than Dr. Earlandson.

"Steve, Bill, I can only say that you need to be patient and meticulous, take your time. This specimen has been frozen for 25,000 years in that block. One or two days more won't make a big difference. I'll be with you the entire time."

Indeed, the chipping away of the encasing ice proceeds slowly, not just because of the meticulousness required but also because of the awkwardness of working in heavy clothes and heavy gloves. Even with that, the cold seeps through the layers making all four shiver at times and require one-hour "warmup" breaks every two hours.

Early Friday morning, the last ice chip falls, an image captured like so many others by Heather's excellent photography and video skills. Throughout, Heather also takes note of the three men's fatigue and annoyance with the constant cold, as well as their dogged drive to get to the Neanderthal despite it all. At times, she feels guilty and offers to help, but each time, Dr. Earlandson turns her away. She thought maybe it was chauvinism or perhaps he didn't want to take a chance on an untrained person who might accidently cut into the specimen. Nevertheless, when the last of the encasing ice falls away, all four fall silent.

There it is, a human-like creature from over 25,000 years ago. Dr. Earlandson circles his prize with a piercing and intense examination. Through his N95 respirator mask, Dr. Earlandson barks out:

"Heather, take notes! A male, about 30 years old, I'd say. Long straight black hair curled at the ends, and a ten-inch black beard. He is covered in an animal skin with short fur. Looks like it came from a deer or deer-like animal. Similar fur and hide wrapped around the lower calf serve as a shoe or boot. The ties, I would assume, are animal tendons. No exposed areas of the torso except the hands and head. The hands are short with the same black hair on all surfaces except the palms. The arms are slightly long for the body height. The skull appears oversized as well. The forehead is protruding and the chin is receded consistent the fossilized specimens thought to be from Neanderthals."

Dr. Earlandson continues to circle the table, making several complete circuits in order to view the Neanderthal from every angle and not miss anything. He takes out a tape measure and carefully measures the Neanderthal as well as he can without touching it.

"The body is about five feet, six inches in height. My best estimate is that his waist is 44 or 46 inches and his chest close to sixty inches. Indeed, a body habitus fit for the cold climate of the last ice age. Heck, he probably would be very much at home in this room."

With that lighthearted remark the other three break out in laughter as the stern seriousness of the occasion is set aside for the moment.

"Look! There are red sores on his face, most are open with ice crystals still on them. And there are some under the hair on his chin and scalp, too. Even his hands have these 2 mm, maybe 3 mm sores. I wonder if it was frostbite. After all, I surmised that he, along with a band of his clan and even some homosapiens, were trapped by an avalanche. Maybe their species had a dermatologic condition. Heather! Take several pictures of these skin sores. Get some closeups."

As Heather obliges Dr. Earlandson's wishes, she removes the strap of her camera from around her neck so that she can move in for a closeup shot of some of the red sores. The strap brushes up against the frozen skin. Unseen and unnoticed, small ice particles carrying millions of frozen viable viruses adhere to the strap, still suspended in ice.

Throughout the next few hours, Dr. Earlandson takes x-rays and a CT scan. A closer examination of the Neanderthal's coverings, mouth and teeth, and at least a peek at his chest will have to wait until tomorrow.

The four gather in the outer control room and are glad to warm up after having spent three straight hours in the freezer room. However, the viruses are now freed from their icy confines of the past 25,000 years and are now alive within the fibers of the camera strap and doing what viruses do best: multiplying. The four view the x-rays then the CT scan with Dr. Earlandson commenting on each finding.

"I see three old healed fracture callouses. They are located on the left humerus, the right radius, just above the wrist joint and the right sixth rib. It seems that this fellow led a pretty rugged life. He also has a deformed left ankle joint. Probably, that's related to an old ligament tear or joint avulsion that healed with a deformity. The CT scan shows all the same internal organs as we have and all in the same place. There is a hyoid bone located between the lower jaw and larynx. It is smaller than we have, but the larynx seems to be the same size so they must have had some speech capabilities."

"Heather, let's see the pictures you took."

Heather queues up picture after picture and passes the camera around for each to view the digital screen image on the screen at the back of the camera, an unintended but fateful error. In doing so, all four come in contact with the camera strap, offering the virus the desirable home of human skin cells on the menu. The die is now cast and the genie is literally let out of the bottle once more as all four go to a local Italian restaurant to celebrate what they think is their best day ever. Actually, it will prove to be their worst day ever.

There begins the exponential rise of an epidemic as their waiter, water boy, bus boy and seating host all come into contact with the unseen virus. Soon it spreads to their coworkers, friends and family.

A little over 4,000 miles away, at the Museum of Archeology just west of Paris, Drs. Morales and Rousseau along with one research assistant, Andre Rindeau, have also finished removing the ice that encased their specimen. In awe, all three gaze upon a very different figure than the one in Chicago. This specimen measures six foot and one inch, and has a chin and a less profound forehead. He is an early modern man clothed in animal skins somewhat thicker than that of the Neanderthal and more finely sewed together. His face is covered with red ochre streaked in black, a type of "war-paint," Morales and Rousseau surmise. His hair is light brown and beaded in a purposeful way with honed and polished antler spikes within it, to hold his hair in a purposeful position. He too has open red nodules and sores with ice crystals on his face and neck, the only exposed skin on this specimen.

The excitement of discovery is as pronounced in this suburb of Paris as it is in Chicago. The same cold temperatures and the same thick clothing slow down the necroscopy. However, Rousseau becomes impatient and takes a scalpel blade to excise one of the neck sores. He cuts through the frozen skin painstakingly and uses a firm pressure to take only a small specimen, which he places into a double-sealed vial and then into a plastic bag. With the cold sapping their desire to continue, they adjourn for the day, planning to CT scan the entire body tomorrow.

Rousseau sends his specimen to the adjacent lab set up to remotely process it for bacterial, viral, and fungal cultures as well as microscopic slides within a sterile, sealed plastic box. However, Andre Rindeau cleans up and dutifully disposes of the scalpel blade in the sharps container in the freezer room. However, he takes the blade handle covered in frozen blood and exudate to the warm part of their lab for autoclave heat sterilization. In doing so, his fingers come into contact with the unseen blood on the handle. So as the viral particles on the metal scalpel blade handle dry, their counterparts on Andre's fingers multiply and spread to Drs. Morales and Rousseau as they shake hands at the end of the day.

CHAPTER 18

DAY ZERO PLUS THREE DAYS

In Chicago, the following two days after the removal of the encasing ice minimally invasive tissue sampling, complete plain radiographs, CT scans, samples of clothing and hair was accomplished. Additionally, the patient was weighed and turned out to be a remarkable 280 lbs. However, by the middle of day three, Dr. Earlandson called a halt to the sampling. It seems all four were fatigued and headachy which he attributed to the intense work and concentration of the expedition in such a cold environment. Since it was Friday anyway, he gave everyone including himself the rest of the day and the weekend off to reconvene Monday at 8:00 A.M.

In the Museum of Archeology near Paris, work continues throughout Friday and half-day Saturday without anyone being plagued with the fatigue, lethargy and headaches experienced by their Chicago counterparts. This team had already removed and categorized the clothing of their specimen, noting several scars on the chest and shoulders suggestive of a fight with sharp weaponry, as well as more scattered red sores. They notice a strange indentation in the contour of his chest and surmise "possible broken ribs" from the ice or from the avalanche that all agree was the likely cause of the entrapment in the glacier. They also weighed their specimen and found it to be a sleek but musculature physique of 85 kg (187 lbs.). They wait for the culture and microscopic slides of their first day's specimen and stored frozen blood in a cup- sized container for later testing. They then adjourn.

Monday (day 0 plus six) finds the Chicago lab empty, save for the Neanderthal still lying on the exam table in the center of the room.

Heather calls her fiancé from the emergency room at Rush Memorial Hospital.

"Bob, something is wrong. I feel terrible. I am weak. I have no energy and my skin is breaking out."

"Heather, when did this start?"

"Just two days ago, on Saturday. I know you tried to call yesterday but I was just too tired to answer the phone. I have no appetite and I have terrible nausea. I just mustered up enough energy to call an Uber to take me to the emergency room. I am waiting to see a doctor now."

"Heather, let's switch to FaceTime. I need to look at you."

"Bob, I am frightful. I didn't have a chance to put my hair up, or put on lipstick or any decent clothes."

"Don't worry about that. This is a medical evaluation, as limited as it will be."

Robert looks closely at Heather's image on FaceTime. He tries to hide his immediate concern. Heather looks gaunt and pale. He can see her skin is dry and can make out small red bumps on her face. As he talks to her, he can tell that not much of his words are being understood. She is obviously fighting back either fever or pain or both.

"Heather, listen to me carefully. Have them admit you to the infectious disease isolation unit. Do you understand?"

"Yes, yes. What is it? You are scaring me."

"I don't know what it is yet. I am just being cautious and overly protective of someone I love. Just do as I say for now, okay?"

"Okay, I will."

"Look, I will get the first flight out tomorrow. You'll be all right. I better get to shifting my schedule for the week and getting booked on that flight. See you tomorrow, bye."

After ending the call, Robert closes his eyes and grits his teeth. His hopes tell him that it is just the flu but his medical training and his senses tell him that it is something far worse. For now, he busies himself with the schedule changes and airline reservation he promised just minutes ago.

CHAPTER 19

Tuesday, Day Zero Plus Seven

A nervous and anxious Dr. Merriweather waits impatiently on the American Airlines flight from Miami to Midway Airport in Chicago as it awaits the clearing of a gate occupied by another plane. His flight out of Miami had already been delayed two hours due to thunderstorms around Chicago and the American Airlines hub in Dallas. Flight schedules throughout the system are in disarray. On one hand, he feels fortunate that his flight was not one of the ones that has been cancelled. One the other hand, it is well past his planned arrival time of 8:15 A.M. It is now 11:30 A.M. and the plane remains awaiting a gate to open.

After finally deplaning and rushing to an awaiting taxi (no time to call an Uber), he arrives at the hospital at 1:00 P.M. He doesn't identify himself as a medical professional, but rather as Heather's brother so as to be perceived as immediate family and avoid a possible denial to visit a patient in isolation. Robert is directed to the third-floor isolation unit where he is instructed on how to put on the yellow Personal Protective Equipment (PPE), including gown, mask, cap and gloves. Dr. Merriweather listens politely and follows their directions playing the role of an inexperienced family member.

Entering the room, Robert is immediately appalled. He sees Heather's state of drowsiness and confusion. She is slow to turn her head and open her eyes. A light smile of recognition comes over her face, but she says nothing. The red sores are scattered in copious numbers and most are weeping a straw-colored liquid that Robert knows is serum mixed with a tinge of blood. Her hair is thinner and recently fallen strands of brown hair are scattered on her pillow and bedding. Her skin is covered by red nodules or open sores, which is pale and dry. As Robert holds her hand, a superficial layer of skin peels off.

His touch and voice, saying, "Heather, it's Bob. Can you hear me?" evokes a response. Heather turns her head toward him and opens her eyes as if awakening from a deep sleep. Her voice is weak and strained.

"Bob, you're here. Why did you come?"

"I'm here to help you get well. What happened?"

"I don't know. We are all sick. Dr. Earlandson is down the hall, so is Bill. I don't know where Steve is?"

Just the effort to speak drains Heather as she slumps back into her pillow with first a sigh then a few deep breaths. She seems to fall back into a stupor.

Robert tries to process the entire scene. He looks at the monitors overhead; low pulse at 57 beats per minute, low blood pressure 94/66, tachycardia (rapid pulse) 111 beats/minute. He thinks to himself, Heather is struggling physiologically. She is on the verge of shock. He thinks to himself: What is this? He saw her on FaceTime just yesterday and now she is lapsing into a coma. This thing is progressing rapidly. He looks up at the IV bags hanging on the stand. Levofloxacin and Erythromycin… those are for bacterial infections particularly Legionnaires' disease. Do they think she has Legionnaires' disease? Her symptoms don't indicate Legionnaires' disease to him. What is this?

Robert's medical diagnostic acumen kicks in. If he can't help Heather directly, at least he can find out what this rapidly progressing disease is. He takes off the PPE gown and accompanying gloves, cap and mask and places them into the contamination container at the door. He exits the room and avails himself of the hand sterilizer at the door.

Robert goes to the nursing station with the ruse of thanking them for the PPE and their instructions, but really takes the opportunity to scan the rack of patient charts. He quickly sees the names he is looking for: "Ralph Earlandson in Room 312 and Bill Reynolds in Room 381." "Yes, Heather was right, both are here."

Hoping to gather further data, Robert remarks to one of the nurses, "It sure seems busy around here."

"Yes, we are completely full and the emergency room is holding six more isolation candidates. It seems we are in the middle of a Legionnaires' disease outbreak."

Before Robert can pump her for any further details, the nurse is called away by her supervisor to help with a Code Blue (cardiac arrest) in Room 322.

Robert knows what that means and the likely outcome. He exits the third floor and hospital, still playing the part of the patient's brother he was supposed to be. Once outside the hospital, Robert hails down a nearby waiting taxi and tells him, "Take me to the nearest Walmart and wait for me while I buy some things. Keep your meter running, I'll pay your full fee. Here's $50 for now."

The taxi driver is curious but gladly accepts the $50 bill and complies. He has taken several couples and individuals hurriedly to a hospital but has never been asked to do an emergency run to a Walmart.

Within seven minutes, the taxi pulls up to the doors of the superstore. Robert rushes out of the taxi and through the doors in search of the sports section. He rushes over to it. There, he sees what he is looking for: first, a cylindrical container housing three racket balls and another, larger one housing, three tennis balls. Both have a screw-top lids. *Perfect,* he thinks. On the way to the checkout area, he picks up a box of quart-sized Ziplock bags and a roll of duct tape, before checking out and returning to his waiting taxi where he instructs the driver to return to the hospital. During the ride, Robert empties both cylindrical containers and donates the racket balls and tennis balls to the driver. He then removes two Ziplock bags from their box and places one inside the other. Finally, he puts the two cylindrical containers and the duct tape in his overnight duffle bag and the two plastic Ziplock bags in his left pants pocket. Minutes later, the well-paid taxi driver, gifted with three racket balls, three tennis balls and another $50 bill, watches his fare enter the same hospital door he picked him up at 30 minutes ago.

"I gotta tell this one to the wife when I get home," he mutters.

Robert checks his duffle bag at the main desk of the hospital, per hospital policy, and proceeds up to the third floor isolation floor. It is now 4:00 P.M. and Robert notices a busier nursing service scurrying about, seemingly overwhelmed. As he dons on the PPE gear again, one of the nurses approaches him.

"Your sister is very sick. I must tell you, she may not make it through the night. She is not responding to her antibiotics. Nobody is responding to this Legionnaires' outbreak. The infectious disease doctors think it is a resistant strain. Even all their cultures are negative."

Pushing back a sense of dread Dr. Merriweather reads her nametag, Robert responds with a short "Thank you, Ms. Aberdeen. I understand."

"I just want you to be prepared. Ms. Bellaire signed a living will on admission. She is a DNR (Do Not Resuscitate), you know."

Robert swallows hard and, fighting back his tears, shakes his head to signal he knows without having to speak.

Robert enters Heather's room fully clothed in the PPE. No exposed skin. He sees that Heather's condition has degraded in the two hours he's been gone. "Heather, it's Bob again. Can you hear me?"

She doesn't awaken. No response this time. Heather is in a coma, unable to be roused. Robert holds her hand tightly, hoping that somehow, in her fading conscious, she knows that he is there and that he loves her.

Robert Merriweather, the tough guy of his youth and the staunch authoritarian surgeon of today, bows his head as tears well in his eyes. Over the next two hours, Robert recalls feeling emotionally drained and asking the same rhetorical question as he did when his parents and two older brothers passed away. Why was this happening? Another hour passes before the inevitable occurs, Heather takes a final breath, announcing the end of her life, and machines register flatlines and emit a sharp tone. Robert remains for another fifteen minutes, still holding Heather's hand, until the nurses come into the room to disconnect the monitors and to console him.

Robert dries his tears and stands up, knowing he has to do what he planned. As he releases his hold on of Heather's hand, he makes sure to abrade some of the skin with sores onto his glove. Then, as he removes the PPE and puts it into the contamination container, he turns his right glove inside out as he removes it to safeguard the specimen that he has collected. He puts that glove into the inner Ziplock bag that he removed from his left pants pocket, while placing only the left glove into the contamination bin. Exiting the room with the contaminated right double-bagged glove in his right pants pocket. Robert once again uses the hand sterilizer from the wall-mounted dispenser, this time cleaning his hands twice as an added measure before proceeding down to the first-floor reception area to reclaim his checked overnight bag.

Once the overnight bag is in his possession, Robert moves to an area hidden by a row of hedges on the side of the hospital, he takes out the two empty cylinders and places the plastic bags containing the glove into the smaller racquetball container. He screws the lid down tight and duct tapes it in place at its edge to seal it. He then places that cylinder into the larger tennis ball can and screws that lid down tightly and once again seals it with duct tape.

That night, in a nearby hotel, Robert washes out all the clothes that he wore with bleach and then bags them in two larger plastic bags to be burned later. He knows that he will need to arrange for Heather's cremation and accepts the difficult task of informing her twin sons, now 22 years old and finishing college, of their mother's death. Meanwhile, his medical diagnostic curiosity flares again.

This is not bacterial. It is not Legionnaires' disease. The damned thing is behaving like a virus, a highly fatal and probably highly transmissible virus, like Ebola or Marburg virus. Holy Jesus! An Ebola outbreak in a major city like Chicago would be devastating. Mega deaths and widespread infections would be unavoidable.

CHAPTER 20

THE OUTBREAK

It is now Wednesday, only eight days after the original contamination of the camera strap. Heather is dead and, although Dr. Merriweather doesn't know it as he sits in a window seat on his return flight to Miami, so are Dr. Earlandson, Bill Reynolds and nine others. Steve Cotini is barely hanging on at suburban Northwestern Medical Center in Naperville, a new epicenter of this strange form of Legionnaires' disease.

Robert is torn between the grief he feels over Heather, the angst about a potential fatal outbreak of an Ebola-like virus, and his practical concern over shipping an infectious agent in the baggage hold of a commercial airline carrier. Robert knows well the risks even though he has quadruple-sealed the specimen. He also knows it is wrong, which conflicts with his straight-laced sense of integrity. Before the plane lands, he decides to put his grief for Heather aside. He will arrange the Memorial Service that her two sons had requested in the months ahead. Now, he must seek out the source and identify the infectious agent of this epidemic for the good of the many. Common sense tells him that the disease must have originated with the Neanderthal specimen that they were working on. Regrettably, Heather, his old college buddy, and his research assistants were patients zero. They let the genie out of the bottle. But what is this genie and how malevolent is he?

Arriving at Gate 47 of Miami International Airport, Robert walks toward Gate 24 and the exit. As he does, he sees a small crowd of about twenty gathered around a television screen. He is drawn over and hears the newscaster, "The latest update on a breaking news story out of Chicago. The recent deaths in the South Side of Chicago, around the University of Chicago, has extended to the surrounding suburbs as well. Hospitals are overrun and emergency medical teams are stretched to capacity. At least 800 deaths have been attributed to what medical science has now identified as another outbreak of smallpox. This outbreak, similar to the recent one in South America, seems to be spreading faster and incurring more fatalities. Public health officials are attributing the deaths to those who have not received the smallpox vaccine after the South American outbreak. They ask that all persons who have not yet received the smallpox vaccine do so immediately and want to reassure the public that those who received the vaccine are safe. There is no need to panic."

Dr. Merriweather moves on and mutters to himself, "Smallpox, smallpox, I should have known it. It was just like the South American epidemic in signs and symptoms but this is worse, much worse. What a bunch of bullshit about the vaccine. I know Heather and Ralph both received the vaccine."

Robert moves to a quiet area, near a vacant gate. He calls his office secretary, starting, "Mishy, it's Dr. Merriweather."

She interrupts him.

"Chief, everyone is asking about you. You have over 200 emails, the stem cell book publisher has been calling you, and the administrator overseeing your clinic expansion project has hit a snag. Oh, and the Department Chair...."

"Mishy, stop! All that can wait. They can fire me later. Just be sure Drs. Torborg and Samanka take care of any of my patients that need attention. What I need you to do for me now is look up Dr. Keith Jeffords on our alumni list. See if his personal cellphone number is there. Is it?"

"Yes, it is, Dr. Merriweather. There is also an updated number for his office. It says here that he works in the Georgia State Governor's Office."

"Yes, that's it. He is one of our oral and maxillofacial surgery alumni. He always said his ultimate goal was to be the first dentally and medically trained Governor of Georgia. Text both numbers to me right now."

While Dr. Merriweather waits for the text, he recalls how Dr. Jeffords graduated and went on to take a fellowship in facial cosmetic and reconstructive surgery at Emory. There, his outgoing personality and uniformly good surgical outcomes opened doors for him in community projects and several state organizations, which in turn led him to shut down his practice and successfully gain a seat in the State Legislature. Then, after an overwhelming election victory to the governorship, he has helped achieve two years of gains in Georgia's economy that has brought out whispers of even a Presidential run.

Receiving the text, Robert, knowing the governor's secretary will be protecting him from outside calls, immediately calls the old cellphone number in the hopes he has not changed it in the past 18 years. Somewhat surprisingly, it rings and Dr. Jeffords answers.

"Governor Jeffords, here. Can I help you?"

"Keith Jeffords, this is Dr. Merriweather. Sorry to use your old cellphone line and sorry to bother you."

"Professor Merriweather, what a pleasant surprise!" responds the 46-year-old, round-faced Governor, clearly remembering his mentor. He is neatly attired in a blue business suit and seated at his desk alone in an office that is a near replica of the President's oval office in Washington.

"Hey, no bother at all. In fact, I'm going over the state budget proposals and upcoming bills. I was actually just thinking about the phrase you taught us – 'Be firm but compassionate.' I can't tell you how often I employ that, particularly now when I am trying to figure out a way to accommodate everyone's public bathroom needs while keeping the perverts out. Now, with a new influx of homeless, I need to find a compassionate way to support them but also keep them off the streets. I do not want Atlanta or Augusta to become another San Francisco, you know? Anyway, what's up with you? It's been a long time."

"It certainly has, but this isn't a social call. I need a big favor from you, if you can even do it."

"What is it? For my professor, I'll be glad to try."

"You know the CDC Committee on smallpox chaired by David Connors and Peter Fowler? Can you pull a few strings and get me on that committee?"

Governor Jeffords chuckles.

"Heck, I thought you would ask for a difficult favor. Consider it done. I know Fowler well and actually have a great deal of influence on their budget. When do you want to start?"

"How about the day after tomorrow, Friday?"

"Okay, I can see to that but why do you want to be on a boring committee? The South American smallpox epidemic is a thing of the past and nearly everyone has been vaccinated."

“Keith, that’s just the problem. There is a new outbreak of smallpox emanating out of Chicago. I just came from there. This outbreak is different, more virulent, more transmissible, more deaths, and the vaccines don’t seem to work.”

“Oh, boy, sounds serious. Are you sure?”

“Look at the breaking news coming out of Chicago, 800 deaths already, including two people I knew. Both received the vaccine.”

“Now, that sounds serious. Should I prepare my state for a medical emergency?”

“Yes, I fear this could go national and even worldwide.”

“Well, then, I better get you on that committee. You have always been a pioneer and a crusader. Just show up in the lobby on Friday at 8:00 A.M. Peter Fowler will be expecting you.”

“Keith – Governor, I can’t thank you enough but I better get going now. I’ve got some packing to do and planes to catch.”

As each signs off and presses the red icon on their cellphone to disconnect, Governor Jeffords reflects on the conversation he just had.

Dr. Merriweather was never one to push the panic button even in the most dire operating room situations, but he is genuinely concerned now, he reflects.

Governor Jeffords puts aside the state budget proposal and picks up the phone to call Peter Fowler at the CDC immediately.

CHAPTER 21

A Warm and Cold Reception at the CDC

After a whirlwind Thursday morning that lapses into midafternoon, Dr. Merriweather collapses in his living room chair in front of a television that isn't on. He holds a glass of the only alcohol he is known to drink, Amarula, the cream liquor from South Africa. He has already packed for his trip to Atlanta, and handled a few of the urgent emails and the phone messages left for him. He also called his colleagues, Dr. Samanaka and Dr. Torborg to handle the continued responsibilities of his residency program. He is sure they are up to the task. Finally, he called Heather's sons and painstakingly tried to explain their mother's unexpected death and to console them as much as himself. The unpleasant task was made more difficult by the necessary pauses for tears from all three. He arranges for his house sitter to return as soon as tomorrow to take care of his three dogs. In fact, all three dogs, the two white labs called Rocky and Tubby and the small chocolate lab named Libby, sensing their master distress, gather around and sit in front of him. Trained as medical therapy dogs by his ex-wife Veronica, all three seem to have evolved an inner sense to console their master. Rocky, in particular, moves forward to lay his head on Dr. Merriweather's left leg but the troubled oral and maxillofacial surgeon is too lost in his own thoughts to respond.

Some would label Dr. Merriweather's state as one of detached reality, others a state of deep introspection, and many as simply a funk. He ponders the death of Heather with misty eyes.

"How? Three weeks ago, we were together. She was beautiful. She was vibrant. She went out of her way to help me to relive part of my youth and even somehow arranged for a Cubs game that included Chucky and Johnny. Now, she is gone. A sad and horrible death, one that I was responsible for, one that I didn't even recognize, and one I couldn't save her from."

Robert stops, his eyes now brimming with tears. He suddenly feels Rocky's head on his lap and gently rubs the soft ears with his left hand while using his right to take the first sip of his Amarula. For the first time, his blank stare focuses forward, seeing not the equally blank television screen, but the University of Miami football autographed by then Coach Jimmie Johnson on the shelf above it. It was given to him after the University of Miami football team defeated then archrival Notre Dame. With a slight smile on his vacant face, he recalls the time when the University of Miami football team was considered the bad boys of college football because of their "trash talk" bragging and their swagger. In fact, the press wrongly labeled the game "Convicts versus Catholics," stirring an outrage from Miami citizens but also creating a heightened national interest. Robert was given the football for his help with some of the players' jaw and teeth concerns throughout the year. He values the gift not only because of his respect for Coach Johnson as a hard-driving coach focused on success and championships but also for his genuine care for his players education, health and future. Robert also appreciates the gift for the inscription that Coach Johnson wrote on it, "If you talk the talk, you need to walk the walk." Translated from football lingo, it simply means don't brag unless you can live up to it. That's something Robert has also passed on to his own team of residents and fellows in oral and maxillofacial surgery.

Now, fully out of his funk, Robert also recalls a worthy quote from the storied and equally successful Notre Dame Coach Lou Holtz. After a disappointing defeat, Coach Holtz in an interview recalled what he told his wife after their house burned down years before, "You have 24 hours to grieve, then we must start to rebuild."

Robert thinks to himself, *That's right, enough with the self-pity, and enough with the self-blame and even with grieving over Heather. She is gone now. You can't bring her back. Your task is to live up to your reputation and walk the walk. You have finished grieving now. Plan to rebuild by making a difference on that CDC Committee tomorrow.* With that mindset, he completes his preparations and heads to the Miami Airport to catch the 7:00

P.M. American Airlines Flight to Atlanta where he has booked a hotel room close to the CDC.

As planned, Peter Fowler dressed in is accustomed college professor attire of gray slacks, blue shirt and a brown vest with a gray bow tie contrasting against his curly red tinged brown hair, is waiting for Robert in the lobby of the CDC when he arrives the following morning.

"You must be Dr. Merriweather. I recognize you from your website picture. Welcome to the CDC."

Peter extends a welcoming handshake.

"Dr. Merriweather, let's get you through the registration process, photo, and badge. It will take a few minutes, then we will be off to Room 202 for the committee meeting. I pushed our usual 8:00 A.M. start time to 8:30 to get you through the formalities. I suspect all 18 members will already be there anxious to hear what you observed from the new outbreak in Chicago."

Fifteen minutes later, Peter Fowler escorts Dr. Merriweather to Room 202, one floor above the entrance foyer and just down the hall from the Director's Office. As he enters, Dr. Merriweather sees a long oval mahogany table where, indeed, 18 others, mostly medical researchers, and other scientists are seated. The room is a typical conference room. The oval table seats two at one end and two at the other curved end with eight chairs positioned on each side of the table for a twenty seat capacity. A centrally located speaker supports conference calls. There are outlets for computers at each of the twenty stations, as well as a ceiling mounted projector directed at a screen, positioned behind the head of the oval table where David Connors is seated. As Peter Fowler seats himself next to Conners, Dr. Merriweather takes an unoccupied seat on the curved oval directly opposite. He looks around the room at the committee members seated around the table. To his right, there is a bank of windows with blinds drawn to shut out the morning sun. To his left is an enclave housing coffee, breakfast rolls and assorted pastries, as well as sodas and ice. Glancing across the faces of the committee members, who have already availed themselves of the coffee and pastries he recognizes several of them either by their reputation, television interviews, or previous medical meetings.

To the left of Peter Fowler sits a stocky man with a round face and thick, mostly gray hair and beard, albeit with some remaining rich black streaks.

He is dressed in a black suit with a white shirt and red tie similar to Dr. Merriweather's attire. Dr. Merriweather recognizes him as Dean Richard Heimbach, the 2017 Nobel Prize Laureate for his development of an HIV vaccine as well as his work with hepatitis vaccines. Going clockwise around the table, he also recognizes Dr. Christine Hargraves, the researcher and developer of the Human Papilloma Virus (HPV) vaccines now in common usage to prevent uterine cervical cancer, seated in the middle of the straight edge to his right. Opposite her on the long side of the table, he sees Dr. Ragnan Olaffson from Sweden's Karolinska institute in Stockholm, Sweden. Dr. Olaffson is noted as Europe's foremost expert on viral diseases. Next to him is Karen Georgeff, the Chief Nursing Officer and authority on research methodologies at the CDC.

Before sitting down himself, Dr. Fowler introduces Dr. Merriweather to the assembled group.

"Today, I would like you to welcome the newest member of our committee, Dr. Robert Merriweather, Professor of Surgery and Chair of the Oral and Maxillofacial Surgery Unit at the University of Miami Miller School of Medicine. You will find his extensive curriculum vitae in the package in front of you. Please review it at your leisure. Dr. Merriweather can help us with the troubling new outbreak of smallpox out of Chicago. I understand he has insights as to the beginning of it and has observed its course in at least one patient."

Dr. Merriweather smiles and shakes his head slightly in an accepting gesture in response to the committee members as they offer soft applause and welcoming words. That is, all but one. As Peter Fowler sits, David Connors stands.

"This is all wonderful and politically correct but this is an important committee where life-and-death decisions are made. I happen to know that the Governor himself used his influence to get you on this committee, Dr. Merriweather, and the only reason you are hear is that your fiancé died in this new outbreak. While I am sorry for your loss, I don't see what an oral and maxillofacial surgeon whatever that is can really contribute to the importance of this committee and I can't imagine you know much about smallpox."

Dr. Merriweather, familiar with the hard questions and challenges designed to impeach his testimony in the drug company scandals involving Bone Protect and/Bone Max from David Connors employer, Apollo Drug Co., is unfazed by the pointed attack. In a calm manner, he retorts:

"Perhaps I can relieve your concerns, Mr. Connors. I do know that smallpox has been reported to be first recognized 12,000 years ago, at the end of the last ice age, when agriculture first came to mankind. I also know that smallpox is a rather small orthopox virus called variola and is in the poxviridae family and that it is only 300 to 400 nanometers (10^{-9} meters) in size. It is transmitted mostly by secretions and also by airborne vectors and it adheres to fabrics like clothing. In fact, the first biologic warfare in history was attributed to smallpox virus laden blankets and a handkerchief given to the immune naïve Native Americans purposefully in 1763 at the British Garrison known as Fort Pitt. Normal smallpox has a twelve-day incubation period after being inhaled, producing lymphadenopathy, fatigue and then finally oozing red sores. There is actually a variola minor and a variola major form of smallpox. The same variola major that history notes was used by Edward Jenner to develop the first primitive vaccine for smallpox in 1798. He used scrapings from the sores of smallpox victims to form an injectable vaccine containing live viruses, which worked on some but caused others to actually develop smallpox. Some of those people died. Because he used a live smallpox virus that caused the development of smallpox as much as conferred protection from smallpox, his initial vaccine fell out of favor."

At this time, the medical researchers and other scientists are smirking and reveling in the bashing medical lesson Dr. Merriweather is giving to David Connors, who is obviously uneasy and realizing that he had overstepped. At this time, Nobel Laureate Dean Heimbach breaks in.

"Well, Mr. Connors, it seems you have your answer. Our colleague here seems well versed about smallpox. I for one want to hear what he has to say about his observations in Chicago. We need to hear everyone on this."

David Connors, seething inside, falls silent and sits down.

"Thank you, Dr. Heimbach. I was about to say that the Chicago epidemic had a much shorter incubation period, producing red open sores in less than three days in the people exposed. Yes, one was my fiancé, and she seemed to have no natural immunity to this smallpox virus, just like the Native American population around Fort Pitt in 1763. They went downhill rapidly and died. The worst of it is that the two people I personally knew had received the recent vaccine."

Dr. Merriweather's report stirs a discussion that continues until David Connors and Peter Fowler together suggest a 15-minute coffee and bathroom break. During the break, the man seated next to Robert introduces himself with an outstretched hand. Ameer Parkesh is in his late 40s, a dark-skinned man of East Indian heritage, cleanshaven with dark black hair neatly combed.

In an East Indian accent, Dr. Parkesh shakes Robert's hand to introduce himself.

"I am so glad to meet you, Dr. Merriweather. You may not remember my niece, Natasha Sandhu. You removed her jaw tumor and rebuilt her bone at the same time with your stem cell protocol."

With wide eyes and a surprised look, Robert responds, "Dr. Parkesh, I do remember her. That was almost ten years ago, though. I haven't seen her for over five years now. How is she doing?"

"Please call me Ameer. She is doing fantastically well. She looks normal and your colleague in Augusta, Dr. James McDonald, put dental implants in the bone graft that you did. Six months later, her dentist put teeth on the implants. She is now an M.D., Ph.D., herself and actually works for me in my immunology lab here in Atlanta."

"Well, Ameer, what a small world. I am glad things worked out so well for both of you and, by the way, please call me Bob or Robert, whatever you like."

The committee reconvenes after more than the 15 minutes originally proposed. It is now approaching 10:00 A.M. The discussion that started before the break continues and centers on how the Chicago outbreak occurred and how serious is it. David Connors perspective is that it is an isolated outbreak and developed in people who had not received the proven effect vaccine from the Apollo Drug Co. While he agrees with Dr. Merriweather that the Neanderthal is the probable initial cause, he disagrees that those who contracted the disease actually received the vaccine. After all, Dr. Merriweather was not present to see them receive the shot.

Christine Hargraves, supported by several others, agrees in principal, knowing that a lack of appropriate vaccination is at least possible, but reiterates concern about the enhanced virulence seen in this epidemic. There have been reports, not just by Dr. Merriweather, but specifically from the initial reports sent to the committee from the treating physicians in Chicago. She suggests a mandatory revaccination campaign, focusing on those who did not avail themselves of the vaccine before.

Of course, this presents the ethical dilemma of forcing a repeat of a vaccination known to have side-effects, ranging from minor headaches and joint aches to a full-blown Guillain-Barre Syndrome, on objecting individuals for the protection of others. It becomes the classic debate brought to the public by the original *Star Trek* series. That is, "The needs of the many outweigh the needs of the few," as uttered by actor Leonard Nimoy in his role as Mr. Spock. The debate focuses on this question until a lunch break is called at 12:30 P.M. with a plan to restart the discussion/debate at 2:00 P.M.

During the lunchbreak, Dr. Merriweather and Ameer Parkesh stand together in the cafeteria line behind Dr. Heimbach.

"Dr. Heimbach, I thank you for your support his morning."

Turning around, but still looking over the lunch choices in front of him, Dr. Heimbach replies.

"David Connors has been a bit of a stone wall to some of the ideas of this committee. He seems to draw his authority from the success of the Apollo vaccine in South America and Peter Fowler's support. He has been somewhat overbearing particularly when you consider that his own science is limited. He certainly seems to have heartburn about you. I am glad you put him in his place. Perhaps, it will take his arrogance down a notch and cause him to have a greater respect for the committee members who are far more accomplished than he."

Dr. Merriweather just shakes his head affirmatively and moves along the line. Not accustomed to eating lunch because of his busy schedule of surgeries, administration, and research back in Miami, Robert takes only a small turkey wrap with lettuce and looks for his favorite drink, a Diet Dr Pepper. However, in Atlanta, the headquarters of the Coca-Cola Bottling Co, Diet Dr Pepper is nowhere to be found. He goes with the flow and takes a Diet Coke with ice and has a quick taste.

"Not bad for a second choice. I can live with this."

Robert and Ameer find a two-person table.

"Robert, I must tell you, this David Connors person is trouble. In all of our meetings, he reminds us of the vaccine success in South America and how Apollo was responsible, not doctors and researchers like us. I tell you, he can't be trusted."

"I am well aware of that, Ameer. However, I am sure he gets his marching orders from Apollo headquarters. I guess I am more surprised by his influence over Peter Fowler. I guess it is because Peter Fowler and the CEO of Apollo, David Epstein, teamed up to gain the governmental support and funding for the vaccine protocol."

"Robert, changing the subject, do you like Indian food?"

"Certainly, I do. In fact, tandoori anything is my favorite but vindaloo is a little too spicy for my American palate."

"Good, then you and I will have dinner at my brother's restaurant tonight. Natasha will come too. You can see how beautiful she is."

"Sounds good. I would like that very much but now it's 1:45 P.M. We should be getting back to the committee room. I want to review the notes I took this morning."

Robert and Ameer are among the first to return to Room 202. Already present and seated is Peter Fowler. Seated next to him is someone in a military uniform. From his years as an oral and maxillofacial surgeon in the Air Force, Robert recognizes the brown-green uniform and the single star on his shoulder epaulet to indicate the rank of U.S. Army Brigadier General. He ponders.

"What is an Army General doing on this committee?"

He asks Ameer, "Has this Army officer been here before?"

"No, not ever. I am as surprised as you."

Over the next few minutes, the other committee members file into the room. As each one enters, they look surprised and curious but say nothing.

Once all are seated, Peter Fowler closes each of the two doors into the room and walks back to the head of the table where the Army General now sits between Fowler and Connors with hands folded on the table in front of him as if in prayer. The room is eerily silent as both stand. Peter Fowler begins.

"I want to introduce Brigadier General Harold Vandenbos who flew here this morning from the Pentagon with some urgent news for us."

The introduction stirs a further curiosity among the committee members, who remain silent but turn their heads to assess the reaction of the committee members seated next to them.

Dr. Merriweather immediately suspects something has changed. A one-star General in the Pentagon is not a particularly high-ranking General, such as a two star (Major General), three star (Lieutenant General) and those with four stars, which are reserved for the "Chiefs of Staff" directly responsible to the President. Brigadier Generals are most often operational officers who head up important missions handed down from one of the Chiefs of Staff or the President directly.

As Peter Fowler sits down, General Vandenbos begins in a firm military tone.

"Members of this committee, the President and I thank you for your service. I come to you this afternoon with new information for you to consider as well as a directive straight from the President."

The only sound in the room is the committee members shifting in their seats and/or reaching for their notebooks or laptops to capture the details of this new development.

"Prompted by the rapid escalation and deaths and, moreover, new cases from the smallpox epidemic in Chicago and the surrounding suburbs, the President has ordered a lockdown of the entire Chicago land area and has declared martial law. Similar to the methods used to contain the South American smallpox epidemic, all commercial and private airports are closed until further notice, all roads are closed and guarded by the National Guard and U.S. Army personnel. The harbors from the Illinois state line to Gary, Indiana, are also closed and blockaded by Coast Guard vessels. Sustainable food, water and medical supplies, among other necessities, will be flown in daily to Midway and O'Hare airports and distributed by Army personnel under my direction. Public gatherings are prohibited without my permission and restaurants, public transports, movie theatres, parks and beaches among other businesses will be closed as well."

General Vandenbos pauses for a short moment as all the committee members, including Robert and Ameer, gasp internally and exchange astonished looks. Several utter a few choice four-letter words. Some start to ask a question but the General ignores them and continues.

"Ladies and gentlemen, this is now a dire and unprecedented situation in American history. The original death toll of 8,000 has risen to 40,000 in just two days. There are now 300,000 known cases which leaves about 20 million in the Chicago land area and Northern Illinois area at risk. And, ladies and gentlemen, the rest of the United States are vulnerable, as well. Isolated cases are now popping up in other cities around the country, most probably from those who have left the area and seeded the disease elsewhere. Of course, those cases are being quarantined and mitigation efforts are being enforced. However, in the Chicago area, it is martial law not just mitigation. I am afraid, though, that we are too late to contain this epidemic in one locality. The genie is truly out of the bottle. The President's directive for you is to come up with a plan, to resolve this crisis by the end of the day."

Peter Fowler gasps, and then speaks up.

"General, that's impossible."

"Mr. Fowler, I and the President expect you to do the impossible. I will be in your director's office for the remainder of the afternoon. In front of each of you, I have placed a data sheet about what we currently know. Please review it and present your plan to me by 1800 hours. Good day, everyone."

The General leaves with a quick purposeful stride, a reminder to all in the room that he is in command.

The wide-eyed and exasperated group of medical and research scientists look to Fowler for some direction but the ever-aggressive David Connors seizes the moment instead.

"Well, it seems to me that our charge isn't that impossible at all. I agree with Dr. Hargraves that a revaccination plan is required but not just for those who missed the first go around but everyone in the Chicago area and even nationwide.

Patrick Goode, a burly statistician with thinning gray hair and an untrimmed gray mustache from Emory University, who is still pouring over the data booklet from General Vandenbos, breaks in.

"I agree that everyone needs to be revaccinated. The graph plot of cases radiating out from the epicenter at the University of Chicago supports a risk to everyone in its path, not just isolated cases where a particular person may or may not have been vaccinated. This pattern and the times between reported cases is very disturbing. It seems that, based on the data, even previously vaccinated people are developing smallpox, just like Dr. Merriweather said.

Nobel Laureate Dr. Heimbach immediately chimes in.

"If this smallpox epidemic doesn't respond to the vaccine then it was either partially inactivated, the dose was too low, or this smallpox is resistant to the vaccine."

Dr. Merriweather speaks next.

"In my observations, the smallpox progression did not show an incomplete response, which would indicate a partially inactive immunoglobulin or a dose of the antigen being too low. Instead, the smallpox clinical signs progressed as if the victim had no immunity at all."

Dr. Heimbach chimes in.

"In that case, we need to produce a new vaccine from a viral specimen taken from a recent victim."

"Wait a minute. Just wait a minute," says Peter Fowler, trying to exert his leadership as Co-Chairman of the committee.

"Obtaining a live viral specimen from one of the Chicago victims is dangerous and risks spreading this disease further. Plus it will take time. Besides, reading the report from Europe, that epidemic from a similar caveman specimen has responded well to the vaccine. Look at page 22 of the General's report. Ninety-eight-point-four percent (98.4%) of those who received the vaccine in Europe did not develop smallpox and those that had the disease already responded to the vaccine if given within seven days of exposure or within three days of developing symptoms. The French used a higher dose of the vaccine for those who were not previously vaccinated and for those who developed symptoms."

Dr. Christine Hargraves speaks next.

"What was the original dose of the antigen in the vaccine? It says here the dose was 78 million plaque-forming units per milliliter. Although that has been a standard dose, it may be too low today. Smallpox has been extinct since 1980. Today's patients may have experienced a decline in their background immunity, which will prevent a complete response to the antigen in this vaccine. I have seen a similar pattern in the mumps, measles, and rubella (MMR) vaccine over the past twenty years that required a minor dose adjustment. Similarly, we now commonly give a higher dose of the yearly flu vaccine to people over 55 in anticipation of an age-related decline in their development of antibodies. I suggest we revaccinate at 156 million plaque-forming units per milliliter. "

Dr. Heimbach adds his thoughts.

"That may be correct, but we can't take that chance and we don't know what the 98% effective dose is. I am in favor developing a new vaccine and reducing the risk of spread outside the area of initial outbreak by developing it in the Abbott Laboratories within the already stricken Chicago area."

David Connors immediately recognizing the business threat to Apollo and to himself that this line of thinking presents and so he jumps right in.

"Developing a vaccine takes time that we don't have. Apollo has stockpiled enough of the vaccine to revaccinate the entire U.S. population three times over. We can double the dose as Dr. Hargrave recommends and start as early as tomorrow."

Dr. Hargrave responds.

"Yes, doubling the dose would likely do it."

Ameer Parkesh steps in.

"Doubling the dose of a vaccine that doesn't work still won't work."

Dr. Merriweather agrees.

"Certainly, two times zero is still zero."

Dr. Parkesh adds his two cents again.

"With our new PCR technology and the use of a primer we could develop a new vaccine within three days, once we have a sample of the virus. We could distribute it immediately thereafter if the FDA would release its regulatory restrictions."

The debate rages on with committee members arguing points and counterpoints. Sides are taken, supporting either the fast response requested by the General or apparently the President. That is, an immediate revaccination program using twice the original dose is weighed against developing a new vaccine that would take at least five to seven days to first develop and then produce in sufficient quantities to vaccinate 20 million people, provided the FDA agrees to suspend its regulatory restrictions.

By 17:30 hours (5:30 P.M.), a polarized committee stands at an impasse with no consensus. Peter Fowler calls an end to the debate.

"My fellow committee members, I see no reason to continue the discussion further. All of the data has been reviewed and everyone's facts and opinions have been heard. We must now vote on a plan that I am tasked to present to the General. While I see the value in each of the two plans, we must now put it to a vote. From my personal perspective, I favor an immediate revaccination plan at a dose double of the original."

The vote proceeds around the table, with Dr. Heimbach, Dr. Merriweather, Patrick Goode, Karen Georgeff, and Dr. Parkesh plus three others voting to develop a new vaccine and Drs. Fowler, Hargraves, and, of course, Connors voting for the immediate revaccination program of a double dose of the Apollo vaccine. It seems Peter Fowlers concluding comment favoring the immediate revaccination plan sways some of the committee member who are on the fence and the vote tips to that plan which passes 12 to 8.

Peter Fowler adjourns the meeting with a final double-edged remark.

"We will meet again Monday at 8:00 A.M. But, please, do not leave the area. We may need to call an urgent meeting this weekend. Also, I must tell you that I pray that we have done the right thing and that our country will look upon our decision with favor rather than with scorn in the final analysis."

CHAPTER 22

DR. MERRIWEATHER'S EPIPHANY

David Connors follows Peter Fowler to the CDC's director's office where General Vandenbos has somewhat taken over to command the quarantine and city lockdown operations, as well as locating and planning logistics to get the needed supplies to maintain the basic services for more than 20 million people isolated from the rest of the world. The General accepts the plan and particularly likes the fact that it can be started as early as the next day. He immediately starts making calls.

First, he reaches out to the Chiefs of Staff at the pentagon to outline Fowler's plan, which of course they will relay to the President. Next, he calls several Army bases and National Guard units. He knows the task ahead of him will be difficult. Policing and containing more than 20 million people, controlling the inevitable civil unrest and probable riots, as well as providing food, medicine and information is no small task. Yes, he also knows that rumors will spread particularly with a media noted for exaggeration and crisis reporting. Conspiracy theories will abound. He knows he must control the narrative and flow of information while appearing to provide a free flow of data.

"General, I need to call Apollo CEO David Epstein. Is the government going to pay for a second vaccination program?"

Somewhat annoyed, the General looks up at Connors over his glasses which had been trained on the pages in front of him. "Listen, Mr. Connors, you just be sure the initial shipment of vaccine at the dose you promised arrives at my headquarters at O'Hare Airport by noon tomorrow or payment will be the least of your concerns."

General Vandenbos shoos both Connors and Fowler away with a brush of his hand. The General has no time for them now.

David Connors immediately goes to the private office afforded to him by the CDC. He calls CEO Epstein.

"David, this is David," he says with a chuckle, bemused by the greeting that uses their shared first name. He then continues, "You owe me big time, David. The committee wanted to develop an entirely new vaccine within the area of the epidemic using Abbott Labs in North Chicago. We would have lost time and dollars, in addition to media coverage. Instead, I convinced them that assembling and delivering more of our current dose would be quicker since it is already available. Do we have that much in stock?"

"Yes, we do and more. Good work, Connors. That's why I got you on that committee. Now, tell me, how much do they need, by when do they want it and how much are they willing to pay?"

"They need at least 20 million double doses of the vaccine with an initial shipment flown into O'Hare by noon tomorrow."

"Connors, did you promise that?"

"I had to. The demand came from a Pentagon, General with direct access to the President."

"Wow, you really committed us this time but another billion dollars now and 20 billion dollars more when the rest of the country is revaccinated will make it worthwhile. Look, I'll get everybody here to load our current doses but doubled into a chartered cargo plane by early tomorrow so that they will get there by noon. We won't have time to add two doses together. The good doctors and nurses will just have to inject each person twice. I'll get our packaging people to put two loaded syringes in one pack with instructions.

"Again, good work, Connors, you can certainly expect a bonus and more, if this works out. Also, you need to go with the General to oversee the arrival and distribution of our vaccine. I don't want any slipups that would come back to haunt us now."

"The committee was concerned about the effectiveness of our vaccine. Several said the Neanderthal virus is different and our vaccine won't work," Connors warned the CEO.

"It doesn't matter, Connors, we will get our money anyway. Just do your job."

A click in Connors' ear indicates an abrupt conclusion to the call. David Connors hangs up the phone with two uneasy thoughts circulating in his calculating mind. The first is that the General didn't guarantee any payment. Perhaps Apollo is expected to provide a re-dosing program at no cost since the initial one didn't work. The other is a concern about going into the center of the smallpox epidemic. Even though he has bought into the belief that the vaccine at an enhanced dose will protect him, doubts about it still linger with the echoes of Dr. Heimbach and Dr. Merriweather's warnings adding to his apprehension.

By 7:30 P.M., Robert, Ameer, and Ameer's niece and former patient, Natasha, are seated in a private dining area at the Indian restaurant owned by Ameer's brother. Dr. Merriweather is indeed pleased to see that Natasha's surgery from over ten years ago has turned out so well and is further pleased that she has become a physician and researcher herself. The meal goes along smoothly with light social conversation as if Robert and Ameer had been lifelong friends instead of being newly thrown together as committee members. However, it develops a serious tone when Ameer changes the subject, "Robert, I don't know about you but I think the committee made a big mistake today."

"You know, Ameer, I think so too. The smallpox that I saw in Chicago was devastating. It was like the victims had no natural immunity, like the native tribes in and around Fort Pitt, the Inca and Mayan cultures of South America, Hawaiian natives, and every other culture into which Europeans insinuated themselves."

"Robert, we could develop a new vaccine ourselves without fresh virus from the Chicago epidemic. I have a stock of the same cowpox antigen used by Apollo and other drug companies before smallpox became extinct."

"Cowpox? Why would you use cowpox?"

"Robert, that may be the only thing you don't know about smallpox. Because of the smallpox disease transmissions from Jenner's live variola virus injections, vaccines for that disease were made from cowpox viruses instead because they are not pathogenic to humans. It eliminated the development of smallpox seen from the injections originally developed by Jenner. The mild disease of cowpox also added to a background immunity in most everyone in Europe at that time due to their association with cattle, as well as by the practice of eating beef that developed over the centuries. The immunity of the vaccine is from a surface marker on the cowpox virus, which is identical to one on the smallpox virus. It is a 100% cross reactivity. This cross reactivity confers lifelong immunity from smallpox. It worked so well that the last-known case of smallpox was in 1977 and the World Health Agency declared smallpox extinct in 1980. That is until now."

Robert is silent, mulling over this lesson. His thoughts are turned inward. He stares straight ahead, his mouth partially agape. His mind races forward. More than 30 seconds elapse.

"Robert – Dr. Merriweather, are you alright?"

As if awakening from a daydream, Robert's eyes focus on Ameer again.

"Yes, yes. Ameer, that's it. Why did smallpox hit the Inca and Mayan indigenous populations so hard? They never came into contact with cattle like Europeans did. They lived off the land. They hunted local game and ate what the land offered them. And why did smallpox hit the Native American populations to the point of near extinction? They didn't come into contact with cattle or eat beef either. They ate deer, bear, wild birds and bison, which are a different species altogether. The same thing happened in Hawaii and the Pacific Islands after Captain Cook brought smallpox to those islands. None of those populations were ever exposed to cows and therefore, to the non-virulent cowpox virus. Therefore, they did not have the cowpox antibodies i.e. immunity or even partial immunity to smallpox conferred by the cross reactivity from cowpox as the European invaders did."

Robert continues, his mind racing.

"It relates perfectly. It actually confirms it. The Chicago epidemic is virulent and spreading quickly. It came form a frozen Neanderthal. The recent outbreak in France was much less virulent and spread more slowly, mostly affecting the young, the old, and the medically compromised just like the epidemic that occurred in South America. Don't you see? That epidemic came from viruses transmitted from Modern Man. My college anthropology friend, Ralph Earlandson, who was one of the two original deaths in Chicago had told me months earlier that early modern man domesticated the Yurok and throughout the centuries bred them into cattle. The reason that the French, South American, and European outbreaks responded to the current vaccine and have been so mild is because the virus from the modern man caveman has been kept in check by the centuries of exposure to cowpox that the native populations in the Americas and Pacific Islands didn't have. And guess what?

Neither did the Neanderthals. Neanderthals never domesticated the Yurok. Their weaponry for hunting was sufficiently primitive that they could rarely bring down such a big animal. Instead, they focused on caribou, deer, boar and other species, rarely coming into contact with enough Yurok viruses to develop a cowpox or you might call it Yurok pox immunity to protect them from or even mute the virulence of smallpox."

"Oh my God, Robert. You are right. You are very right. It makes sense. It is the only explanation that fits the pattern of facts."

Natasha breaks in.

"Dr. Merriweather, Uncle Ameer, from what you are saying, the revaccination program your committee approved has no chance of working then. This smallpox virus, because it originated from the Neanderthal, has not been modified by the cowpox driven evolutionary pressures over the centuries. It is like a completely new virus to 21st-century mankind. That's a terrifying thought."

"Robert, what are we going to do? The current vaccine won't work on this smallpox, any more than it would work on mumps, measles or chickenpox."

"Ameer, did you say that you could make a vaccine in just three days if you had a fresh sample of the virus?"

"Yes, making a vaccine is quite easy with the new primer technology I developed. One that has been sitting at the FDA for the past two years. First, you need to kill the virus without changing the structure or chemistry of it. That will keep it from transmitting the disease to others like Jenner's first vaccines did but will still allow our immune system to recognize the virus and synthesize neutralizing antibodies specific to it. Today, I can accelerate the process by restricted fragment enzymes, which would isolate a vulnerable chemical sequence of the viral coat. Then I could multiply that sequence by Polymerase Chain Reaction (PCR) to gain millions of copies of that sequence. From there, it is routine to make larger batches."

"Can you do what you just said from a frozen sample?"

"Yes, of course."

"Then we have a chance."

With that, Robert takes his cellphone out of the pocket of his sport coat and dials a number. He nervously taps his finger on the restaurant's table, already cleared of its plates. The intervening seven to ten seconds seems like seven to ten years to Robert. Finally, he hears a voice.

"Hi, Chief. What's up? Is something wrong?" Cathy Ellyn, Robert's

Surgical Coordinator and Nurse back at his clinic in Miami, greets him.

"No, nothing is wrong and I am sorry to call you on a Friday night. I hope I am not interrupting anything."

"Only the laundry, Chief, and I can certainly use a break from that."

"Cathy, I need a huge, huge favor from you. It could save millions of lives."

"Chief, is this one of your jokes, like that visit from the Queen of England that we all fell for on April Fool's Day?"

"No, I am dead serious this time. Listen carefully. It's important. Drive over to my house tonight, but, first, stop at Publix and get two pounds of dry ice and put it in a small cooler, like the ones that our tissue bank specimens comes in. Buy some duct tape, as well. When you get to my house, my house sitter will let you in. I'll let her know to expect you. In my garage, you'll find a 4x4-foot freezer that I usually keep fishing bait in. It's empty except for a tennis ball can wrapped in duct tape. Don't remove the tape or attempt to open the can. Instead, put the frozen can directly in the cooler with the dry ice and tape the cooler shut to keep it frozen. And Cathy, the next part will be the hard part. As soon as you're fully awake, tomorrow morning, I want you to drive to Atlanta and bring the box to the Atlanta Immunology Center. I will text you the specific address for your GPS after we hang up. Are you okay with that?"

"Yes, of course, but what is it? And why does it need to be frozen?"

"It's too long a story. Let's just say it is biologic material that is critical to saving the lives I mentioned. We need to get it as soon as possible and it is something we can't trust to overnight shipping."

"Chief, I don't understand, but I'm glad to do it. In fact, if you need it that quickly, I'll come up with my friend Denise tonight. I've driven there before. It's only a ten-hour drive from Miami. We'll take turns driving. We'll drive straight through and have it there before noon."

"Are you sure? That would be great, if you really want to do it."

"For a mission of mercy like this, heck, yeah. Remember, we are nurses you know."

"Okay, you and Denise are just fantastic. Thanks. See you tomorrow and, Cathie, drive safe."

Ameer and Natasha have remained silent throughout the entire call, anxiously waiting for it to conclude. Ameer interjects as soon as Robert presses the red end call button.

"Do you mean to tell me that you have a frozen virus specimen from the

Chicago outbreak?"

"I do. It is actually sloughed skin and some blood from my fiancé, I have to admit."

Realizing what he just said, Robert fights back the emotion that is about to overtake him and gets back to the important task ahead of him.

"The specimen will arrive at your lab before noon tomorrow. You talked the talk, now you'll have the chance to walk the walk."

Unfamiliar with the reference, Ameer looks quizzically at Robert who immediately rephrases it.

"It means you said you could turn out a vaccine in three days. Now, you will have the chance to do it."

"We will do it, Robert. Natasha and I will get all our technicians together. We will make the vaccine, a lot of it. I promise."

After an hour of introspection, vacillating about what to do Robert looks at the CDC list of committee members. Finally, he calls the only one he thinks will understand how quickly developing a new but untested vaccine against a new and virulent virus against which modern man has no natural defense is the only hope.

"Hello, Dean Heimbach, here."

"Dr. Heimbach, this is Dr. Merriweather, along with Ameer Parkesh. Sorry to call you late on a Friday night."

"Hey, that's okay, I'm doing nothing at the moment. I suspect you're calling about the committee's decision to overrule us and proceed with their revaccination plan?"

"That's right, Dr. Heimbach."

Robert reiterates his hypothesis of modern man's evolution in Europe and his ascent to the present today. He explains how it was associated intimately with cattle that was domesticated form the Yurok and therefore the nonpathogenic cowpox virus which gave us a background cross immunity to smallpox. He emphasizes that the Neanderthal virus is actually a different, more ancient form of the smallpox virus we know today and that modern humans currently have no such background immunity to it and no effective vaccine.

"So, Dr. Heimbach, the revaccination program has no chance of working."

"You know, Dr. Merriweather, I suspected the same but couldn't put a clear rationale in such evolutionary terms as you have put it. From my experience with viruses, you are spot on. Indeed, we need to develop a new vaccine. It is now absolutely necessary."

"That's why I am calling you. I am having a frozen specimen of human tissue from the Chicago outbreak (don't ask me how I got it) brought in tomorrow by noon. And also, don't ask me how it is getting here. Dr. Parkesh will start making a vaccine as soon as it arrives. He has an advanced technology that can produce it in just three days. The advice that I need from you, sir, is advice how to get the support of Peter Fowler and the committee so as to put it in the hands of the community?"

"Well, Dr. Merriweather, we are both scientists, aren't we? We are trained to advance a hypothesis then test it to either prove it or disprove it, right?"

"Okay, but how can we do that?"

"Simply, my boy. We take a blood sample from each caveman and test it for antibodies. If the modern man specimen has antibodies that react with the current cowpox vaccine and the Neanderthals blood specimen does not, it validates your hypothesis. I am sure David Connors wouldn't accept even that but I can assure you Peter Fowler and the rest of the committee will. Heck, I can call Michel Fortin, my colleague in France who started working on the modern man specimen to take a new blood sample and test it. That will give us one half of the answer. Does the specimen you have coming to Atlanta have blood on it or in it?"

"Yes, but I don't know if it is enough to run protein electrophoresis for antibodies."

"If it is not degraded by the freezing-thawing cycle we may be able to concentrate it. I'll try to do that."

"Now, I know why you won the Nobel Prize in Medicine. Come over to Ameer Parkesh's lab tomorrow at noon. We can start right away. I will text you the address."

"I'll do just that but, first of all, we need to be strategic and bring Fowler into the loop. If we want his support, we do not want to appear that we are working behind his back. I'll call him now and get him to come to his office at 8:00 A.M. tomorrow. We can run it by him then."

"Good idea, Dr. Heimbach. You could also be a politician."

"Oh, no, no, my boy, God forbid, God forbid."

They end the call with each scientist chuckling.

At 8:00 A.M. Saturday morning, while Cathy and Denise are more than halfway to Atlanta from Miami carrying the frozen, bloody skin tissue from Heather, Peter Fowler is listening to Dr. Merriweather's and Dr. Heimbach' s plan.

"From what you are saying, we are re-vaccinating 20 million people who will still die and essentially millions more after that. That is a pretty big and dire prediction. Look, I'll meet you halfway. We will continue with the revaccination program at the higher dose. In fact, the first shipment of the double dose vaccines will arrive at O'Hare later today with immediate distribution to the vaccination teams set up throughout the Chicago-land area. If as you imply, this dose of vaccine shows the first sign of ineffectiveness, we will use the new vaccine Dr. Parkesh is producing. It is just a shame we don't have enough time to test your vaccine on animal models or even on a few human volunteers."

"Do you mean we have your support to start producing a new vaccine from the tissue being sent?"

"Dr. Merriweather, Dr. Heimbach, I don't know whether you're right or you're wrong but we have no choice. If you're wrong, we only waste money. If you're right, we save millions of lives. It's a dilemma but a no-brainer. Go ahead as fast as you can. I'm with you on this one."

CHAPTER 23

A TRUCE OR A CLASH?

"Connors? What are you calling me about at 9:00 in the morning? I have a tee time at Mt. Tabor Golf Club at 9:30."

"Sorry, I didn't know, but this is important. I don't know what it was about but Fowler met with Merriweather and Heimbach less than an hour ago. They're planning something that may change our plans. I suspect they're planning to develop a new vaccine, instead of using ours."

"Well, that is important. How the hell can they produce a vaccine that quickly? Nevertheless, if their vaccine works better than ours, it will not only cost us billions but discredit the Apollo Drug Co. again, just when we are the top dog. It is time for me to finally get Merriweather on our side, whatever it takes. You be sure to get to Chicago and represent the noble efforts of Apollo and let everybody know it."

"David, I am already at the airport."

"Good, I will work on Merriweather after my golf outing today."

David Epstein addresses his research director and two of his marketing directors, who make up the golfing foursome of the day.

"Gentlemen, today. We will only play nine holes. I have some important negotiating to do today."

Almost exactly at noon, Cathy and Denise arrive with the all-important frozen tissue. After gratefully hugging both women, Dr. Merriweather takes the frozen can out of the cooler and hands it to Ameer and Dean Heimbach. All are now on a comfortable first-name basis. They take the can off to the lab to slowly dethaw it in a sealed sterile clear plastic box with rubber gloves sealed to the inner wall to allow the contents to be manipulated from the outside. They first need to test it for viable virus. After that, they will try to do Dean Heimbach's concentration of blood antibodies and Ameer's attenuation of the virus and expansion of its protein coat sequence as the first step in rapidly developing a new vaccine from scratch.

As Robert turns to thank Cathy and Denise, as well as write a check to cover their expenses for an overnight stay to rest up in Atlanta, his cellphone rings.

"Hello, this is Dr. Merriweather. Can I help you?"

"Dr. Merriweather, this is David Epstein. You know me but don't hang up until you've heard me out. I know that you and I have been adversaries for a long time. However, with the crisis going on in Chicago and the global threat it represents, I think it is time for us to set our differences and perhaps even our animosities aside. I need your help to develop a new vaccine that more directly targets the plague going on in Chicago. If you understand me and you are willing, I would like you to visit me personally tomorrow to discuss a working relationship. No tricks, no false promises. I will send a limo to pick you up at 8:30 A.M. at your hotel. My corporate jet will fly you to my office in Morris Plains, New Jersey. You'll be back in Atlanta by 2:00 P.M. I think you will be excited by what we can do together. It will certainly be worth your while."

Dr. Merriweather removes his cellphone from his ear and gives it a curious look and a wry smile of suspicion but answers.

"Okay, I'll be ready. If we can somehow work together to prevent a global plaque and help so many, it will be worthwhile to declare a truce."

As David Epstein sees the screen on his cellphone return to the time page indicating the end of the call, he leans back in his cushioned office chair. Speaking to no one he muses, "Everyone has their price. Everyone is a whore. It is just a question of what price. Everyone has a weakness. Old Dr. Goody Two-Shoes is no exception. Hey, Dr. Goody Two-Shoes, let's save the world together. He took the bait, hook, line and sinker. Now all I need to do is reel him in."

Conversely, Robert dials Andy Molinaro, his friend who is a detective and now fiancé of his former secretary Isabella Ruiz, who now partners with him to solve cases.

"Andy, this is Dr. Merriweather. I need a big favor from you."

"Nice to hear from you. You sound pensive. What's up?"

"Do you recall the involvement of David Epstein the CEO of Apollo Drug Co. in the Bone Protect scandal and in the scam about supporting a suspended animation drug to NASA?"

"I sure do. That scum got away both times. Why do you ask?"

"Well, he just called me about working with him and Apollo on the recent new smallpox outbreak from Chicago. While I would be glad to work with any drug company with the technological and manpower resources that exist at Apollo, there isn't an honest bone in that man's body. I suspect he is up to something."

"Okay, what you do you want me and Izzy to do?"

"I am not sure. First, can you do a background check on Epstein and his appointee on a CDC committee named David Connors? I smell a scam and I think they want to drag me into it."

"Okay, I'll put my feelers out."

"Look, Andy, I have to run. Give my best to Izzy and tell her that her daughter Mishy is *almost* as great as she was."

"Okay, Doc. I understand."

The curious conversation ends with a laugh.

While Robert is on the line with the detective, David Epstein remains gloating in his office. He leans back in his cushioned office chair, lights up a Cuban cigar, and puts his feet up on the desk, staring up at the ceiling towards nothing in particular.

"Yeah, some people have it and some people don't. The gift of persuasion."

Epstein, a multibillionaire at only forty-six, is the spoiled son of rich parents. His father, a successful importer/exporter of diamonds and gems, and his mother, a socialite among the well-to-do of Westchester, New York, had little time for their only son. Raised mostly by nannies, he learned early on how to "get his way by just asking and sometimes bending the truth, if you know what I mean" as was his motto. He recalls his lifetime of continual success: How he got a driver's license at the age of 14 and his own car for his 16th birthday; how he got into Harvard on a scholarship by falsifying his parents income and address. There, he became president of his fraternity and president of the student council. He learned each position brought a connection and, with that, money. Yes, money, something that was actually easy for him to come by. It was as easy as organizing a fundraiser and keeping most of the money for "expenses." Just organize a social event and pocket even more. With his connections, he got into the Harvard MBA program, which opened doors for their graduates at major companies. Indeed, at Apollo, he rose to the top, introducing the term "blockbuster drug." That is a drug that everyone needs and, even if they don't need it, an advertising campaign would work to convince the populace of the drug's vital importance and then convince doctors to prescribe it.

Now, smiling broadly, he clicks off the drugs that brought him to the pinnacle of his success: osteoporosis drugs, cholesterol-lowering drugs, painkillers, blood thinners, sleep medications, the list goes on and on.

Satisfied with himself and his daydreaming, his last thought, *You know, I should run for President. With my money, I'll bet I could win.*

As promised, a chauffeur-driven limousine picks up Robert at 8:30 A.M. sharp on Sunday morning and he soon finds himself in the office of Apollo CEO David Epstein by 10:30 A.M. Robert is not surprised to see the spaciousness of the office nor the silver embossed plaques on the wall boasting "Man of the Year" and "CEO of the Year," as well as several encased magazine covers heralding the success of the Apollo smallpox vaccine used in the South American outbreak.

Both men are dressed casually in khaki slacks and dress shirts, Robert in blue and Epstein in a maroon. Neither wears a tie. Each hides his suspicion of the other as Epstein extends out his right hand for the traditional and expected welcoming handshake. As Robert sits in a chair of plush fabric and cherry wood opposite Epstein, he recalls the legend of how the handshake became popular. The gesture allowed adversaries to prove to each other that neither was carrying a weapon. Robert smirks at the thought. However, the thought lingers since he knows all too well that the weapons of today are very different, being of the mind and the word, rather than the hand.

"Dr. Merriweather, I'll get straight to the point. The horrible and preventable deaths in the Chicago area outbreak have made me realize I and my company need to be more oriented to people and society rather than profits. That's why I need a person of your reputation and humanistic commitment to help me turn it around. We can start with this new smallpox outbreak. I want you to lead a team and be a consultant to produce a new vaccine specifically aimed at ending this new outbreak. For that, I am offering you a 10-million-dollar consultant fee. After that, if you are willing, I can give you a position in Apollo as "Director of Special Research," specifically tasked to start anew the two projects you are working on at your university; the Human Papilloma Virus initiation of oral cancer and the use of bone marrow-derived stem cells to regenerate bone. You see, Dr. Merriweather, I have read about all your projects and followed your publications. Consider the progress you can make with my company's technology and financial support without all the onerous obstacles academia puts in your way. With the directorship comes a 5-million-dollar annual salary and I'll even donate a 3-million-dollar research chair in your name to the University of Miami Miller School of Medicine. What do you say?"

Robert responds slowly and without any show of emotion. "Mr. Epstein, I am shocked and honestly overwhelmed. You are talking about a major change in my career, albeit for a very worthwhile purpose that speaks to my core values and goals. You are also proposing a major change in your company's direction, as well as mine. I am accustomed to being an academic surgeon treating patients with serious problems. I will need a few days to digest your very comprehensive and generous offer."

"Fair enough, Dr. Merriweather. I'll have my legal team draw up a contract that I am sure you will like."

"For that purpose, we can get at least the preliminaries started today, if you don't mind. If you agree, we can finalize it when we next meet. If you don't agree, we just tear it up unsigned. I'll have our HR Director walk you down to her office to gather the specifics we need. No commitment or formal agreement for now. Are you okay with that?"

"I am familiar with contract development, Mr. Epstein," Merriweather answered dryly.

"We should meet by the end of the week to get after the Chicago-based outbreak right away."

"That's affirmative, Mr. Epstein. Thursday or Friday, at the latest."

Robert stands and both shake hands once again perhaps indicating that neither had a hidden weapon. Or did they?

Patricia Carpenter from HR arrives at the very conclusion of the handshake and escorts Dr. Merriweather to the HR office.

"Dr. Merriweather, I have developed a profile for you in our employee database. Please have a seat at this computer station. You'll need to choose a login and password. Everyone's log in is their first initial and their last name. The password can be anything that you will remember. Most of us use a capital of our middle name, the numbers corresponding to the letters of our last name followed by the pound sign."

"Wow, that seems complicated."

"Not really. It is actually quite easy."

"It has worked for us and everybody that forgot it was able to figure it out without having to develop a new password. Go ahead and log in. It may take you a few minutes but fill in all the blanks on the form. I'll be back later."

Robert logs in with a more simplified password and quickly completes the standard demographic questions on the three-page form, as well as a medical history and current medications questionnaire. Out of curiosity, he tries something. David Epstein's middle name is Horatio according to his silver-embossed wall plaques. Robert then calculates E=5, P=16, S=19, T=20, E=5, I=9, N=14. He then logs out of his own login and tries -e-p-s-t-e-i-n H5, 16, 19, 20, 7, 9, 14#. It doesn't work.

"Well, it was worth a try."

Then Robert remembers seeing the center plaque above Epstein's desk that sports a big star. Certainly, it was something Epstein thought added to his luster. His desk blotter also had a big star on it. On a hunch, Robert tries again H51619207914*. It worked. Robert is in. He mutters to himself, "I just can't believe this, shows me once again how worthless the HIPAA law really is. I wonder what a real hacker could do."

As Robert looks over CEO David Epstein's demographic data, he sees nothing that everyone doesn't already know. He then delves into his medical history. Perusing it for two to three minutes, Robert eyes widen. He sees something unusual for a man who grew up in the 1970s and 1980s, something useful, a vulnerability. A plan begins to hatch in Robert's mind. He commits the new information to memory. He then quickly logs off and logs back on to his own page just as Patricia Carpenter returns.

"All done, Doctor?"

"Yes, it was quite straightforward as you said. I guess I'll head out now. I can see Mr. Epstein's limo waiting for me down below through your corner office window. Mr. Epstein must think highly of you to give you such a nice office."

As Robert heads toward the Morris Plains private airstrip in the company limo, David Epstein calls in his marketing director Richard Bloom who heard the entire conversation from an adjacent room via a hidden intercom disguised as a computer mouse on Epstein's desk. "Well, Richard, what do you think?"

"David, you were magnificent again. You sure have a way with words and were very persuasive just like you were with the congressional committee. Of course, he bought it. The schmuck is an idealist. You hit him in all of his vulnerable areas: saving lives, research discoveries, rebuilding bone from stem cells with a person's bone marrow. He never even talked about the money you threw at him. He may be an accomplished surgeon, researcher and all that stuff but he is very naïve about money and the real world we live in."

In the back of the limo, Robert looks out the window as they pass a field with about 20 cows grazing aimlessly. Closest to the fence, Robert notices a more concentrated group of cows around a bin stacked with hay eagerly eating away. However, instead of the scene reminding him of the association of cowpox with cattle, it conjures up a different thought. As cows are ruminants, they often eat and defecate at the same time. Robert remarks to himself, "How appropriate. I was fed more bullshit today than these cows could ever produce. That bastard knows that his vaccine doesn't work. He may not know why but he doesn't even care about the millions that are dying. He only wants to use me to save face and get the credit and profits for a vaccine that really works."

It seems that Robert was not as naïve as Epstein and Bloom think. Surely, if they knew, they would wonder why he went along with it.

Robert returns to the lab that Sunday afternoon to find that the frozen tissue specimen, once thawed, indeed contained numerous live viruses suitable for killing the viruses without changing its chemical coat. Production of a vaccine is already underway. Indeed, Ameer proudly announces, "Robert, I'll have the first batch of vaccine by Tuesday. I am walking the walk."

Both Ameer and Robert laugh at his remark while Dean Heimbach looks on, confused.

Monday morning finds the CDC Committee meeting again, this time without David Connors. Fowler apprises the committee members of his decision to support the development of the new vaccine in Ameer Parkesh's local lab, a safeguard if the higher-dose revaccination plan fails. A similar discussion and debate ensues with Christine Hargraves advancing that smallpox has historically responded to the current vaccine and the only reason to doubt its effectiveness is most likely due to a sub-therapeutic dose or that fewer people availed themselves of the first round of vaccinations than previously thought. She dismisses Merriweather's theory of an ancient virus from the Neanderthals, saying that the idea that they never domesticated the Yurok is pure speculation. Ragnar Olaffson and Patrick Goode back up Dr. Merriweather's assertions with a statistical model demonstrating the outbreak is following a geometric growth rate that can only be explained by a new disease. The committee remains at an impasse with nothing more to do than to see what unfolds over the next few days.

In Chicago, there is no impasse but there is a growing unrest among the citizens unaccustomed to the restriction of freedoms in a democratic society. General Vandenbos, in the prototypical style of military Martial Law, has put troops on every street. His team of 50,000 healthcare workers are instructed to revaccinate 400 individuals each over the next two days to reach the 20 million individuals under his responsibility. He places several teams at major sites in the center of Chicago, including Grant Park, White Sox Park, Wrigley Field, the University of Chicago, The University of Illinois and Northwestern University Medical Schools. He also dispatches workers to the entrance steps of the Field Museum and the Museum of Science and Industry. Further, he has teams in the suburbs at major parks and all schools, as well as injection teams giving injections door to door. General Vandenbos is running this as a military exercise from his "war room" in a hangar at O'Hare Airport. Every injected person will receive a permanent tattoo with the initials RV, indicating revaccination, on his or her wrist so that no one will mistakenly be injected twice. More importantly, his team can readily identify anyone who has not received the second dose of the vaccine as they go house to house.

General Vandenbos has covered all logistical bases including supplying food, fuel, and normal healthcare, masks, hot lines for smallpox updates, open communication lines to entertainment, free access to all radio and TV channels as well as sports and news from the outside world (that he carefully curates). He wants to keep at least a semblance of normality. He also has his communications team sending out several daily messages that indicate the outbreak is under control and that Martial Law will be lifted soon. He does not release numbers for either death or infection rates. Those are only passed on in code to the Pentagon and forwarded only to the White House and the

Surgeon General. The CDC Committee is the only "civilian" group to be apprised of the growing numbers in each category, figures that support that this is a geometric spread of a new disease.

CHAPTER 24

Cracks in the Dike

By early Tuesday night, General Vandenbos' goal of revaccinating nearly all 20 million people has been accomplished. At this time, the General should be relaxed and proud of his mission's success. Yet, he is uneasy. He sees that the make-shift morgue in the empty hangers at O'Hare Airport now contains more bodies than yesterday. In fact, more bodies are coming in each hour. His assigned leaders at Midway airport and Soldier Field report the same results in their newly constructed morgues. However, he is even more concerned about the medical staff reports that indicate five percent of his own troops and even a few of his medical staff have developed what maybe the early signs of smallpox: fatigue, weakness, lumps in the neck and small red sores. He knows all his personnel received the first vaccine before deployment and received the revaccination booster on Saturday. The first doubts about the effectiveness of the entire vaccination program creeps into his thoughts. He briefly contemplates the chaos and breakdown of societal norms, as well as the mega deaths, that would result if his troops could no longer control and contain the populous for which he is responsible. He is aware of the many conspiracy theories circulating around and how all of them are accusing him and the government of a cover up. He is like a good soldier, he fights back the momentary panic that his thoughts bring to the surface.

In the Chicago suburb of Naperville, third-grader Richard Snyder rubs his left arm, which is a little sore from his revaccination "booster shot," as it was described to him. He is proud of the fact that he again didn't cry and presented a brave face even though this time it was two shots. Meanwhile, his father Harold Snyder, the 42-year-old section captain of Local 21 of the International Brotherhood of Electrical Workers (IBEW), is on the phone finishing the last call to each of his 24 lieutenants in the IBEW covering the entire Chicago land area under quarantine.

"That's right, Bill, I want all of our members in the area to meet on the steps of the Art Institute on Wednesday at 9:00 A.M. sharp. This has to be a peaceful rally and protest. I have instructed all lieutenants like yourself to have our members brings signs and placards but no firearms, bottles, mace, Tasers, Molotov cocktails or weapons of any kind. The signs should demonstrate our solidarity and have our IBEW logo. No threats on the signs. I got the marching permit by personally guaranteeing that it would be a peaceful demonstration. In particular, no one starts a confrontation with the army, the National Guard troops or the police. We just want to show our concern for our families and let them know that we want real answers. We want to gain their confidence. That's the only way we will find out when this shit ends and when we can get back to our normal lives."

"Harold, I got it. You can count on a 100% participation from my members."

"Great! We got the truckers union, the machinists, the airport workers union, and others to join us. We will be over one million people strong. We'll march from the Art Institute on Michigan Avenue southward to the Soldier Field parking lot. That's where we will hold the rally and demand answers. I have secured a permit for both the march and for the rally afterward."

Harold Snyder is about to continue when Richard's 14-year-old older brother Jerry comes in from shooting baskets in the driveway and announces, "Dad, I don't feel so good."

Harold looks at his son and sees that he looks pale. He has small red acne spots on his cheeks, beads of perspiration on his forehead, and a vacant expression on his face. The young man slumps down on the sofa chair, places his head in his hands, and looks downward as if exhausted.

"Bill, look, that's it for now. I've got to go."

The rugged 42-year-old union captain in his usual blue jeans, tan work shirt, and tan working boots, already primed to expect the worse from the little medical details made public, rushes to his son. The stocky union captain with short brown hair, graying at the temples, contrasts with his thin, diminutive son who has long black curly hair that is currently slick with perspiration.

Harold brushes the damp hair aside and feels his son forehead, which is hot not just warm. He first rationalizes it as the expected sweat and fatigue from shooting baskets out back. He then notices the red spots not only on his sons face but on his arms as well. A wave of panic overtakes him.

"Jerry, you get right to bed. I'll get some ibuprofen and orange juice. You rest up for a while, then I am taking you to the emergency room at Edwards Hospital."

"No, Dad, I'll be alright. With no school, I've just been playing with the guys too much today."

Harold only hesitates for a moment then responds, "You're going to the ER anyway. We can't take any chances."

Harold goes about getting the orange juice and ibuprofen, as his wife Judy comes in through the back door from grocery shopping. She immediately notices the concern registered on Harold's face and the ibuprofen in his hand as she sets her packages down on the nearby kitchen counter.

"What's wrong?"

"Nothing."

"Don't tell me it's nothing. I can tell something is not right. What's wrong, Harold? Tell me."

"It's Jerry. He's got a fever and red spots."

"Oh, no, no. But he got both rounds of vaccinations. He had the booster just yesterday. It can't be smallpox. He never had chicken pox... Maybe it's just chicken pox. Chicken pox gives you red spots, too."

Harold and Judy hug each other in the kitchen next to the counter where she put her grocery bags down. Out of sight of Jerry and also Richard, who is now playing a video game in the living room, both break down in tears of fear.

The rugged union captain dries his tears quickly and kisses his wife's forehead.

"We'll take him to the emergency room. He'll get the best treatment, I promise."

While Harold and Judy's wrestle with overwhelming fear and apprehension, a group gathered in a corner of Mike Ditka's Sports Bar in Oak Lawn south of Midway Airport are grappling with suspicion and anger.

"Casey, this rumor that the smallpox epidemic is from some Neanderthal is a bunch of bullshit. Neanderthals have been extinct for thousands of years. Viruses can't live that long."

"Ron, you're so right. This is bioterrorism. I'll bet some of them damned rag heads from the Middle East poisoned our drinking water," rages Casey in a moment of racism fueled by helplessness and fear.

"Ron, Casey, you're both way off. It's our own government. They've been playing around with biologic warfare stuff for decades. This smallpox must be one that has gotten out of control. I tell you, there's been some funny stuff going on around at Fort Dearborn and also at Fort Arlington in Arlington Heights. Heightened security, late-night deliveries and whatnot. It's the Army, I tell you. They lost control of biologic warfare stock piles and are now covering it up."

"Yeah, it's another damned coverup," all three blurt out in unison.

"Yeah, a coverup."

In Atlanta, Ameer Parkesh breaks the good news and the bad news to Dr. Merriweather. It seems that his production of a vaccine that directly targets the ancient smallpox virus that is unmodified by the evolutionary pressure of time is proceeding at an even faster pace than originally hoped. However, the small amount of blood on Heather's skin was too degraded to test for antibodies.

Dean Heimbach looks at both of his colleagues.

"Well, I have some news for you too. The scientists in France tested the blood from the homosapien caveman and indeed found neutralizing antibodies against cowpox and regular smallpox. That's why the outbreak in Europe was so mild and confirms the first half of our theory. Gentlemen, I'm going to Chicago to get blood from that damned Neanderthal. If it turns out that the Neanderthal doesn't possess any similar antibodies, it places this new vaccine on solid scientific grounds even if it is untested. It will confirm your theory, Dr. Merriweather. It also could be the most important scientific finding concerning the evolution and changes in the immune system of modern humans like us."

"I'll go with you," announces Robert.

Ameer follows with a "Me, too."

"Ameer, I am afraid you have to stay here and oversee the production of your new vaccine. It will save millions of lives."

"Dean, Natasha can do that. I'm going with you."

"No, you're not! You are critically needed here. That's an order from an old Nobel Prize Laureate."

Robert interjects.

"Dr. Heimbach, I agree we need Ameer to produce as many doses of the vaccine as possible and as quickly as possible, but I also want to go with you. Are you going to pull rank on me, too?"

Dr. Heimbach smirks slightly.

"Heck, no. I need another person as crazy as me to prove our point. In fact, I am counting on you. You know your way around Chicago. Look, Ameer, inject us with the first batch of your vaccine right now. I pray that it will work. I'm going to call Fowler and get him to give us clearance from Vandenbos to fly to O'Hare tomorrow."

By 9:00 A.M., Robert and Dean Heimbach are seated in a military cargo plane at Atlanta's Hartsfield-Jackson Airport, ready for takeoff. They were the very first to receive the untested experimental but hopeful new vaccine. The plane is also loaded with the first 200,000 doses of the new vaccine. That's enough only for General Vandenbos' troops, the National Guard troops, police, and critical support staff. Back in Ameer's lab, new vaccine doses are being produced as rapidly as possible but they can only make two million doses per day. However, Dean Heimbach is carrying a container of the primed killed viral chemical sequences from Ameer's pioneering technique. He plans to deliver it to Abbott Labs in North Chicago. He has used his reputation and influence to have their molecular and immunology sections already prepared and geared up to produce the new vaccine in greater quantities. With their greater capacity and manpower, they can likely produce five million doses per day.

Three hours later, the C-130 cargo plane lands at O'Hare Airport. General Vandenbos himself greets Robert and Dean Heimbach. He immediately shuffles them into his make shift office and "war room," located in one of the hangers.

"Okay, doctors. Update me on your plan. Dr. Fowler has already briefed me that you have a new vaccine that is going to work this time. Good Lord, I hope so. New cases are occurring fast. The death rate continues to climb. My morgues and all those in the various hospitals are filling up. My troops are actually developing smallpox too, God damn it! Without the reinforcements I have already requested, our containment will break down in just four days. After that, complete chaos and infection will spread across the entire country."

Dean Heimbach answers.

"General, here's the plan. Dr. Merriweather and I have enough faith that this vaccine will work that we received it ourselves just last night. Get your troops vaccinated with the new vaccine that we loaded on your plane this morning. Transport this container to Abbott Labs in North Chicago via helicopter right away. They know all about it. They will produce the new vaccine, which the lab in Atlanta will supplement daily. Begin revaccinating everyone and, I mean everyone, as soon as you receive each new shipment of vaccine."

General Vandenbos is speechless. He's not used to receiving orders from a civilian. But this is not just any ordinary civilian. It is a Nobel Prize recipient, a doctor with a strategy that is almost military in nature, and one that promises victory. Yes, victory, the goal of any military leader.

"Oh, and General, we need one thing from you."

"What is it?"

"A helicopter to get us to the University of Chicago where the Neanderthal remains frozen and a return back."

"Doctors, I would normally say no to such a crazy request. But, you two seem to have your act together and you brought along a workable strategy. Permission granted. Be ready at the entrance of this hanger at 1400 hours."

Promptly at 2:00 P.M., General Vandenbos' helicopter takes off from the helipad at O'Hare Airport with the two doctors, the pilot, and two Army Rangers as "mission support." Since no one else knows of the mission nor the exact place and the importance of the "patient zero" for this epidemic, they expect no resistance. The chopper takes off and first heads east toward the Lake Michigan lakefront then turns south along the outer drive which parallels the lake shore. On the way, Dr. Merriweather gets a close overhead view of Wrigley Field. The stands are empty now but, near second base, he sees a field hospital with Army doctors and nurses present milling around. Robert thinks back to the packed stands with cheering fans for the Cubs-White Sox City series just a little more than a month ago. He momentarily pictures Heather as she sat next him. He also thinks back to his two cousins Chucky and Johnny Burger. They were at the game too. How are they? Did they contract the virulent form of smallpox? As Heather had? A wave of guilt ripples through Robert. With the horrible death of Heather, the CDC Committee, the meeting with CEO David Epstein and now bringing a new vaccine to his former city, he forgot all about the two cousins he grew up with. He recalls their hockey games on frozen lakes in winter, racquetball tournaments and, yes, walking together on a Saturday to good old Wrigley Field for a daytime game like they did last month. He feels like a derelict and vows to call them as soon as he gets back to O'Hare.

As the chopper proceeds south along Lake Shore Drive and its branching where Michigan Avenue begins and enters the heart of downtown Chicago, both Robert and Dean Heimbach remark how normal the activity seems to be from their overhead perspective. Indeed, only about one-fourth of the citizens are milling about in contrast to the usual congested and frenetic activity of the Michigan Avenue downtown area. However, the activity seems quite orderly under the circumstances. Both doctors see that most stores are closed while parks, movie theaters and entertainment areas remain open. They also see some military posts in parks and vacant lots and then are startled to see tanks. Dr. Merriweather and Dr. Heimbach break away from viewing the terrain. They face each, other shaking their heads just before Dean Heimbach asserts.

"Tanks in a U.S. city, unbelievable, Robert. However, it is a reminder that we are at war. Not with a foreign adversary but with a microbe, one that may be more threatening and deadly. One that our military might is not be able to defeat. It may even turn our citizens against one another. I pray the new vaccine we received last night works, not just for us, but that it will work for the rest of the country. In effect, we are human guinea pigs."

"We wouldn't be the first, Dean. You know, in my own profession, Horace Wells was the dentist who first discovered anesthesia. He had a colleague pull one of his teeth while he was under nitrous oxide. Indeed, the tooth was pulled, no pain. After that, he used nitrous oxide on numerous dental patients successfully before Novocain was developed. He then attempted to take his discovery national by introducing it to the Harvard Massachusetts General Hospital. There, he made the fateful mistake of agreeing to follow the hospital's strict policy to have the hospital's anesthesia team administer the nitrous oxide instead of doing it himself. That patient was significantly underdosed due to the inexperience of the Massachusetts General Hospital anesthesia team. The man screamed out in pain, discrediting Horace Wells and nitrous oxide, as well."

"But Robert, nitrous oxide is still commonly used in anesthesia today. Is it not? And isn't it actually a mainstay?"

"That's true, but Horace Wells experienced a worse fate. He dealt with the rejection by pursuing chloroform as an alternate anesthetic. After weeks of daily self-administering the chloroform, its cumulative toxicity caused him to become psychotic. He then committed suicide."

"So you are saying Horace Wells testing on himself produced, on one hand, a long-term durable success that we still use today and, on the other hand, caused him to take his own life."

"Exactly. I wonder what fate has in store for us, Dean."

With that sobering thought, Dr. Merriweather and Dr. Heimbach abandon their conversation and continue looking down at Michigan Avenue below. Going south toward the University of Chicago, the chopper passes the Art Institute where they see a sea of people some carrying banners marching slowly southward. Both doctors are impressed by the size of the march, which they estimate to be a mile long. They fly low enough to make out that about two-thirds of them are wearing masks, some industrial masks, medical masks, and just a few N95 respirator masks. About 200 feet behind the throng, several hundred fully equipped Army soldiers march at the same pace all wearing N95 masks. As the chopper continues, they pass the Field Museum and Soldier Field where the NFL Chicago Bears play. In the huge parking lot south of Soldier Field a small collection of people are gathered near a stand with microphones. Several hundred Army and National Guard troops form a perimeter around the parking lot and the four tanks at the very south end. Both doctors surmise correctly that the march will end there with a rally. The chopper continues past the rally point with an ETA of eight minutes.

IBEW Captain Harold Snyder heads the march. He is relieved that, although boisterous, it has been the peaceful march he had hoped. He begins to walk backwards to view the mass of his marchers, most wearing medical masks as they have become accustomed to do. He reads some of their signs and placards: "When will this end?" "A pox on smallpox!" and even one attempt at humor "Three vaccinations? That's acupuncture."

Harold Snyder turns back around to face forward unaware that at the very culmination of his leadership, his life will be turned upside down.

When the march is just about to pass Soldier Field and with the parking lot in sight, Harold's cellphone rings. He is just barely able to hear the voice above the din of shouts and chants from the marchers. He moves off to the left side of the marchers near the side entrances to Soldier field. He cups one ear as he presses the phone to his other ear. He sees from the screen that it's Judy.

"Harold, Harold, Jerry's worse. He's for sure got smallpox. The hospital put him in isolation this morning. Now, he is struggling to breathe. He has red sores all over. They want to put a tube into his airway and put him on a ventilator. Harold, I'm scared. I don't know what to do. Please come home right now."

Harold can hear her sobbing. Just then he hears gunshots and a small explosion coming from the edge of the marchers across from him. He sees people scattering with screams and shouts.

Harold dismisses his initial gut reflex to abandon the march to head home when he sees smoke arising from the west end of the street and his marchers running toward him and the entrance ways into Soldier Field like a panicked herd of antelope.

It seems that, despite Harold's best efforts and organizational planning for a peaceful march and rally akin to the Dr. Martin Luther King organized Civil Rights marches in the 1960s, he did not account for a wild card. It seems that a group of several hundred paid activists joined the open march intent on creating chaos for motives uncertain and unknown at this time. Nevertheless, igniting small explosives, firecrackers and smoke bombs and using handguns to shoot live rounds into the air, they were successful in disrupting the march, creating chaos and, as was most likely their prime objective initiating a response from the Army.

The situation worsens as the marchers attempt to get inside Soldier Field to escape the perceived threat and initially engage a collection of troops at every entrance point. Although ordered to use non-lethal force if necessary to resist any attempts to enter the building, the sheer numbers of marchers soon overwhelms the troops, who are reluctant to use tear gas, Tasers and blunt force on their fellow citizens. The marchers soon push past the troops to enter the building and scatter about the internal walkway ramps and concession areas. Despite the troops attempting to hold them back, the throngs now angry and blaming the Army and the National Guard for attempting to stop the march and for the chaos, they break down the door to the players' locker room and ransack it as well as the concession areas and bathrooms. A large group runs down the stairways of the lower deck toward the field where they are met by a large military force with water cannons at the ready and six full-armed tanks behind them. The military, National Guard, and some of Chicago's police force reach a standoff with the marchers. The marchers stop. They do not enter the field.

The marchers see a large Quonset hut made of canvas that runs nearly the length of the football field and spreads out about half of its width.

The soldiers, ironically stationed in "Soldier Field," see the stands rapidly fill to become fully packed with standing angry citizens. Neither side makes a move.

Unit Commander Colonel Holgate grabs a bullhorn, but before he attempts to address the crowd. He sends a message to General Vandenbos: "Riot at Soldier Field. Viable threat to morgue facility and personnel, request reinforcements immediately."

Harold Snyder having reluctantly disconnected from Judy finally makes his way to the edge of the field. As he does, he hears the whole group picking up the slogans and threats from the paid activists.

"They lied to us. The Army is part of a coverup. They are getting the real vaccine and letting us die."

He fears that they will incite the marchers to storm the field, giving the Army and National Guard no choice but to shoot and probably use the tanks. He must try to calm the crowd down.

As Harold makes his way down the cement stairs through his marchers, who are packed together in the stands and on the stairways down to the field, he notices that a large number of them have now taken their medical masks off and are either shouting or grumbling to themselves or others. Harold also sees some have the red spots like the ones he saw on his son Jerry. Harold's mind turns to thoughts of his son in peril but he can't go to him now. He is too immersed in the situation. Harold also shudders at the potential for exposure and spread of the smallpox with so many of his union member closely packed together with their masks off. He keeps his on. He tries to focus his attention on the task of snaking through his marchers, moving them aside gently without causing them to turn their already pent up anger on him. As he does so, he sees the stadium Jumbotron flicker and then come on. It focuses on Colonel Holgate. Harold sees him standing in the infield facing the very field edge he is moving toward. Harold continues to move through the throng. He hopes to persuade the guards to speak to him. He struggles past each marcher one by one. As he does, he hears Colonel Holgate's message.

"Marchers, fellow citizens. You are on federal property illegally. My troops do not want to harm anyone. Our mission is to protect this facility and will do so, as ordered. I request and actually beg you to exit this military facility and reconvene in the South Parking Lot, as your permit to march and gather indicates."

Harold finally makes his way to the edge of the field. He has now taken off his mask and shirt perhaps as a sign that he is not wearing a weapon or as a symbol of peaceful intent. He engages a group of four Army Rangers guarding the field entrance. The Jumbotron is now turned on him. The packed stands at Soldier Field begin to chant, "Coverup! Coverup! Coverup!" The chants get louder and louder, as the crowd sees Harold gesturing but cannot hear any of the words spoken.

While Harold is trying to explain his leadership role with the marchers, telling them that he was actually the one who requested and signed the marching permit, Colonel Holgate receives a return communication from General Vandenbos. He reads it with a lump in his throat as the chanting gets louder and louder.

"Reinforcements are on the way. Protect the facility using any means necessary. You are authorized to use lethal force."

Unaware of the potential breakdown of societal control and the possible deaths that may occur from a conflict at Soldier Field, Drs. Merriweather and Heimbach land at the University of Chicago hospital's trauma helipad on the roof. They are met by the Hospital's CEO who has been instructed to cooperate and escort them to the location of the frozen Neanderthal. Using his authority under Martial Law, General Vandenbos instructed the CEO to open any doors required to enter the Neanderthals location and to stand by to assist as necessary. Although very willing to follow the instructions, the CEO pretends to be calm but is uneasy about opening the door to the very room and its contents that started the epidemic. Disquising his reluctance to open the door or even stand close by, he looks down the short stairway while waiting for Dr. Merriweather and Heimbach to don the traditional yellow Personal Protection Equipment (PPEs). Such PPEs are constructed from a repellent yellow fabric gown, boots, mask, and cap used in most every isolation area in hospitals today. The CEO descends five steps to open the first door, which accesses the below-ground room. He reaches around the door to turn on the lights to the foyer and the glass enclosed room with a desk, computers, viewing screens, and control panels where Dr. Earlandson, Heather, Bill and Steve once gathered to discuss their observations of the Neanderthal and where Heather's viral laden camera strap began the re-plague of the 21st century. The CEO goes no further and hands the keys off to Dean Heimbach pointing to the door just ahead. It is the door to the still below freezing room containing the Neanderthal now referred to as "Patient Zero."

As Dean Heimbach fumbles with the keys, Robert, carrying a compact metal surgical kit the size of a child's lunchbox, peers into the workstation. It is exactly as Heather described. For a brief moment he pictures her there, entering important points for the planned story of Dr. Earlandson's great discovery. However, his daydreaming ends abruptly when Dean Heimbach opens the door and both are hit with an icy blast. Although they prepared for the cold by wearing several layers of clothes under the PPE, they realize that it is still "damned cold" anyway, as muttered by both men. Robert removes the tarp-like covering over the Neanderthal and gets his first glimpse of the 25,000-year-old member of an extinct species that ours somehow overtook and replaced. His college buddy, anthropologist Ralph Earlandson, tried to find out how that occurred. This was his proof that it occurred by war and a forced extinction by a better mind and larger numbers. Was he right? We will never know.

Robert knows that the Neanderthal blood is frozen and therefore cannot be drawn through a needle. He prepares his surgical kit. He tells Dean Heimbach to isolate the area of the femoral vein for a cut down as he searches through the small metal surgical kit for a Betadine sterile prep sponge and a container for the specimen. Robert looks up and sees Dean Heimbach examining the upper arm instead of the groin area where the large femoral vein is known to be somewhat close to the skin surface. Robert points out the appropriate site. Sensing that his ignorance of human anatomy has been revealed, Dean Heimbach blurts out, "Well, these damned Neanderthals have all screwed up anatomy." Both doctors chuckle as Robert goes about the serious business of preparing the area and cutting into the 25,000-year-old specimen. It is something that his friend Dr. Earlandson never got to do.

The seriousness of what they must now do causes both men to focus intently and ignore the cold. They know that as Robert removes a four-inch length of the large vein to be thawed out later in order to get blood the very opening of the skin and tissue will result in small, frozen blood particles that will cling to their PPEs, particularly their gloves. Since they plan to remove and burn their outer clothes that would not be much of a problem, except that taking them off runs a high risk of these same particles getting onto their skin, hair and or face. They hope the new vaccine really does work.

Robert finds cutting through frozen skin and underlying tissue much harder than excising normal skin and tissues during the head neck surgeries to which he is more accustomed. Nevertheless, with greater force and manipulation, but not greatly assisted by the brilliant but surgically naive Nobel Laureate Robert manages to isolate the femoral vein. The blue cord is the size of an index finger. With the cold now seeping into his body and becoming uncomfortable to the point of shivering, Robert crushes his #10 scalpel blade through two sections of the frozen femoral vein, four inches apart. Small ice chips fly into the air landing on each doctor's PPE. Robert extracts the frozen vein segment containing blood and begins to suture the area closed, more of a matter of habit than because it is necessary. The entire effort takes only ten minutes. The two are now more than anxious to exit the room mostly, due to the cold. They seal the specimen in a container and carefully remove their PPEs, as well as all of their outer clothing, which they place in doubled plastic bags for incineration later. Outside the foyer door, in the warm and bright sunlight of an August day in Chicago, the naked forms of two scientist is momentarily a strange sight to the CEO and the two accompanying Army Rangers. Immodestly, with the attitude "at our age, what have we got to hide," each sprays the other with skin disinfectant and begins to put on the replacement clothes they brought along.

At Soldier Field, a shirtless Harold Snyder shows the Army guards his ID and tells them he wants to address the crowd of marchers who are continuing their cover up chanting. Col. Holgate checks out the name on the ID and compares it to the printed name and signature on the marching permit. They match. He tells one of his soldiers to bring Harold to him. Harold is relieved to be allowed to talk with the officer in charge. As he walks toward the center of the 50-yard line in front of the Quonset hut morgue, he turns around to face the crowd and, with the large screen focused on him, he motions with his hands. It is not a motion to incite the crowd but rather to calm it down. With arms outstretched over his head and palms down, he lowers them in stages, a clear sign to calm down. The chanting gets softer and softer, then finally ceases altogether replaced by the low buzzing sound of individuals and groups talking together trying to figure out what is happening. They anxiously wait and glance periodically at the large screen.

Out of range of the microphone, Harold speaks to the Colonel Holgate.

"Colonel, I am really sorry for this. This was not our intent. Just the opposite, we wanted to show that today's unions are not the disruptors and agitators of the Jimmy Hoffa era. We wanted only a peaceful rally and to voice the recurrent questions that we all have. I was told it was only a few agitators who started this riot. It was not any of us, believe me. Let me talk to my marchers. I think I can get them calmed down."

"Okay, Mr. Snyder, but no tricks, neither of us wants this to escalate. See what you can do."

Colonel Holgate turns the microphone back on and gives it to Harold. Still shirtless, Harold Snyder begins, "Fellow union workers. I am Harold Snyder, Captain of IBEW Union Chapter 21. This is not what we are all about. We came here for a rally to show our solidarity for our brothers and sisters and the worry we have for own families. We want only to bring our questions to the Army. We can't do that with a riot. Hear me. There is no coverup. So let's go out the South exit and begin our rally, as we came here to do. Then, we can all go home safe to our families."

While the packed stands at Soldier Field goes silent, Harold reflects on what he just said, "Then we can all go home safe to our families." His mind is thrown back to his wife's frantic phone call. While he desperately wants to get back to her and Jerry, he has irreversibly committed himself to the rally. Indeed, he sees the packed crowd slowly moving toward the exits. The tension in the air lessens. Both Colonel Holgate and Harold let out a cautious sigh. They look at each other with new-found respect.

"Mr. Snyder, well done. We may have escaped a disaster here today. My men will escort you to the speaker's platform in the parking lot."

As the marchers and Harold slowly file out and enter the south parking lot, few notice the twenty attack helicopters filled with elite Army Rangers approaching from the north. Few also notice them turning back abruptly in response to Col Holgate's emergency call to General Vandenbos to "Cancel the reinforcements, unrest satisfactorily resolved. Escalation averted."

While the rally proceeds without further turmoil, Robert and Dean Heimbach are returning in the chopper. They pass over the Soldier Field parking lot and observe the rally in progress, unaware of the near disaster and bloodshed akin to the Kent State Shooting of unarmed college students by Ohio Natural Guard troops in May of 1970. This one had the potential to be equally tragic, but on a much greater scale.

However, before landing, Robert takes out his cellphone and queues up the number of Charles Burger and presses the green start button. Several rings. No answer. He then punches in the number for Johnny Burger. Once again, several rings bring no answer. Reminding himself to call again later, he places his phone back in his pocket.

As soon as they land at O'Hare Airport, Dean Heimbach asks the general's medical staff to draw a sample of his blood and one from Robert. Robert obliges the nurse and holds out his left arm while a second nurse places a tourniquet around the Dean's left arm to draw his blood.

"What are these samples for, Dean?"

"Well, my boy, I am going to take the Neanderthal's sample to Abbott Labs. We planned to test his blood for any antibodies to the smallpox virus, right?"

"Yes, that is right, but what about our blood?"

"While I am up there, we will also test for the early antibodies against the live virus from the Neanderthal that you and I hopefully formed in just the past eighteen hours. We'll see firsthand how many and how neutralizing those antibodies are. From there, we can project when the latest time from the onset of symptoms that the vaccine can be expected to reverse the infection and prevent death."

Referring to him now as Dr. Heimbach, Robert responds.

"Dr. Heimbach, once again now I know why you won the Nobel Prize in medicine. However, I cannot figure out why you were not nominated for some sort of a prize in clever advanced thinking. You go do your thing at Abbott Labs and call me as soon as you get any results. I am going to head back to Ameer's lab and then to Apollo headquarters to take care of some unfinished business."

CHAPTER 25

A Lot of Good News, Then Some Bad News

Returning to Ameer's lab in Atlanta Robert is onboard one of General Vandenbos Army cargo planes. He is unaware that another Army cargo plane passes him going in the opposite direction to O'Hare Airport. This plane carries two million doses of the new vaccine from Ameer's lab. After landing and on his way to Ameer's lab by cab, he also receives a phone call from Dean Heimbach.

"Robert, are you in Atlanta yet?"

"Yes, Dean, just got off the plane. What's the news, I hope it's good."

"Absolutely fantastic, my dear boy. The Neanderthal had no antibodies to this ancient form of smallpox at all. In fact, his immune system was very underdeveloped. His immunoglobulins were much lower than ours. He could never survive in our current world of millions of microbes and crowded cities."

"Wow, Dean, that really does say something about the evolution of our immune system. What about our blood samples?"

"That's even better, our immune systems recognized the vaccine and produced antibodies directed against this ancient smallpox virus. I found adequate titers of IgM, the first responding antibody, and even a few IgG antibodies, the second and most profound antibody produced by a vaccine. I'm going to recheck my results but I'd say our new vaccine will protect anyone exposed to the virus with no symptoms and resolve early smallpox, if administered within four days of symptoms."

"Dean, that is great, just great!"

"Want to hear some more good news?"

"Dean, you're on a roll. Of course I would."

"Abbott Labs ramped up their antibody production system and can now crank out four million doses per day starting tomorrow already. We will be able to vaccinate the entire quarantined population in five days or less.

"You know, I also tested my own antibodies from the Apollo vaccine that was effective in the South American outbreak that they produced, and the one that we used twice here in Chicago. It doesn't react at all with the Neanderthal virus, just as we suspected. It caused an unfortunate loss of time and lives. Wait till I tell that to that bastard, David Connors."

"I am speechless, sad and elated all at the same time. Horace Wells would be proud of you. Look, the cab is pulling up to Ameer's lab now. Continue your good work there. I need to attend to some details here."

Arriving at Ameer's lab, Robert is greeted with a jubilant hug from Ameer and then one from Natasha.

"Robert, we are so glad you are back. Are you all right? Dr. Heimbach emailed the good news about our vaccine. It will work. I knew it. I just knew it."

Peter Fowler, hearing Ameer's greeting, emerges from a back office in Ameer's lab, where he was checking on the vaccine production data.

"It seems you and Dr. Heimbach were right all along. I am embarrassed and ashamed that I let myself be influenced too greatly by David Connors and David Epstein. I wonder if they know that their vaccine was ineffective."

Before Robert can expound on his meeting with David Epstein and his past dealings with him, his phone rings. It is from a number with the 312 Chicago area code, but he doesn't recognize the number.

"This is Dr. Robert Merriweather. Can I help you?"

"Yes, this is Medical Attaché, Dr. Joseph Myers. Did you recently try to call the cellphones of a Mr. Charles H. Burger and Mr. John F. Burger?"

"Yes, I did. They are my cousins."

"I am sorry to inform you that they were both early victims of the smallpox plague. Their remains are in the morgue at Soldier Field. Are you a next of kin?"

Robert's heart sinks. First Heather, now the two cousins he grew up with. The great joy of the past half-hour gives way first to grief, then turns into anger focused on the Apollo Drug Co. and its CEO. Disguising his anger for now, Robert tells Dr. Myers that he is not the next of kin and gives contact numbers for each of their wives, who, fortunately for them, were away when the epidemic started.

Robert talks to himself, with both teeth and fists clenched. "It is time to put Epstein and his big pharma arrogance in their place." Seething, Robert heads out to do a little shopping, but first stops at the back of Ameer's lab.

CHAPTER 26

Dr. Merriweather Hatches a Plot

"Ameer, when you first gave me a tour of your lab, I saw incubators with stored culture plates and vials in certain growth mediums."

"Yes, I keep a reference stock of many microbes, bacteria and viruses mostly but a few fungi too. I don't keep smallpox or bacteria of potential biologic warfare like anthrax or E. Coli 157. The law doesn't allow those. I do have all the old childhood diseases though and many others."

"Oh, really? Show me where."

Robert looks upon more than twenty vials each labeled with one of the childhood diseases that he remembers having himself prior to the mumps-measles-German measles (also known as Rubella) vaccines known as MMR now given to most everyone today. He sees what he is looking for and emits a slight smile.

"Ameer, you're amazing. You have a virtual microbiology museum and zoo here, in addition to your lab. You keep up the vaccine production I have to go shopping."

Ameer shocked and quizzical at Robert's abrupt statement is nearly speechless, uttering just a soft "Okay" as he watches Robert head out the door.

Robert takes his cellphone from his sportscoat pocket and does a search for novelty stores nearby to Ameer's lab. He sees that there is one just 4.2 miles away and calls himself an Uber.

Arriving at the novelty store, Robert sees that it is a rather large one and seems to focus on all of the gag gifts he remembers from his youth. He mutters to himself, "This place should have it."

Robert gazes around the store and sees the traditional items such as the whoopee cushion, the fake dog poop, the dribble glass, the spring-loaded can of snakes, the bug in a fake plastic ice cube, itching powder and more. He is reminded of the times he and his now two dead cousins bought most of those at one time or another for pranks on their friends or parents. His initial smile, recalling those innocent days of his youth, soon gives way to a frown and a few tears as he remembers that Chuckie and Johnny are now gone too.

Robert forces himself to concentrate on his purpose for being there as he looks intently into each glass showcase until he sees what he is searching for. There, next to the itching powder, is a small metal cylinder labeled with the contents. The label also has a cartoon picture on it depicting the person's reaction to the prank. With a wry smile, exposing a revengeful mindset, he calls over the sales person behind the counter to show him one so that he can read the ingredients.

Talking to himself, he reads, "veratrum album alkaloid," and "helenalin from chamissonolid."

Robert now mutters loud enough for the salesperson to hear, "Oh, boy, that ought to do it."

"It works alright, but be careful with it. It should not be taken into the mouth or swallowed. Read the directions and you'll have a lot of fun with this."

"I know. I remember this stuff. I used it once as a kid and earned a good spanking for it. I also know that it was banned by the FDA in 1919 and that this kind of shop are the only ones allowed to sell it. That's why I came here."

Robert pays for his item and takes his purchase outside. Rather than immediately calling for a taxi or Uber, he takes out his cellphone and queues up a recently entered number.

"Hello, this is David Epstein."

"Mr. Epstein, this is Dr. Merriweather. Do you have a moment?"

"I certainly do, Dr. Merriweather. I am glad you're calling. Have you read over the contract?"

"I did and after a lot of thought and some soul searching, I realized that I am just spinning my wheels in academics. Your contract offers a lot of opportunities that will greatly expand what I can do for patients compared to my treating them one at a time. How about if I come up there tomorrow? We need to correct a few spelling errors and typos in the contract. I also want to show you two specific research projects that I want to add to the contract. I'd like you to commit to supporting them if you approve. We can do lunch, as they say."

"I am sure I will be able to support any initiative of yours. We'll have lunch in our corporate dining room. It will be great to have you on board, Dr. Merriweather. I'll have my limo pick you up at 10:00 A.M. as before and our corporate jet will fly you to my office. We can do whatever we need to do with the contract and have lunch after that. How's that? "

"Perfect, just what I was hoping you would say."

Tuesday morning, Robert has a private conference with his former patient and now medical researcher herself, Natasha Sandu. She hands him a small metal container. Twenty minutes later, while Robert waits for the Apollo limo in front of his hotel in Atlanta, David Epstein receives his second call from David Connors in Chicago.

"Well, hello there, David. Things still going well in Chicago? Have you used up the 20 million double dose injections packages we sent? When are they going to send payment?"

"That's just it. The General and everyone around here is telling me that our vaccine doesn't work. The Nobel Laureate Dr. Heimbach has been pushing the idea that this strain of the smallpox virus is not sensitive to our vaccine and he is pushing a new one from Abbott Labs that they are now giving to everyone. And, you know, David, I believe him. I woke up this morning tired and headachy. And I got red blotches on my arms and face. David, I had both rounds of our vaccine."

"Don't panic now, Connors. They have already bought both rounds of our vaccine and used them. I'll call Peter Fowler. He'll get them to pay. "

"David, you don't understand. I'm getting smallpox. The vaccine doesn't work. The body count I overheard General Vandenbos talking about is over 1.2 million. He's got all his troops vaccinated with Heimbach's new vaccine and almost all of the Chicago area already. By Wednesday, they'll have everyone vaccinated and you know that goddamn Merriweather guy is hooked up in this somehow too."

"Again, don't worry about that. I talked to Merriweather just yesterday. He bought it. He's coming up here today. He will be one of us. We can take credit for this new vaccine by our association with him as one of our employees. Our marketing department will make everyone think we helped Merriweather develop the new vaccine together with Heimbach and we got Abbott Labs to produce some of it under our direction, of course."

"Okay, okay, but I'm getting the new vaccine. It is supposed to work if injected within four days of developing the red sores."

Tuesday morning also finds Harold and Judy Snyder sitting anxiously and nervously in the waiting room of Edwards Hospital's isolation unit in Naperville, Illinois, a western suburb of Chicago. Jerry is now in a coma with red sores across his body, some of which are weeping a fluid (exudate) the color of tea. Jerry is too weak to breath and is, therefore, on a ventilator. He is given medications to reduce the fever (antipyretics), but they only work for one or two hours. The doctors have tried several antiviral drugs but this smallpox virus seems to be resistant to them, just as it was to the two rounds of vaccines he received.

Sitting in the waiting room with medical masks on, they wait for the okay to put on the PPE clothing and visit their son. Although they long to be with him, they dread seeing him in this quickly deteriorating condition. Their worries are multiplied because their younger son, nine-year-old Richard, woke up this morning with red sores. While his grandmother is staying at home with him at a distance, he too is in isolation in his room with his Xbox. Both parents cling to the hope that the new vaccine that they heard about will really work this time. It is their only hope but it is not due to be distributed to the Chicago suburbs until tomorrow.

From his command post hanger at O'Hare Airport, General Vandenbos sends out his report to the Chiefs of Staff and the President in curt military language. He also copies Peter Fowler.

"Initial reports from the field indicate a positive response to the new vaccine. The death rate has slowed by 50%. The troops are all vaccinated and 92% are duty ready. No further unrest reported. Quantities of new effective vaccine arriving daily. Should complete third revaccination mission by Thursday and have sufficient vaccine to begin nationwide revaccination program."

By noon Tuesday, Robert finds himself placing his light cloth duffle bag on the security belt at Apollo headquarters. The two small metal cans that appear on the security scanner screen are explained as medication bottles by Robert without further investigation. After all, it is a pharmaceutical headquarters.

Robert arrives in David Epstein's outer office and glances at the star on most of his awards and grins slightly recalling it was the key to Epstein's password and his unauthorized entry to his medical records. David Epstein himself greets Robert, coming through the door with an extended hand. Robert thinks, *The handshake. Who is hiding what weapon now?*

Robert and Epstein go over the corrections and Robert's requested monetary support for a second stem cell project and a tumor-suppressor gene project related to his human papilloma virus study. He requests fifteen million for each project. He thinks the amount that he is asking for is way too much. He is mentally prepared to bargain but David Epstein agrees to it without hesitation. With that final piece to the puzzle complete, they shake hands once again with the agreement to add these requests and mutually sign the contract a week from Friday. Robert will begin officially working for Apollo in three months, on January 1st.

David Epstein escorts Robert to the Executive Dining room, which is exquisitely decorated with tasteful pictures and several mahogany tables set with fine China and sparkling silverware. The maître d' greets them and seats them at David Epstein's reserved table. He offers a choice of sparkling or distilled bottled water. David Epstein's personal waiter comes over and relates that all things are available on the menu card today, recommending the seared Chilean Sea Bass with a Vietnamese-avocado pesto sauce as the best of the best. Both Robert and Epstein agree and order the sea bass with a small salad and young asparagus, after which Robert excuses himself for the men's room. Taking the two small medical metal cans from the duffle bag with him, he offers the explanation of "It's time to take my own pills. You, of course, understand that."

David Epstein smiles and nods. "Of course."

Robert then subtly takes his cloth napkin with him and enters the men's room. He is alone. *Good,* he thinks. He looks at the cartoon on the can, which depicts a wide-eyed victim violently sneezing and puffs of air coming from his nose and mouth.

Robert opens the first can, keeping it far away from his nose. With the aid of a small toothbrush, he spreads some of the sneezing powder onto one side of the cloth napkin. He completes his task, closes the can, and places it back into the duffle bag while sliding the second canister into his right front pant pocket. He then call Natasha at Ameer's lab and tells her to "Make the call." As he returns to the table, he is sure to hold the inside of the folded napkin to avoid getting the potent powder on his own hands. As planned, as soon as he approaches the table, he sees David Epstein answering his cellphone. David excuses himself and moves several feet from the table to hear the details of the call. On the other end, he hears a nurse from a Chicago hospital telling him that his employee, David Connors, is gravely ill and wants Mr. Epstein to call him tonight. While David Epstein is away from the table, Robert exchanges Epstein's napkin for the sneezing powder-laden one that he carries.

Epstein returns with a concerned look on his face, not so much about David Connors' health as about what it might reveal about the Apollo vaccine. At the same time, Natasha Sandu disconnects the phone and puts her prepared script aside.

Indeed, the Chilean sea bass and the avocado pesto sauce are exquisite. As expected, the inevitable use of the napkin by Epstein brings about repetitive sneezing. One, two, three, four sneezes in a row with watering eyes and a runny nose. Robert opens the second can in his right pants pocket and pulls out a neatly folded new appearing handkerchief.

"Here, David, use this. It is the least I can do for my soon to be employer."

"Thanks, Dr. Merri—"

His response is interrupted by another sneezing episode.

As Epstein takes the handkerchief, he first sneezes into it but then another sneeze overtakes him as his sneeze causes him to inhale deeply. He does this several more times to Robert's hidden delight. Robert's thinks to himself, *That's for Heather, Chuckie, and Johnny,* even as he expresses outward concern.

The sneezing episode gradually abates with Epstein excusing himself to the men's room this time, in order to clean up and recompose himself. During that time, Robert pushes the sneezing powdered napkin to the floor and out of the way and takes up the second napkin and replaces it in to its original metal can.

The remainder of the lunch goes on smoothly with Robert saying, "Let's let whatever went on in the past stay in the past. A new era begins today."

Epstein smiles broadly. They clink water glasses together. He couldn't be more pleased. He forgets about the sneezing episode and is self-assured that his planning and skills in communication have turned an enemy into his obedient servant, just as he has done so many times in the past. He is smug enough to decide that he won't call Connors tonight. Connors has served his purpose. He can be replaced. Now, Merriweather is more useful to him.

Robert returns to Atlanta and goes directly to Ameer's lab where vaccine production is in full swing. Natasha comes out of the lab into the office area and smiles knowingly at Robert. Robert winks and holds up his index finger to his lips as a sign to keep it quiet for now but simply says, "It worked."

CHAPTER 27

HOPE

Wednesday morning, it is 8:30 A.M. in Atlanta and 7:30 A.M. in Naperville, Ill. In Atlanta, the CDC Committee meeting is about to begin, nearly fully represented with the return of Dean Heimbach last night but still absent David Connors, who is quarantined in Chicago. In Naperville, Harold and Judy Snyder, along with Richard, are already at Edwards's hospital in anticipation of the new vaccine injections planned to begin at 9:00 A.M., which have not yet arrived. Near the front of a line that is already two blocks long, Harold answers his ringing cellphone. It's the isolation unit, asking him to come up immediately. Harold's heart sinks with an expectation of what is likely bad news. He tells Judy that they want him to come up to the unit, explaining that they hadn't said why. Judy starts to cry. She knows. They both abandon the line with Richard tagging along with them.

When they arrive on the second floor, the nurse immediately summons over the attending physician. By the expression on his face, their greatest fears are realized and only confirmed by the words that follow.

"I am so sorry to tell you that Jerry passed away 20 minutes ago. We did all we could but he didn't respond. His body was just too weak from the smallpox."

Judy crumples to her knees, sobbing and crying out, "No, no, no, it can't be." Although still standing, the tough union captain breaks out in tears as well. He is followed by their youngest and, now, only son, also with red sores too. He doesn't fully understand the impact of the moment but his primal fears are heightened. He is there to bravely face needle injections for the third time, but this is worse. A grief counselor, assisted by several nurses, escorts them into a nearby empty room normally used for chart completion. It takes all of ten minutes for the red-eyed, red-faced threesome to regain a semblance of composure, albeit with tears still trickling down their cheeks.

The grief counsel advances, "Do you want to see him before we take him out of the room?"

Harold doesn't answer right away. He stares straight ahead with mouth open, unable to respond. After more than 15 seconds, he answers.

"No, we want to remember him as he was before last week, not as he looks now covered in red sores."

Judy looks up at her husband and nods in agreement and begins sobbing uncontrollably again.

The meeting at the CDC begins with Peter Fowler introducing U.S. Surgeon General, Dwayne Hudson, who is seated to Fowler's right, in the seat previously occupied by David Connors.

"Committee members, I have asked Surgeon General Hudson to this meeting to brief him on the latest findings in this epidemic. He plans to address the nation tomorrow evening, as he did to the local Chicago area a little more than a week ago. Hopefully, this time, he'll be equipped with a more reliable vaccine to report. Dr. Heimbach will now update all of us. Dr. Heimbach, please begin."

"Thank you, Peter. Surgeon General and fellow committee members, we now know that the two previous vaccines had no chance of working. With the help of Dr. Merriweather and Dr. Parkesh, we discovered the Neanderthal carried an ancient smallpox virus for which we as a species had no background immunity and no effective vaccine. My own blood tests and that of Dr. Merriweather indicated that the antibodies formed by the two rounds of injections from the Apollo vaccine did not neutralize the Neanderthal smallpox virus. However, the vaccine produced by Dr. Parkesh from tissue obtained from one of the early Chicago victims rapidly produced both IgM and IgG antibodies that killed this virus."

The mention of the ineffective Apollo virus causes Dr. Hargraves and those who voted for the double-dose revaccination campaign and against a new vaccine to frown and bow their heads in a small gesture of regret. Dr. Heimbach's mention of "tissue obtained from one of the early Chicago victims" causes Robert to swallow hard and fight back his own emotion.

Dr. Heimbach continues, "By the end of today, the revaccination program with this effective vaccine will be complete in the Chicago area. The latest report indicates very few new cases. Better yet, those individuals that had developed initial red papules and were vaccinated with the new vaccine were seen to be free of those papules after just two days."

Surgeon General Hudson breaks in. "From a practical standpoint, when do you think we can end Martial Law and lift the travel ban into and out of Chicago?"

"Dr. Heimbach, there are still infected people in the Chicago area even with the revaccination being done. When enough vaccine can be produced to vaccinate the entire country and maintain a backup supply for isolated outbreaks throughout the world, the bans can be lifted."

"How can that be accomplished, Dr. Heimbach?"

Robert breaks in before Dean Heimbach can respond. "Dr. Hudson, the problem with the two previous vaccination programs was that a single, somewhat autocratic supplier produced the vaccine. May I suggest that we give attenuated virus samples made by Dr. Parkesh to several pharmaceutical companies to produce the new vaccine? With Abbott Labs and Ameer's lab up and running already, adding several more labs capable of vaccine production will rapidly produce the amount Dr. Heimbach says we need."

Dr. Heimbach gives an affirmative smile and a nod of assent but says nothing.

"Well, I like that. This gives me something positive to give to the American people: results, a plan and hope. Thank you, gentlemen."

In Naperville, there is no hope for Jerry Snyder. He is gone. One of the 1.2 million victims of a disease for which medical science was unprepared and a greedy drug company, all too willing to put profits over humanity. Harold and Judy Snyder and their remaining son were given the new vaccine. They now cling to the hope that this new vaccine really does work and that the only child they have left will not experience the same fate as his older brother.

As planned, on Thursday night, Surgeon General Hudson backed by the President, Vice President and Peter Fowler goes on national television and is on radio and public address systems, as well.

"My fellow Americans, as your Surgeon General, I have shared with you the concern and uncertainty that this truly deadly epidemic has brought to the city of Chicago and the fear that I have had that it will spread to threaten us all. I fully realize the disappointment and added fear that two rounds of inadequate vaccinations has created. However, the Center for Disease Control has developed a fully tested and proven vaccine. It has already halted the spread of this disease in Chicago and has actually cured early cases. With this reality, I am asking each and every one of you to cooperate with yet another round of vaccinations. It is then and only then that we can lift the quarantine on the Chicago and Northern Illinois area and all of our lives can get back to normal without the fear of this menace occurring elsewhere."

More than a politician, the words of an established physician such as the Surgeon General are believable and respected. He outlines a plan to begin revaccinations for the entire country over the next three weeks, starting with the area around the Midwest and branching out in all directions so that areas closet to Chicago, such as Southern Illinois, Michigan, Wisconsin and Indiana are in the first phase. From there, vaccinations will progress radially outward, finally spreading to the East and West coasts last.

Listening to the broadcast, Dr. Merriweather couldn't be more pleased, not just from the now likely resolution of the smallpox epidemic but from what he knows is going on inside of David Epstein and the fact that the vaccination program won't get to him for more than 10 days. That's enough time for symptoms to appear.

CHAPTER 28

SPRINGING THE TRAP

On Friday, back at his office in Miami, Robert meets face to face with his friend, Detective Andy Molinaro.

"Andy, are you up-to-date on the Chicago epidemic and the failed vaccines from Apollo Drug Co.? Did you find out anything about David Epstein and David Connors?"

"Oh, boy, I sure am and I sure did. I remember their largesse when you were up against them in the Bone Protect scandal. I found out that they could be in big trouble. I hear rumors about a growing interest in a class-action suit over the failed virus, as well as a coverup. You know attorneys are like sharks, they can smell blood a mile away."

"I'm not interested in any class-action suit, but David Epstein is a narcissistic monster, who knew and didn't care whether his vaccines worked or not. He actually planted David Connors as one of his stooges on the CDC to sway the committee."

"So, what are you leading up to?"

"What if I told you that I can get him to confess on tape?"

"You can really do that?"

"I am sure I can. I will be meeting with him later this upcoming week. I need to let a few little gremlins work on him first."

"Gremlins! What are you talking about?"

"Never mind that for now. The reason I called is that I need your help and advice on wiring me up when I see him next week at his office and get him talking about the Apollo vaccine. I also want to know if whether any of what I might get him to say can be admissible in a court of law."

"We can certainly get you wired. Today's microphones and transmitters are more discrete. It would actually be wireless and nearly impossible to detect. Can you get him to meet you on a Saturday when his headquarters are almost empty and the security is lax? That way we can arrest him on the spot. We will be just outside in a van listening. When we have enough, we come in. Do you think you can get by security with a bug on you?

"Yes, I am sure. By Saturday, he will be desperate and I will be carrying three syringes with me. I'll call him before I enter and get him to let me pass security without a search because of the needles, which would otherwise be confiscated."

"Sounds like you have planned every detail."

"I hope so. This guy and his company have caused a lot of deaths and grief due to this man's greed. Because of his money and connections, he has avoided accountability. I want to be sure that he won't this time. Now, what about the admissibility of a confession from this taped conversation that he obviously hasn't agreed to?"

"That's where I come in. There has already been talk of a federal wiretap of his office under the antiracketeering act from the Bone Protect scandal that he somehow dodged. I am sure my contacts in the FBI can get one by next Saturday, particularly now that their vaccine has not worked after two tries."

"Great! Where do we go from here?"

"We will arrange to meet in a hotel close by his headquarters an hour before your meeting. We will have a separate vehicle for you to drive to his headquarters from there. We will follow in our van five minutes later."

"Good, I'll be ready."

While Dr. Merriweather's unknown "Gremlins" are working their magic on David Epstein, the results of his greed are played out at Jerry Snyder's burial service. After the young man receives his too early in life eulogy and his casket is lowered into a grave, the graveside guests slowly disperse. As they leave, each of the many from Harold's union associates fumble with words of condolences as best they can. Harold and Judy, both dressed in black as would be expected, force a tearful acknowledgment to each and then find themselves left alone, feeling empty. Richard's grandmother takes the boy back to their car. Standing over the open grave, Harold and Judy just look at each other. They say nothing. They can't. Tears, and the finality of their loss, won't let them speak. Yet, they know they must keep it together for Richard's sake and raise him now as their only child. On a broader scale, many others throughout the area are playing out scenes similar to this, struggling with devastating emotions like these. It seems that no family was spared, including Dr. Merriweather's.

As the weekend lapses into Monday, David Epstein gets a surprise visitor.

"Connors, what are you doing here?"

"I came to collect my pay and bonus. I'm quitting. You bastard, you hung me out to dry. I got smallpox and would have died had I not been given the new vaccine. Our damned vaccine didn't work the first time and didn't work the second time. You knew our stocks were old and were not sufficiently potent and you didn't care. You didn't even try to get our dammed scientists to make a new vaccine or even use a new cowpox antigen."

"Connors, stay where you are. You're probably still contagious."

David Epstein gets off his office chair and backs up, positioning himself behind the back of his plush office chair as if it were a protective shield.

"Don't worry, I'm cured and not contagious, as if you even care."

"But your clothes may be contaminated with the virus. I've read about that. How did you get out of Chicago anyway?"

"You're not the only one who can bullshit your way through life. I got the General to believe I was called back to the CDC urgently. He had my blood tested for antibodies against what they are now calling the 'ancient smallpox' virus. And guess what? I am fully immunized. He let me hop on one of his cargo planes for Atlanta. When I got there, I rented a car and drove up here."

"Connors, you can't tell anybody about this. I got Merriweather on our side now. We'll claim his new vaccine was secretly made here and that Apollo saved the day again."

"No dice. I am out of here. You're on your own now. Good luck with Merriweather. I hope he is the idealistic chump you think he is."

"Okay, okay, just go. Stop by HR. I'll have them cut you a sizeable check on the spot."

Connors takes off the tie he is wearing and throws it toward Epstein.

"Here, test that for viruses, if you want."

After David Connors leaves, nervous to the point of panic, Epstein goes over to the corner of his office where he stores a golf putter and a few golf balls for office putting practice. He takes the club by the handle and uses the putter's surface to engage the tie and deposit it in his wastebasket. He then calls housekeeping with an unusual request.

"Housekeeping, this is CEO Mr. David Epstein. Please come to my office to dispose of a contaminated article and have a lab decontamination team decontaminate my entire office. I'll be in Mr. Bloom's office the rest of the day."

On Thursday, Dr. Merriweather begins the final phase of his plan.

"Dr. Merriweather! Thank God you called. I need your help."

"Mr. Epstein, I was just calling to tell you that I am ready to come up to Morris Plains tomorrow and sign the contract. You sound worried. What's wrong?"

"Dr. Merriweather, I am getting smallpox. I must have gotten it from David Connors."

Although confused by the fact that he thinks David Connors is still in Chicago, Robert goes along with it.

"Why do you think you have smallpox?"

"I woke up this morning feeling awful. My head was hot and then I looked at my arms and then in the mirror. Dr. Merriweather, I have red sores all over and most of them hurt."

"It certainly sounds like smallpox. You need the new vaccine."

"I know but the Surgeon General's plan is to distribute it out from Chicago. It is not due to get here to New Jersey until next week. Then it will be too late. Do you think you can use your influence to get me to Chicago or close by like Indiana or Michigan at least?"

"Don't panic, Mr. Epstein. I can help you. I can get the vaccine to you and inject you myself but I can't get it to you until Saturday. If you first saw the red sores this morning, Saturday should be in time but it will be cutting it close. I'll bring needles and the vaccine in a metal box. It would be best to clear your facility that day and have your security team stand down, so that they don't confiscate the vaccine or the needles I'll be bringing."

"Consider it done. I'll be alone and we can sign the contract at the same time."

Robert concludes, "Okay, but to avoid getting your pilots and chauffer to become suspicious, I'll drive up to Morris Plains in a rental car to your headquarters myself. I'll be there at 10:00 A.M."

"Okay, great, great. Just get here. I'll make it worth your while."

Robert ends the call and wonders what David Connors had to do with it. In any event, it was more helpful to his plan than he could have hoped. He then ponders, "Instead of any more research awards, I might qualify for an academy award. One more performance to go."

At 9:00 A.M., Detective Andy Molinaro is busy getting Dr. Merriweather "wired up." His microphone is hidden in his tie clasp and the receiver transmitter is cleverly concealed in a little larger than normal belt buckle, which has a Texas star and motif on it to explain its larger size.

Robert receives last-minute instructions from the recording team and Andy Molinaro's three FBI buddies.

"Look! Be natural. Speak clearly but casually. Don't let your voice make him suspicious. Get him talking. Try to get him to admit that he knew his second vaccine wasn't going to work. That will cinch it. Anything else you get will be gravy. We'll come in when we have enough. Got it?"

"Got it, guys, but don't come in until I say 'It's okay now' real loud. That will be my signal. Is that okay with you four?"

"It's your show, Doctor."

"Now, let's go and get one bad guy, one very bad guy. I want to expose his greedy empire today."

They head out in separate vehicles as planned.

As hoped, the Apollo Drug Co. is nearly a ghost town on Saturday. After being let in at the main gate by seemingly the only security guard, Robert finds the metal scanner abandoned. There is no one at the reception desk or security. There is an eerie quiet as Robert's footsteps echo down the hallway to the bottom of the staircase leading up to the second floor and David Epstein's office. When Robert reaches the second floor he goes through the outer office where Epstein's assistant usually sits. As he opens the door, he sees David Epstein dressed in his usual Khaki slacks, but this time with a green button-down shirt. Robert can see red weeping sores in clusters on the skin of his cheeks and a worried expression on his face.

"Well, you sure look like you have smallpox, Mr. Epstein. What are those papers in your hand?"

"That's the contract. I need you to sign it before you vaccinate me. It's for legal purposes."

Before Robert takes the 34-page contract from Epstein, he gently but purposely grabs Epstein's left arm, unbuttons his shirtsleeve and rolls it up to the elbow.

"David, you have smallpox up this arm. I suspect the other arm looks similar."

"Yes, and so does my back. They hurt like hell. I have to take oxycodone every three hours. The only areas that are spared are my legs and groin, thank God. You brought the vaccine, didn't you? Hurry up and sign the contract."

Robert immediately smells a rat. He had no intention of signing the contract before injecting Epstein. Why does Epstein insist on signing the contract now? He should be more focused on receiving the vaccination. He knows from his courtroom experiences against Apollo that as an employee he could not testify against Epstein in court and the upcoming recording may even be deemed inadmissible.

"David, let me review the contract first. Then, I'll need about ten minutes to prepare the injections. The whole process will only take 25 minutes tops."

"Okay, but get started. I don't want it to be too late."

While Robert pretends to read the contract, Detective Molinaro and the two FBI agents approach the front security gate. Showing their badges to the guard, they proceed to take his radio phone away and explain to him that he is not in any trouble but that they will need him to take them into the headquarters building. The guard complies, not knowing what is going on or figuring out that he must be watched so as to prevent him from alerting Epstein.

Robert sits down and stares at the contract, not to look through the fine print as he told Epstein but to quickly think of a way to not sign the contract while seemingly signing the contract. Soon Robert breaks out in a hidden mischievous smile. As somewhat of a history buff, he recalls the story of World War II Army General, Anthony Clement "NUTS" McAuliffe. As Commander of the U.S. 101st Airborne Division, his troops were heavily outnumbered, out gunned, and completely surrounded by German troops as they were defending the Belgium town of Bastogne. On Dec. 22, 1944, the German Commander sent a written ultimatum that offered an "honorable and safe surrender" of his troops that encircled the town. If he didn't surrender, the German troops would descend on them and show no mercy. They gave McAuliffe only two hours to answer. Upon receiving the note, McAuliffe recalled that his orders were to hold on to Bastogne at all costs until reinforcements arrived. McAuliffe crumpled the note tossing it aside saying "NUTS." His underling, Lt. Colonel Kincaid, picked up the paper and gave it back to McAuliffe encouraging him to write "NUTS" on it as his answer. The paper ultimatum was returned with the only answer of "NUTS." By the time the confused German commander found somebody to translate and figure out what was even meant by "NUTS," the United States 4th Armor Division reinforcements arrived, dispatched the German forces and saved McAuliffe's 101st airborne troops.

Robert smiles and signs "NUTS" in the signature block, while muttering under his breath, "Thank you, General McAuliffe. I am glad you were awarded the Distinguished Service Medal for it."

As hoped, Epstein, in a hurry to receive what he perceives to be the lifesaving vaccine, doesn't check the contract when Robert lays it down on a chair to his right. Robert then ushers Epstein in the opposite direction to his desk where Epstein is more than anxious to get started with the vaccinations.

While Robert pretends to be preparing the injections, he starts off, "You sure you don't want the Apollo vaccine used in the South American outbreak?"

"Very funny, Merriweather. Just get on with it."

"Mr. Epstein, now, seemingly as your employee and your doctor, I need to ask you whether you are allergic to eggs or chicken products."

"I'm not allergic to anything except incompetence."

"I also need to know if you received the original vaccine."

"I did, Merriweather. At first, I thought it would work in Chicago, but shortly after I changed my mind."

As Robert slowly continues the task of drawing several syringes of purported vaccine out of separate vials, he continues to lead Epstein on.

"Oh, really, what changed your mind?"

"Heck, David Connors was giving me daily reports. When he told me how you and that Nobel Prize Winner were coming up with a new vaccine because it was actually a different virus, I knew ours wouldn't work. My own scientists, like you're going to be, already told me that."

"Then why did you go ahead with the second round of your vaccine?"

"Merriweather, you've got a lot to learn. There are 20 billion reasons why I told Connors to move towards a revaccination program. It was a great garage sale of my old stock-piled virus vaccine at a great profit."

"Didn't the deaths in Chicago bother you?"

"Look, it's a dog-eat-dog world out there. The world is overpopulated anyway. Hell, there were only a little over one million deaths out of Chicago. In a nation of 400 million and a world population of seven billion, that's small potatoes."

"So you knew that the Apollo vaccine wouldn't work and you didn't care?"

"I had no doubt you and that Nobel Prize guy were right. What's his name?"

"Dean Heimbach."

"Yeah, I knew you guys were right and that the Apollo vaccine wouldn't work. But why should I care? It was the CDC's responsibility not mine. And, now that you are my employee, Apollo will be linked to the new vaccine. So how about giving me the injection. Stop wasting time."

Robert knows Epstein's last remarks were a virtual admission of guilt. Robert got what he came for. He could signal Andy Molinaro and the FBI to come in but Epstein's callous answers and demands infuriate him. He is seething inside. He wants something more. As Robert prepares the last of the three injections, Detective Molinaro and the two FBI agents quietly make their way into Epstein's outer office where his secretary usually sits and continue to listen through their headphones.

"David, roll up both of your sleeves. I must tell you that, due to the red sores you already have, I need to give you three injections to fully immunize you. Each one will sting quite a bit. But I have found that giving each injection a name and having you concentrate on it takes our mind off of it and helps ease the pain. Are you ready?"

"Go ahead and do it. What's a little pain?"

Knowing he was using 95% alcohol instead of any vaccine at all, Robert is sure each injection will cause more than "a little pain."

"Okay, let's call this one Chuckie. Concentrate on the name Chuckie Mr. Epstein."

Robert injects Epstein in his left deltoid region (shoulder area).

"Ow! God damn it! That hurt more than you said. Oh my God, WOW."

Epstein leans forward and almost doubles over rubbing his shoulder.

"Well, there are two more to go. Do you want me to stop?"

"NO, NO, go ahead."

"Let's call this one Johnny. Concentrate on the word Johnny, Mr. Epstein."

This time Robert injects Epstein deep in his right deltoid region and once again Epstein yells out in pain and this time rolls over onto the floor. He kneels down as Robert vengefully smiles behind him, unseen by Epstein. Epstein picks himself off the floor and senses something is out of the ordinary, but he remains desperate to "get immunized."

Now, not disguising a sinister smile any longer, Robert tells Epstein, "This one will be the worst of all, since I need to give it to you in your abdomen."

With a worried expression on his face, a wide-eyed Epstein braces for the pain he knows is coming and tenses his abdominal muscles which only makes it worse.

Robert takes the syringe and needle in front of Epstein and grabs him by the shirt collar. He pulls Epstein closer and with a snarl says, "David Epstein—look at me, you coward."

David Epstein now looks at Robert with terror in his eyes. Robert, with a continued snarl, forcibly jabs the alcohol-loaded needle into him and says to Epstein, "This one is for Heather."

Now, a person visibly afraid of Dr. Merriweather and in terrible pain rolls onto the floor again and looks incredulously up at Robert. Robert, in a calm reassuring voice, says, "It will be alright, Epstein," softly followed by a loud "It's okay now."

That's the signal Andy Molinaro and the three FBI investigators are waiting for. They quickly open the door and move in to arrest David Epstein, CEO of Apollo Drug Co. a recent hero to everyone now soon to be exposed as a villain. However, they stop short.

"Hey, he's got red sores. He's got the smallpox. We can't be exposed to him."

"Not to worry. It's not smallpox at all," Robert says reassuringly. "It's actually chicken pox. I gave it to him myself twelve days ago with a contaminated handkerchief, just like Captain Trent did to the American Indians. In fact, he is even beyond the contagious stage for chicken pox. Go ahead and arrest the scum, he can't harm you."

"You bastard, Merriweather, you fucking bastard. You traitor. You're fired and you won't be able to testify against me as my former employee particularly with the restrictions I put in the contract."

"Here. Read your damned contract, Epstein, particularly the signature page."

Epstein's eyes widen. He reaches for the contract that Robert tossed at him and nervously fumbles to the last page, the signature page. Probably similar to the 1944 German commander with is troops surrounding the town of Batstone, Epstein is confused and unaware of its meaning of "NUTS," but realizes that he has been duped.

Robert quietly gathers his empty syringes into his small leather doctor's bag as the three FBI agents escort the handcuffed Epstein away. Andy Molinaro wants to tell him something in the quiet aftermath but cannot come up with the words. He merely gives Robert a thumbs-up and follows the captive and FBI agents out the door leaving Robert alone with his thoughts.

Robert is quiet. He looks down, not at all proud of his actions as exhausted relief overcomes him.

"What have I become? Did I have to go that far? The hate, the anger for that scum. The primal emotion of revenge. He deserved it alright but has this whole thing brought me to his level—the dark side?"

CHAPTER 29

THE AFTERMATH: A WORRISOME FUTURE?

The last CDC committee meeting gathers at 8:00 A.M. on the Monday following the arrest of David Epstein. Dr. Merriweather has returned from Morris Plains, New Jersey, and Dean Heimbach returned from Chicago days before. All are present with the notable exception of David Connors and Dr. Christine Hargraves. Peter Fowler begins.

"This will be the last meeting of this committee for now. Remember, you are not to discuss the inner workings of this committee or the discussions that have occurred. Also, you all may be recalled at any time if this outbreak rears its ugly head gain or a new one emerges.

"On a practical note, you all have spent weeks and most more than a month away from your home and work place for this committee. You will be reimbursed for your travel, hotel and ground transportation and provided a per diem at government rates. I know we can never fully compensate you for your time, but I hope you know what a great service your input and sacrifice provided."

"On a personal note, I want to especially thank Drs. Heimbach, Merriweather and Parkesh for their extraordinary innovative thinking, work and personal risk that helped bring this epidemic under control. To that point, I am pleased to inform you that no new cases have been reported in the Chicago area since the completion of the revaccination program using the vaccine developed by Dr. Parkesh. And incidentally, Dr. Parkesh, your vaccine has the lowest reported rate of side-effects than any other vaccine we track, including the MMR vaccine. Your newly developed technology will likely become the standard for vaccine development in the future. "

The committee members give a round of applause to which Ameer smiles broadly but makes no comment.

"Additionally, the small outbreaks in other cities resulted in minimal fatalities due to a rapid quarantine effort and the vaccinations of what is now being called the Parkesh vaccine."

Another round of polite applause is given this time with Ameer openly blushing.

"The Surgeon General informed me early this morning that if no new cases of smallpox are found in the Chicago area by Wednesday, the quarantine and Martial Law will be lifted."

Now all committee members burst out in a more robust applause led, by Dean Heimbach with a boisterous "Hear! Hear!"

"To that end, the Surgeon General also told me General Vandenbos is being recommended for the Army's Distinguished Service Medal and will probably receive his second star."

This time, Dr. Merriweather, an ex-Air Force officer himself and with great respect for those others who also served in the military, leads the applause and adds, "We may not have liked the General's authoritarian commanding attitude but he did what he had to do to control a nearly impossible situation. He also supported our efforts to prove the vaccine's effectiveness and get everyone vaccinated. He saved many lives."

The committee members shake their heads in agreement but do not applaud. Peter Fowler then continues.

"I also understand that both David Connors and his boss David Epstein, whom I personally trusted and together approached Congress for support, have been arrested on racketeering charges. The law will handle their future but I hope their guilt will be just as big a part of their punishment.

"The Neanderthal specimen will be brought here to the CDC and will be stored in its frozen state. Both he and Inca Indian Chief from Peru will remain here until their fate is determined. They will either be incinerated as a precaution against releasing other diseases from antiquity that they may harbor or, as I have implored our government to do, allow us to study these rare findings under absolutely controlled conditions to learn our past and perhaps our future, as well.

"Lastly, I have requested that each of you receive a Presidential Letter of Merit from the President. So now, I am officially adjourning the committee. God speed to all of you."

The Committee members file out slowly with the exception of Dean Heimbach, Robert and Ameer who seem to be lost in a daze of exhaustion. Then, statistician Patrick Goode remarks, "Don't look at me. I'm hanging around because my wife, Teri, won't be picking me up for another hour. Anyway, why are you three so glum? You are heroes. You should be celebrating. You should be happy."

As Patrick Goode leaves the conference room to wait for his ride home, Dr. Heimbach looks at Robert.

"I know, I'm not particularly happy. What have we just lived through and witnessed, Dr. Merriweather?"

Robert does not answer the rhetorical question but allows Dean Heimbach to continue.

"While I am happy to a degree, over a million people still died. I fear that this country and this planet, for that matter, are very ill prepared to deal with another similar epidemic. We were very lucky on this one because patient zero was identified early and was frozen and isolated from everyone else. Three of the first four patients were confined to the same hospital, slowing the transmission rate. And lucky for us, you knew one of the patients. As a trained professional who recognized it as a new disease it alerted us all. This has been a warning and should be a lesson for the future of mankind. We have now seen the SARS epidemic and the more recent the COVID-19 pandemic with all of its hysteria and its economic impact in the trillions, just like this recent smallpox epidemic. In both of those everyone ran out to get N95 masks and the government-issued travel restrictions and warnings. Countries that reacted slowly and less completely suffered the most. Then, when each subsided either by nature's seasonal changes or mitigation tactics and unapproved or approved treatments along with and the marshaling of medical personnel and medical technology, we all went back to being complacent again. We are not prepared as a people, as a government, or even economically for a global pandemic with the heightened virulence that this one had . We certainly do not have a coordinated medical plan either. This epidemic was treated on the fly, so to speak with Draconian quarantine measures, military Martial Law, and a committee infiltrated by special interests. We need to prepare now for the next one that is sure to come. One that may very well be as lethal as or even more lethal than this one."

Dr. Merriweather replies.

"Dean, one of the biggest fears I have comes from the revelation it has brought to us that our own immune systems evolved gradually to deal with the microbes our species has been gradually exposed to over the millennia. Like the immune systems of our Native Americans and Hawaiian Islanders centuries ago, our modern-day immune systems are ill prepared to cope with a new virus or even a new bacteria. Whether that microbe comes from an extinct species recently unearthed like this one did, from a meteor, from a zoonosis like Ebola virus or due to a spillover from an animal species or even an escape from a research lab, such as occurred with the coronavirus, it poses a real risk that will come about again. With the population increasing and global travel commonplace, the next epidemic could threaten our entire species."

"My college anthropologist friend who unearthed the Neanderthal we now refer to as patient zero did so to gain evidence that the extinction of the Neanderthal species was due to competition and war rather than by mating and assimilation. He may have been right to a degree but he may have just stumbled upon the real reason Neanderthals became extinct; a disease their immune systems could not cope with. A disease brought to them when our ancient homosapien ancestors migrated out of Africa and brought with them smallpox or other similar deadly diseases. Perhaps the question we should ask is; if the Neanderthals became extinct because their natural immune systems were inadequate to protect them from a new disease, will our own species become extinct because our own immune systems are ill prepared to cope with a new or mutated virus? Will our science be able to react fast enough? Our arrogance on these points, our sureness that it won't happen to us, may be our biggest failing."

With that sobering thought, each remaining member offers a heartfelt goodbye while exchanging their business cards with their contact information and promising to keep in touch. In particular, Dean Heimbach tells Dr. Merriweather, "Before this, I had no idea clinicians or surgeons like yourself knew and even cared about science and its place in the world. I now have a greater respect for your kind, Dr. Merriweather."

"Dean, as a bench research scientist wannabe, you have reinforced the image and respect I have for your kind as well. Perhaps we should combine our efforts again on a less threatening cause."

"Indeed, Robert, indeed."

Turning now to Ameer who has been silent throughout Drs. Heimbach and Merriweather's lament, he continues.

"And you, Ameer. I can only say that you indeed talked the talk and walked the walk."

Each of the three exhausted men laugh as they finally shuffle out the door leaving the committee room, the site of debate and decision uncharacteristically empty and quiet.

Robert tries to catch an early afternoon flight back to Miami but, due to weather delays from lightning and rain between Atlanta and Miami, the plane doesn't take off until 6:00 P.M. Even then, the flight is one of continuous turbulence, eliminating his hope of catching up on some much needed rest and sleep. Instead, seated in a window seat, his mind mulls over the loss of Heather and his two cousins over and over again. As each flash of lightning lights up the surrounding clouds and the plane jolts in response, the images of each appears to him in fitful half-sleep. He arouses himself and tries to focus on the expected mound of emails and correspondence he will face upon returning to his office, not to mention the patient backlog, neglected research studies and teaching assignments which only makes it worse for him. The draining nature of the past three weeks and the loss of Heather, Chuckie, and Johnny overwhelms him.

Arriving in Miami at 8:30 at night, he realizes that he told his house sitter to leave last night in anticipation of an early afternoon return.

"Boy, the dogs must be starving. They're going to be all over me when I get home."

Robert finally gets a taxi and is home by 9:15 P.M. Indeed, his house sitter's car is not in the driveway. Robert opens the front door and pushes his suitcase forward to keep his three dogs from jumping on him in their delight. However, instead, all three dogs nervously go to the back of the house then come running back to Robert tails wagging, only to return to the back of the house again. Robert takes a few steps down the hallway and senses he is not alone. There is someone else in the house. He thinks, *Is it Miriam the house sitter, a burglar?* Then out of the master bedroom around the corner appears a pretty blonde mature woman of 52 years.

"Veronica!" Robert stares at her. Five second pass, ten seconds pass. Robert still stares. Neither speaks. Then Robert finally composes himself enough to say, "What are you doing here?"

"I know somewhat about what you've been going through. I know you. I know how you immerse yourself into these projects and how it drains you. I came back because I know you must be hurting."

Robert looks into the blue eyes of his ex-wife, the mother of his three sons, the woman he loved. The one he never could completely get out of his thoughts. He answers.

"I am."